A SPY in the HOUSE

THE AGENCY

A SPY in the HOUSE

Y. S. LEE

CANDLEWICK PRESS

Copyright © 2009 by Y. S. Lee

First U.S. edition in this format 2016

The Library of Congress has cataloged the hardcover edition as follows:

Lee, Y. S.
A spy in the house / Y. S. Lee. —1st U.S. ed.
p.   cm. — (The agency ; bk. 1)
Summary: Rescued from the gallows in 1850s London, young orphan and thief Mary Quinn is offered a place at Miss Scrimshaw's Academy for Girls where she is trained to be part of an all-female investigative unit called The Agency and, at age seventeen, she infiltrates a rich merchant's home in hopes of tracing his missing cargo ships.
ISBN 978-0-7636-4067-5 (hardcover)
[1. Mystery and detective stories. 2. Swindlers and swindling—Fiction.
3. Household employees—Fiction. 4. Sex role—Fiction. 5. Orphans—Fiction.
6. London (Eng.)—History—19th century—Fiction.
7. Great Britain—History—Victoria, 1837–1901—Fiction.]   I. Title.
PZ7.L591173Spy   2010
[Fic]—dc22   2009032736

ISBN 978-0-7636-5289-0 (paperback)
ISBN 978-0-7636-8748-9 (reformatted paperback)

16 17 18 19 20 21 BVG 10 9 8 7 6 5 4 3 2 1

Printed in Berryville, VA, U.S.A.

This book was typeset in Palatino.

Candlewick Press
99 Dover Street
Somerville, Massachusetts 02144

visit us at www.candlewick.com

To Nicholas Woolley

Prologue

August 1853

The Central Criminal Court
at the Old Bailey, London

She should have been listening to the judge.

Instead, Mary's attention was focused on the flies swarming around her ankles in the prisoner's dock and their primary interest: the pool of stale urine at her feet. It wasn't hers. Some poor fool must have lost control of his bladder earlier in the day, but the puddle would remain until . . . well, until long after her case was finished, at any rate.

It was odd how her senses shifted. In the late afternoon heat, the flies' buzzing was the loudest sound in her mind. The judge's nasal tenor was far down the list, well after the persistent cackling of someone in the gallery. If she squinted in just the right way, she could make out a halo of loose, grayish hair. Mad? Or merely relieved that it was someone else in the dock?

The prosecutor—deformed by his wig, white powder drifting off it every time he turned his neck—had enjoyed himself hugely. He'd made much of her youth—

"How much more depraved is one so young, who has already trod so far and so fast through the thorny thickets of evil?"—and her dangerous looks—"Such pitch-black hair is a token of her pitch-black soul. Such evil should be nipped in the bud"—and by that cliché, he meant to hang her. She had not spoken in her own defense. She had nothing to say.

The judge's voice, threading its way amid the excited droning of the flies, loomed suddenly close and intimate. "For the crime of housebreaking, Mary Lang, you are hereby sentenced to hang by the neck until you are dead. May God have mercy on your soul." The last sentence sounded like mockery. How could it not?

There was some minor shuffling in the room but no murmurs of surprise. Mary lifted her chin and gazed steadily into the gallery, where the spectators looked uncomfortable in the late summer heat. Only one figure—a woman dressed in light mourning, her veil rolled back—met her eyes. And winked.

Mary blinked. When she looked again, the lady was gone. Then the wardress was dragging her from the prisoner's box and leading her out of the courtroom, down the long, dung-and-onion-smelling corridor toward the cool damp of the cellar.

The wardress flung a brawny arm round her shoulder and jostled her roughly. "Don't you faint, now, young woman." Her voice was hoarse, with a West Country accent.

Caught off guard, Mary stumbled. "I won't," she muttered, but the woman shoved down onto Mary's shoulders again, hard enough to make her knees buckle.

"May the Lord have mercy on your puny weak soul, indeed!" Under the cover of her petticoats, the wardress kicked Mary's foot, sending her stumbling once again. "Lawsamercy, you scrawny brat, none of this nonsense!"

They had nearly reached the turnkey. Behind her back, the wardress administered a sharp twist to Mary's left wrist. The iron cuffs cut into her flesh, causing her to hiss in surprise. The woman shook her shoulders roughly, gabbling the whole time at the turnkey. "The bloody girl's fainting! I'm not having these fine-lady airs, that's for certain!" Her strident voice drowned out the responses of the nearby jailers. "A good ducking in the horse trough will sort her out!" cried the woman furiously.

Mary chose to go limp. What was another quarter of an hour's bullying to her? She was dragged outside and across the cobbled yard, the wardress still scolding and shaking her vigorously. The men clustered about the door, grinning at the spectacle. As she approached the trough in the corner of the courtyard, lugging Mary under her arm, the wardress produced a coarse handkerchief from her pocket and clamped it over Mary's nose and mouth. A new smell, sweet and cold, flooded her nostrils. She struggled for a moment, briefly bewildered by the expression in the woman's eyes.

And then the sky went black.

* * *

Was this death? Her mouth felt thick, as did her head. Her fingertips were numb. She twitched them experimentally and realized with a small shock that her wrists were no longer shackled. Indeed, she was floating, swaddled in linen and soft blankets. She turned her cheek to one side and rubbed against the pillow, catlike. The scent was pleasant and totally unfamiliar. No lake of burning fire so far. No heavenly choir, either. She saw no reason to move or even to open her eyes.

"Mary?"

She hadn't considered that God might be female. Slowly, reluctantly, she raised heavy eyelids and focused on the speaker. The woman had changed her lavender mourning dress for something darker, but it was she: the lady who'd winked at her from the gallery. That meant this was neither hell nor heaven.

"How do you feel?"

The question seemed irrelevant. Mary let her gaze slide around the room — large, simply furnished, lit by candles — and back to the Winker. "I don't know."

"Your head might ache; chloroform sometimes has that effect, although we use as little as possible."

Chloroform: a fancy word for a dangerous substance. She'd heard whispers of potions that knocked one out but always dismissed them as wishful lies.

"You must be thirsty." The Winker offered a glass of something pale and cloudy. At Mary's hesitation, she

4

smiled. "It's quite safe to drink." To demonstrate, she took a sip.

Mary's first taste was tentative. Then, as the cool liquid filled her mouth, she guzzled it greedily. Lemonade. She'd had it once before, a couple of years ago. Now she was sorry when it was all gone. Wiping her mouth, she looked at the lady. She still felt fuzzy-headed, but her curiosity was strong. "Why?"

"Why don't I begin with who and where? Then I'll get to why and how."

Mary nodded. She felt mocked.

The lady sat down beside the bed. "My name is Anne Treleaven," she began, "and I am the head teacher here at Miss Scrimshaw's Academy for Girls. Our founder was an eccentric and wealthy woman whose desire was to help women achieve a measure of independence. Education for girls in our country is generally very inferior, even for the rich, and many girls receive none at all. So Miss Scrimshaw founded a school."

She spoke quietly, but her eyes were sharp, and they rarely left Mary's face. "We are a little like a charity school, since most of our students would not normally be able to afford our fees. However, we are a very unusual institution in that we often select our students instead of waiting for them to come to us. We search for girls who would most benefit from the special training we offer." She paused. "We have chosen you."

Mary scowled. "I suppose you think that's generous.

What makes you think I want to be chosen? Suppose I *want* to hang?"

Instead of shock and outrage, Anne's face showed mild amusement. "Don't bristle. We don't intend to keep you here by force. You may leave at any time and go directly to the gallows, if you wish. But I hope you will at least listen to me for a few minutes before choosing."

Mary felt both churlish and childish. She shrugged.

"My colleagues have been watching you for some time. You know one of them as the wardress at the Old Bailey, of course; another observed you in Newgate prison during the weeks before your sentencing. They were both struck by your intelligence. They were also intrigued by the fact that you pled guilty instead of insisting upon a trial. Most people charged with capital crimes insist upon their innocence, whether they are truly innocent or not. But you didn't. Why not, Mary?"

After a pause, Mary shrugged again. "Maybe I was fed up."

Anne's eyes glinted. "With lying? Stealing?" She refilled Mary's glass and passed it to her. "Or perhaps with living?"

Mary's blink was the equivalent of a full confession from another, less hardened, girl.

"You are surprisingly resigned to death, for one so young."

"Twelve years is enough for me," she said. Well-meaning strangers—women, especially—were forever trying to coax her into a tearful confession of her life's sufferings. She hadn't fallen for that sort of rubbish in years.

Anne raised one thin eyebrow. "That is what my colleagues suspected, and that is why we brought you to the Academy: in the hope that you might find the prospect of a different sort of life more tolerable."

"As an honest little maid-of-all-work, you mean? So that fine ladies can have the joy of beating me, all for eight quid a year?" She spat on the carpet. "Not I."

Anne's expression hardened. "No, Mary, not that. Not ever that."

"You're mad, then. There's nothing else—not for my sort."

"You're wrong about that."

"Am I?"

"You're clever, Mary. And fierce. And ambitious. There are a few professions open to women; you might join any of these." Anne paused and inclined her head. "And there are one or two other possibilities available to women of exceptional abilities . . . but to speak of these now would be somewhat, shall we say, premature."

This was absurd. Nobody ever got a second chance. Mary knew that much, at least. Oh, Lord—was the unexpected praise going to her head? "What's your angle?" she demanded.

Again, Anne appeared unsurprised by the question, the rudeness. "As I explained before, our aim is to offer girls an independent life. Too many women feel forced to marry; even more lack that choice and resort to prostitution, or worse, in order to survive. We believe that a sound education will assist our graduates to support themselves." She paused. "Not all our pupils succeed. Some girls prefer the idea of marriage to hard work, not realizing that marriage to a brute or a drunkard is more difficult than any profession. But they choose their paths. We cannot force our ideas upon our pupils.

"But I digress. My colleagues see that you have a taste for independence and the desire to make your own way in the world. You are accustomed to making decisions and caring for yourself. Here at the Academy, we can give you a better chance of achieving that independence. We can help you to escape your life as a thief—to reinvent yourself, if you like. A chance to improve your expectations . . . to become what you might have been had fate been kinder in the first instance."

Mary swallowed hard. This woman's ideas were extraordinary—a giddy, improbable revelation. How was it possible for her feelings to change so quickly? Five minutes earlier, she'd been cursing the woman who had snatched her out of jail and away from the certainty of death. Now she was terrfied that all this glowing promise might be merely a cheap confidence trick. "You still haven't answered my question," she said gruffly. She feared that her voice was shaking. "What's in it for you? What's the catch?"

Anne's eyes, she noticed suddenly, were steel gray. "I hate to see girls become victims," she said with quiet intensity. "You very nearly were. That's what's in it for me." Suddenly, she folded her fingers round Mary's cold hand. "And the catch, my dear, is that you must be willing to work hard for it. That is all."

That handclasp shocked Mary more than a sudden blow. When was the last time she'd been touched? The wardress, of course, had knocked her about a little—all for a good cause, apparently. Men had tried to grope her skirts in the streets. Drunks had reeled against her in mobbed alleys and public houses. Small children had bumped against her as they careened through crowds. But the last time someone had touched her, Mary, with affection . . . that had not happened since her mother had died.

Shaken, she pulled her hand away. *This can't be true,* she said to herself. *This must be another dead end. There is no hope. You learned that years ago, you little fool.* She drew a steadying breath and opened her lips to snarl all this. Instead, one word came out in a faint voice.

"Please. . . ."

One

Good Friday, 2 April 1858

Miss Scrimshaw's Academy for Girls
St. John's Wood, London

Mary took the attic stairs two by two. It was tricky in a steel crinoline and buttoned boots, but she needed some sort of outlet for her nervous energy. Since requesting a meeting with the head teachers earlier that day, she hadn't been able to concentrate on much. Her first attempt at a knock was shaky, her knuckles barely scraping the heavy oak door. She overcompensated with a pair of rugged thumps and cringed. It sounded as though she were trying to break down the door.

"Come in," came the crisp command.

She swallowed, wiped her palms on her skirts, and turned the polished brass knob. The door glided silently on its hinges, revealing a bland scene: a pair of middle-class women taking afternoon tea. While the ladies looked conventional enough, Mary had quickly learned that between them, they controlled everything about the Academy. "G-good afternoon, Miss Treleaven," she managed to murmur. "Mrs. Frame."

Anne beckoned her forward. "Come in, Mary. Do sit down."

"Th-thank you." She dropped into the nearest seat, a slippery horsehair chair that immediately attempted to deposit her onto the floor. She didn't normally stammer. Never had. This was a devil of a time to begin.

Anne poured a third cup of tea and handed it to her. It was a very warm day, especially up in the attic. As a curl of steam reached her nostrils, Mary blinked, her nervousness doubling. She was holding a cup of Lapsang souchong, a tea the ladies generally reserved for special occasions.

"Would you like a slice of cake?" Anne indicated the seedcake on the tray at her elbow.

The idea made Mary's stomach clench. "Thank you, no." The more she tried to steady her nerves, the more her cup rattled in its saucer.

"You wished to speak with us." To Mary's surprise, Anne rose and began to pace restlessly before the cold fireplace. Mary's glance flicked toward Felicity Frame, who remained seated. The two women seemed opposites in all ways: Anne was thin, plain, and quietly serious, while Felicity was tall and curvy, a striking beauty with a rich laugh.

Mary moistened her lips. "Yes." When they remained silent, she supposed there was nothing else to do but begin. "I am very grateful to you for rescuing me from the gallows and for the education you have given me. I owe you everything, quite literally. But I have been thinking of my future, and I wish—that is, I do not think . . ." Mary faltered. Her carefully rehearsed speech was evaporating before their grave, curious faces.

She took a scalding sip of tea. *Why serve a special tea today?* A strong sense of guilt prompted her to speak quickly and bluntly. "What I mean to say is that for some time I have been questioning my position as an assistant teacher. While I enjoy living here at the Academy, I know that I'm not very good at the work. I do like the girls, but I lack the patience to be a teacher."

She hurried on without looking up. "I'm afraid it gets worse. Two years ago, I took lessons in shorthand and typing, but I do not find the repetitive life of a clerk appealing. Last year, I began preliminary medical training with the idea of becoming a nurse. But the matrons did not have confidence in me, and I was not invited to continue." She swallowed, the taste of that humiliation still strong in her mouth. "Recently, I have been wondering: Is it not possible—is it even reasonable—to expect something more from my work?"

Anne looked mildly curious. "What do you mean, 'something more'?"

Mary writhed inwardly. "It sounds foolish, I know. . . . I mean a sense of pride and active interest in work . . . even enjoyment. Perhaps satisfaction?" There. It was out. Ungrateful as she was, it was out.

There was a short pause, but not a flicker of surprise or disappointment showed on either face. Anne spoke first. "How long have you been teaching the junior girls now, Mary?"

"For a year; I began when I was about sixteen."

"And you have lived here at the school since you were twelve, of course."

"From the day you rescued me from the Old Bailey." Mary flushed. "At least, I was roughly twelve . . . as you know, I've no birth certificate. But I'm certain I was born in 1841."

"Nearly one-third of your life, then, has been spent with us."

Mary nodded. "Yes. I know I must sound terribly selfish."

A faint smile passed over Anne's lips, but it was gone in a moment. "Let us leave the question of gratitude to one side. You have reached the age of seventeen. You find yourself . . . stifled . . . by the routine of the schoolroom."

Mary nodded. "Yes."

"Do you wish to return to your life as it was before you were imprisoned? Housebreaking and picking pockets?"

"No!" Mary realized that she had half shouted the word. She moderated her voice. "Not in the least. But I long for a little independence . . . for a different sort of work."

"Ah." Again, that satisfied gleam passed over Anne's features. "What sort of work do you envision?"

Mary shook her head miserably. "That is what I do not know. I hoped you would be able to advise me."

Felicity spoke for the first time. "Are you quite certain that you wish to work at all? Many girls try to marry in order to escape poverty."

Mary shook her head firmly. "No. I have no desire to marry."

"Other women find lovers to provide for them."

Mary nearly dropped her teacup in amazement. "Mrs. Frame? You are surely not recommending . . ."

Felicity smiled faintly. "I am not recommending anything. But I wish to set aside conventional morality and speak of practical possibilities. You are not beautiful, but you are intelligent and rather . . . striking. Exotic, even. Being a mistress is a possibility."

"I hate being looked at! People are forever asking whether I'm foreign, just because I haven't got yellow hair and round blue eyes."

"That's my point: unusual looks are sometimes better than mere prettiness."

What a preposterous thing to say. And just what was Felicity suggesting, talking about her "exotic" looks? Did she suspect . . . ? Mary struggled to find her point. "Besides, a mistress is just as dependent as a wife." As the words left her mouth, she remembered hearing a rumor about Mrs. Frame's own colorful personal history . . . but it was too late to retract her remark—were she so inclined.

Felicity arched one eyebrow. "You have been well trained in the philosophy of the school, Mary. We do

14

not encourage girls to build their lives on the whims of men."

Anne spoke again. "Very well. That is your view. Tell us, now, about your early life and your family." At Mary's look of surprise, she smiled. "We do know the details, but I should like to hear it from you once more."

So this was a test of perspective. "I was born in east London—Poplar," she began. She spoke slowly, choosing her words carefully. Could she trust these ladies with the full truth about her past? About her family? How would they respond? They thought they already knew everything about her. . . .

"Is everything all right?" asked Felicity.

Mary blinked, unaware that she'd halted. "Of course." She took a deep breath and forced herself to continue. "My father was a merchant sailor and my mother an Irish-born seamstress. Although my father was frequently at sea, I remember that my parents were happy together. Their only real grief was that my two younger brothers both died in infancy." She paused and swallowed hard. "When I was seven or eight years old, my father's ship was wrecked and the entire crew reported dead. The shock and grief made my mother very ill, and she lost her job as a seamstress through her illness. She was expecting another child at the time, and she lost that, too.

"When she was a little better, Mother tried to get piecework so that she could work at home. But the piecework paid next to nothing. She then tried going out as a charwoman, cleaning houses, but she only got twopence a day for the work. It wasn't enough to keep us both." Her voice was detached now, toneless. "Mother didn't care about herself, but she had me to look after. She soon had no choice: she became a prostitute. Late at night, when she thought I was asleep, she brought men back to our lodgings. That is how I learned to steal. Sometimes they would fall asleep, and I would take coins from their pockets." She drew another long breath and looked up at the two women defiantly. "It was never very much; I never took notes—only coins. I must have thought . . ." She shook her head. "I don't know what I thought.

"It's an old story, I suppose. Mother soon became ill. We didn't have enough money for medicine from the apothecary, and the neighbors kept away. All I know is that even with the bits I'd stolen, we hadn't enough money to live." She paused. "I don't remember much about the time immediately after Mother died. A few months later, I had learned how to pick pockets properly, and then someone taught me to pick locks as well. I dressed as a boy; it was easier and safer.

"I became quite good at housebreaking for a time. Then I began to take larger risks, foolish risks, really, and I was not terribly surprised that I was caught. The only mystery is that I was not caught earlier. And you know the rest—that I was sentenced to hang." Mary flashed the ladies a grateful look. "You saved me."

There was a minute's pause. When Anne spoke again,

her tone was unusually gentle. "Thank you, Mary. It is to your credit that you are able to tell the story of your early life so clearly and without extreme bitterness." She half smiled. "As you know, we at the Academy place great emphasis on strength of character.

"Well, my dear?" Anne turned to Felicity, her voice crisp once more. "How do we assess Mary's professional prospects? That she is intelligent and ambitious is evident."

"She is loyal and capable of great discretion," Felicity added with approval. "She is also brave, tenacious, and decisive. And she strives to do what she believes is right."

Mary glowed under their warm and wholly unexpected praise.

"However, she has a bad temper," Anne noted coolly. "She dislikes correction and goes to great lengths to avoid being in the wrong. She is shy of strangers, particularly men. That is understandable, given her childhood, but a fault nevertheless."

Mary's proud glow became a flush of shame. They were all too correct.

"Mary, you look heated," observed Anne. "Do you wish to continue this conversation?"

Mary swallowed hard. "Yes," she whispered.

"Very well. We understand your philosophy and know your character." Anne looked at Felicity, who nodded once, very slightly. "As it happens, Mary, we have a post in mind that we think will suit your abilities very well."

Mary looked up eagerly.

"But before we continue," said Anne sternly, "you must give me your solemn word that you will never reveal any part of our conversation, or hint thereof, to any other living being. Do you understand me?"

She swallowed and nodded. "Yes."

"Swear it."

"I give you my solemn word that I will never reveal any part of what you are about to tell me to another soul."

Anne's features relaxed, and she nodded with satisfaction. Stepping to one side of the fireplace, she slipped her fingers behind the polished oak mantel. There was a barely audible click. Then, on the wall to Mary's left, one panel of faded wallpaper swung aside to reveal a dark, narrow opening in the wall.

Mary's mouth dropped open in amazement, and she dragged her fascinated gaze back to Anne's face, which wore a small, triumphant smile.

"Let us enter the headquarters of the Agency."

Shaking with excitement, Mary rose and followed the women into the narrow opening and through a short tunnel. Although the tunnel was not lit, its bricks were dry and free of cobwebs—evidence of regular use. They emerged in a large, plain room containing a round table with four straight-backed chairs. Anne and Felicity set down the oil lamps they had been carrying. The yellow light flickered over the exposed bricks and rough wooden floorboards, making the room seem oddly cozy.

The women each took a seat round the table, and Anne smiled at Mary warmly. "I always hoped you would come to us one day, my dear—and you did. But I have talked too much already, perhaps giving you the impression that I am in charge. I am not; the Agency is a collective, although only two of us are present this evening. Felicity, would you care to explain to Mary what we do here?"

Felicity cleared her throat; she had been unusually quiet thus far. "As you know, the goal of Miss Scrimshaw's Academy for Girls is to give young women the means to achieve some form of independence. Marriage is an uncertain gamble, and the primary types of work open to women depend upon the good nature of one's employer. That is why most governesses and domestic servants are so shamefully abused."

Anne vigorously nodded her agreement. "Precisely. Although a few professional opportunities for women exist, it is our aim to train women to do more than teach children and serve meals. But you know this already, and you have been helping to prepare young women in this way, too." She paused and glanced at Felicity. "I beg your pardon, Flick. Do go on."

Mary bit back a smile on hearing the affectionate nickname. She had never before heard the grave, thoughtful Anne Treleaven speak so informally.

Felicity turned her marvelous eyes on Mary, her gaze almost hypnotic now. "The Agency complements the Academy. Here, we turn the stereotype of the meek female servant to our advantage. Because women are believed to be foolish, silly, and weak, we are in a position to observe and learn more effectively than a man in a similar position. Our clients employ us to gather information, often on highly confidential subjects. We place our agents in very sensitive situations. But while a man in such a position might be subject to suspicion, we find that women—posing as governesses or domestic servants, for example—are often totally ignored."

She permitted herself a small smile. "We also find that well-trained women tend to be more perceptive, as well as less arrogant, in their observations. They are often, shall we say, less prone to error—not because they are cleverer or more fortunate but because they make fewer assumptions and take less for granted. And, contrary to stereotype, they are often more logical." She looked at Mary keenly. "Have you any questions thus far?"

Mary nodded. Her fingers clenched hard on either side of her chair. "How many members does the Agency have? Do your clients know that your agents are female? When was the Agency founded? And by whom? Is Miss Scrimshaw involved?"

They laughed at her eagerness, and again it was Felicity who answered. "The Agency was founded some ten years ago, and Anne and I were among its first operatives. We are now its official heads and daily managers, although major decisions are made collectively. However, for reasons of security, you will almost never meet other agents face to face.

"We do not discuss our operatives with our clients. They are attracted by our reputation, but we disclose to them very little beyond the information they seek. We find that to be in the best interests of all involved. We are also highly selective in our clients. We decline to work for criminal organizations or those whose activities we find undesirable or dubious. And no, Miss Scrimshaw is not involved with the Agency . . . although we believe she would approve of our actions."

Mary's eyes were wide. "And you really think I might be fit for this sort of work?"

Felicity's voice was deep and rich. "We had been debating for some time whether or not to approach you. We were each convinced that you had the potential to become an agent, but we were equally concerned that the work might remind you too much of your past. We had no desire to make you unhappy, and we did not want you to attempt the work simply to please us." She smiled brilliantly. "But you have come to us, instead."

"Let us not congratulate ourselves prematurely," Anne announced in her usual brisk manner. "Mary, you must still listen to the assignment we propose and decide whether or not you wish to undertake it. And before that, we must turn to the question of skill."

"Skill?"

"We are interested in your skills of observation, Mary. Close your eyes and picture the room in which we received you. Can you tell me how many lamps there were?"

Mary found it easy to summon a detailed image of the room and her employers. "Three," she said with confidence.

"What are the dimensions of that room?"

"Roughly eighteen by twelve; the ceiling is about ten feet high and plastered smooth."

"And the table that was to your left?"

"It is round and made of walnut—about three feet high and eighteen inches in diameter. It has three legs. There was nothing on it."

"What jewelry am I wearing today?"

Mary paused to consider. Again, a mental image of Anne clicked into place. "An oval brooch made of gold and amber. It has a filigree border."

"And what time do you estimate it to be now?"

"I came to meet you at half past four. It must now be a little after five o'clock."

"Thank you, Mary." Anne nodded as though checking off an item on a list. "You did well—unusually so. I also believe you know something of the art of pugilism."

"Boxing?" Mary smiled at her employer's delicate phrasing. "I have no technique, and I fight dirty. But growing up near the docks, I learned to protect myself. I believe that all young women should know how; that is why I began teaching some elementary maneuvers to the older girls."

Anne nodded briskly once more. "The first phase of training, involving observation skills, self-defense, and a few other useful techniques, normally lasts for several months. However, given your background, this may feel like unnecessary repetition. Mrs. Frame and I have agreed that you may—if you choose—compress the initial training period into one month. It will mean a great deal of intensive work, and you may prefer to undergo the usual training period, which allows for a little more leisure and a greater margin of error. The choice is entirely yours."

Mary paused, suddenly dizzy at the prospect. In the space of an hour, her entire life had been transformed by these women, much as it had five years ago. She gazed at them but couldn't read their expressions. Felicity appeared casually unconcerned. Anne's gold-rimmed spectacles hid the expression in her gray eyes. And Mary thought she understood: their expectations didn't matter. It was entirely her decision. "I should like to begin as soon as possible," she said, her voice firm and clear. "I choose the intensive, one-month training."

"If we start tomorrow morning," said Felicity suddenly, "you'll be ready to commence practice fieldwork in May. The timing is excellent!"

Mary sat bolt upright. "Why is that?"

A look of amused resignation rippled across Anne's face. "Felicity, you're getting ahead of yourself."

Felicity bit her lip. "I'm sorry; I thought we talked about this: that if Mary knows what she's training toward, she'll be better able to focus and prepare."

A sharp tingle ran up and down Mary's spine, making her scalp prickle.

There was an appreciable pause. Then Anne began to speak, her voice dry and dispassionate. "During the mutiny in India last year, a number of Hindu temples and homes were robbed of precious jewels and sculptures. In at least two instances, these very unique items have made their way into private British collections. We have been asked to investigate a merchant who is believed to have handled a significant number of the smuggled artifacts. He is suspected of selling them to crooked antiquities dealers in London and Paris."

Mary frowned, disciplining her thoughts away from the sheer excitement of the situation and toward the problem described. "This task is beyond the scope of the police?"

"Yes and no," said Felicity. "These crimes did not occur on English soil and there is still no evidence linking our suspect to them. As such, Scotland Yard cannot act. Instead, the Yard has engaged us to find the connection and retrieve the evidence. It is a freedom available to us, as an independent agency.

"Our suspect's name is Henry Thorold. He is connected with the East India Company, the Far East Trading Company, and a number of American interests. Although he has warehouses in Bristol, Liverpool, and Calais, his operations center primarily in his London warehouse, located on the north bank of the Thames.

"Thorold has, in the past, been suspected of financial crimes—evading import taxes, some eight to ten years ago and, more recently, defrauding his insurers—but nothing was proven. We believe that our agent will be more effective. She describes it as a straightforward job that is likely to take a month or so. Of course, international trade is always precarious and subject to extreme weather conditions; ships might be long delayed, and our priority is to collect a significant and conclusive amount of evidence."

Mary nodded, trying to appear calm and patient. "I see. But you—you did mention that there might be a role for me in this case?"

Felicity smiled. "Not a major role, certainly. We already have an agent on the case who is conducting the bulk of the investigation. But there is a second post we thought might serve as a training ground for a new agent." She glanced at Anne. "Perhaps, Miss Treleaven, you could describe the post?"

"Certainly. Mrs. Thorold is an invalid who believes that her daughter, Angelica, requires a companion. She would prefer to engage a younger woman—not so much a chaperone as a paid friend, close to her daughter's age. The daughter, I gather, is rather spoiled and accustomed to having her own way." Anne paused, a glint of humor in her eyes. "I expect your classroom experience will prove useful to you, in that respect."

Mary thought of the month long training period. "But won't the post be filled by someone else in a month's time?" she asked.

"I think not. I'm due to meet Mrs. Thorold next week in my capacity as head teacher at the Academy. The negotiations will take some time, and Mrs. Thorold appears to be fairly slow-moving, in general."

Hmm. It sounded as though the ladies had been thinking of her all along. "And if I hadn't chosen the one-month intensive training . . . ?"

"If, at the end of the month we deem you unready, another agent will take the post and you will meet with an equally useful training assignment once your training is complete," said Anne firmly. "You mustn't think that this assignment depends upon you; that would be a gross overstatement of the importance of your role."

Mary nodded, blushing.

"However," said Felicity a little more gently, "you may train with this particular assignment in mind. It will be an opportunity for you to practice being insignificant and meek."

Mary digested that. The Academy trained its pupils to think rationally, to carry themselves with confidence, and to stand by their opinions. Presumably, a stereotypical lady's companion would have little use for those skills. "May I know more about the assignment?"

Anne studied her for a moment. "I don't suppose it could hurt. You'll receive a more thorough briefing before you begin the assignment—*if* you receive the assignment. But, in essence: the agent posted in the Thorold household will listen for news of a particular shipment coming from the Malabar Coast. There is a secretary living in the house—a young man who has been with the family for less than a year, named Gray. There is a chance that Thorold and Gray might discuss illegal business at home."

Mary nodded. "That seems straightforward enough. Is there anything else that I—that the agent, I mean—should do as well?"

Anne smiled at her disappointment. "You did mention that you're impatient. No, Mary. This is to be your first experience of fieldwork. We've chosen it precisely because it's a safe place in which to learn your craft."

"I understand," Mary murmured. "I'm a quick learner."

"I am sure you have further questions, but before we continue—" Anne leaned forward, her eyes intent. "Mary, at this time, you are still free to choose your course. You may leave us now and attempt to forget that this conversation tonight ever took place. Or you may choose to join the Agency. But should you choose to enroll, we must know that you are fully committed to the Agency and to its principles."

Felicity folded her long, shapely hands together. "The Agency is a covert organization, and we require absolute discretion from each of our members. Being a secret agent carries with it many known risks, as well as the constant possibility of unknown threats. Think carefully before you choose." She straightened her posture, seeming to grow more majestic with each moment. "In becoming a secret agent, Mary, you become part of a new family. When you are on assignment, we will be the only people who know where you are and what your purpose is.

"We will support and assist you in any way possible, and we will never ask you to go against your conscience. But there are times when you will feel very alone indeed. Don't rush, Mary, and consider carefully. We will not think less of you if you choose to return to the schoolroom."

Mary took a deep breath and sat tall. Her decision was already made. Her voice was perfectly steady as she said quietly, "I am ready to choose. I accept your terms, and I will carry out all assignments to the best of my abilities."

There was a moment's silence. And another. And a third. Then came the sound of chairs scraping against wooden floorboards as the ladies stood and clasped Mary's hands in theirs.

Anne beamed, pride ringing in her voice. "Mary, welcome to the Agency."

Two

Tuesday, 4 May

Number twenty-two, *may-dams*." The carriage juddered to a halt and the cabman tipped his hat with an ironic flourish to the two primly dressed women who descended.

Anne paid him with fussy precision, counting out the tuppences and ha'pennies under her breath. The cabman rolled his eyes, as if to say, *Bloody spinster governesses.* Once he was gone, Anne shot a small, encouraging smile at her companion. "Ready?" she murmured.

Was she? Mary felt a surge of nausea. It seemed as though all the vigorous instruction of the past month was evaporating before her mind's eye. All the physical training—self-defense, disguise, fitness—seemed irrelevant here, a short flight of whitewashed steps away from her first assignment. And what sort of spy craft could she need? Would there be scope for lock picking and knot tying, not to mention sleight of hand and questioning suspicious parties? The assignment entailed only listening and tea drinking. Perhaps she wasn't prepared at all. . . .

But Anne was still looking at her with a steady, watchful expression.

Mary lowered the handkerchief she'd raised to her nose. "Ready." Here beside the river, the smell of putrefaction was so strong she could taste it. Vegetation. Flesh. Sewage, both human and animal. All rotting. Add to that coal smoke and, beneath it all, the tang of salt water.

Anne pressed her lips together. "Ghastly, isn't it? Once this hot spell lifts, it ought to be quite a lot better."

"I hope so," Mary muttered. Her attention was focused on the house. Number twenty-two Cheyne Walk was a strange choice for a businessman. The Chelsea district was famous—perhaps notorious—for its bohemian atmosphere, but it was still rather seedy.

The house itself was a tall slice of Georgian wedding cake. Being so close to the Thames—it was right across the street from the embankment—its whitewashed façade was an uneven gray, frescoed with lumps of bird guano and soot. The steps, however, had been scrubbed that morning, and the door was promptly answered by a footman. Mrs. Thorold was expecting them; would they walk up?

It took several moments for their eyes to adjust to the dim stuffiness of the interior. The staircase leading up to the second floor was lined with oil portraits: a golden-haired girl, pretty but overdressed; a pallid boy in a sailor costume; a portly middle-aged woman displaying a splendid ruby necklace; and last, a middle-aged man with puffy eyes and the jowls to match. Mary studied this one with special interest.

The drawing room was at the front of the house. Its large windows were swathed in elaborate velvet drapes that excluded all daylight and any possible breeze. The air inside, still and stale, nevertheless held a definite suggestion of the river's stench, overlaid with rose potpourri.

"Misses Treleaven and Quinn, madam." The footman's voice was rather nasal.

Anne advanced and bowed. "Good afternoon, Mrs. Thorold. May I present to you Miss Mary Quinn? She is the young woman I mentioned in my last letter."

"I hope you will excuse my not standing, my dears." The lady's voice was flabby and tremulous. "I feel rather weak today."

Mary bowed, then raised her eyes cautiously. Despite the heat, Mrs. Thorold was wrapped tightly in a lace shawl, her face pale beneath an old-fashioned lace cap. Her blue eyes blinked shortsightedly at Mary and Anne. She was like a faded version of the woman in the oil painting, except that the painter had tactfully ignored her pockmarks, which were pronounced.

"This heat must be very trying for you, Mrs. Thorold." Mary's voice was hesitant.

"Yes indeed." The older lady nodded. "Enervating, that's what my medical men say." Her gaze wandered over Mary's face and plain, unfashionable dress. It was unclear just how much those unfocused eyes could make out in the gaslit gloom.

"Do sit down." Mrs. Thorold indicated the sofa immediately facing her armchair and turned to the footman. "William, you may serve tea. And—and tell Angelica I wish her to meet Miss . . ." She struggled briefly.

"Quinn," Anne suggested. It was Mary's mother's surname, adopted during her early days at the Academy. Mary Lang was still a wanted woman, having escaped her fate at the gallows—and besides, Mary preferred a less conspicuous surname for reasons she refused to name, even to herself.

Anne skillfully led the small talk, describing Mary's abilities as a paid companion—letter writing, reading aloud, good French, genteel taste in literature—and providing Mrs. Thorold with opportunities to quiz Mary on these subjects. Mary was just describing her current reading (a collection of sermons) when the drawing room door opened and Mrs. Thorold's face brightened.

"Angelica, darling. Come and meet Miss Treleaven and Miss Quinn."

It was the girl from the portrait—still pretty and still overdressed, although the eyes were now narrowed and hostile. Her gaze swept from Anne to Mary. "So you're *it*?" she demanded.

"I should like to be your companion, if your mother thinks it suitable," Mary replied.

"I don't want a companion." Stony blue eyes raked her over, taking in her meek posture and unflattering dress. "Especially a foreigner. Where are you from?"

"London."

Angelica snorted. "With those eyes and that hair?"

Mary couldn't prevent a defensive blush. "My mother was Irish. Some Irish people have dark eyes and hair."

"Only half English. . . ." Angelica twisted her mouth in distaste. "How old are you?"

"Twenty." The lie felt strange in her mouth. Mary knew she looked nothing like twenty, but no one was going to hire a seventeen-year-old.

Angelica's obvious disbelief was preempted by her mother's anxious quaver. "My sweet girl, where are your manners? Miss Treleaven will think you so rude."

The sweet girl dropped her gaze to the carpet and muttered a barely audible "How d'you do."

"It is a pleasure to meet you at last, Miss Thorold," murmured Anne. "I understand you're a musician."

Mary took her cue and jumped in with a gentle question about music. Between them, she and Anne cajoled Angelica into something like an ordinary conversation and eventually persuaded her to play for them. Mary braced herself for a syrupy popular ballad executed with a simper; instead, Angelica gave them a Bach prelude, very fast and stormy, and then pretended not to hear their startled expressions of admiration.

When the tea tray arrived, Angelica took charge automatically. She dealt out the cups with a clatter, deliberately stirred too much sugar into Anne's cup, and all but hurled the plate of biscuits at the guests. One or two tipped onto the carpet, but Mrs. Thorold seemed not to notice.

Despite the efforts of Mary and Anne, tea was drunk mainly in silence. Mrs. Thorold settled drowsily into her chair, smiling absently from time to time, while Angelica simply shoved a biscuit into her mouth and shrugged whenever a remark was directed at her. Through persistent questioning, though, they learned that Angelica was eighteen; had left her finishing school in Surrey last year; did not miss her schoolmates, as they were a dull and stupid lot; had no particular friends in London; took pianoforte lessons twice a week at the Royal Academy of Music; and otherwise filled her time with boring parties. It was difficult to tell whether she disliked Anne and Mary especially or if she was angry at the whole world.

When the tea tray was removed, Mrs. Thorold seemed to awaken. She struggled to sit upright in her armchair and sighed, "Well, my sweet girl?"

Angelica flicked a glance at Mary. "No."

Mary tensed. She had failed just like that? She fought an impulse to look at Anne.

Mrs. Thorold blinked twice, then sighed again. "Oh, my dear. We cannot continue this indefinitely, you know. It is so very tiring, for one thing."

"We can. Until you understand that I don't want a bloody companion."

Mrs. Thorold blanched. "Language, my darling!"

"Mama, I will not have a paid companion. Do you understand me?"

The silence stretched for several seconds, with all four women frozen in their chairs. It was Anne who finally broke the impasse. "Mrs. Thorold, I shouldn't like to force Miss Quinn's company upon Miss Thorold; that would be most uncomfortable for both."

Angelica smirked.

Mary inwardly slumped.

"But perhaps," continued Anne, "Miss Thorold would appreciate a different sort of companion? Someone older, perhaps, who could act as a steadying influence? I have in mind a senior teacher at the Academy who is—"

"Oh no," interrupted Angelica. Her eyes flicked from Anne to Mary to her mother. "Not an old biddy."

Anne turned her cool gaze on Angelica. "It's merely a suggestion, Miss Thorold. But as your mother wishes you to have some sort of companion and knows your best interests . . ."

Angelica scowled. "Oh, no, you don't." She turned to her mother. "Mama, tell her! Tell her we're not having anybody at all!"

A slight gleam appeared in Mrs. Thorold's faded eyes. She gingerly moistened her lips. "Er . . . that is, Miss Treleaven . . . I see the wisdom in your suggestion."

"*Ma–MA!*" It was more a howl than an exclamation. Mary half expected Angelica to throw herself onto the carpet and beat it with her fists.

Mrs. Thorold glanced at Anne. "Yes . . . I see now. Angelica, you must choose. Will it be Miss Quinn or an older chaperone?"

"You can't be in earnest!"

"But I am, my dear." Her voice was still soft, but Mrs. Thorold seemed to gain conviction from Anne's lead. She met her daughter's angry glare with a placid blink. "Miss Quinn is the eighth candidate we have considered for this position. She seems entirely suitable and very pleasant as well. You must choose, unless you wish me to choose for you."

Angelica was still sulking. Did she get that temper from her father?

Anne turned to her. "Perhaps a trial period might be best," she said calmly. "To see how you get on. If at the end of, say, a month's time, you find that you cannot tolerate Miss Quinn's company, I shall introduce you to Miss Clampett. She's a very brisk, efficient lady with many years of schoolroom experience. She's a great proponent of early morning constitutionals and cold baths."

"You're only trying to frighten me." But Angelica didn't sound certain.

Anne merely shrugged and consulted her watch. Turning back to Mrs. Thorold, she said, "I have enjoyed our meeting, madam, but regret that I must be on my way."

She paused, then asked casually, "Shall I try to keep Miss Quinn disengaged for a few days? We've another client who requires a young lady companion, but I *might* be able to put her off. . . ."

Three heads swiveled toward Angelica, who threw up her hands in disgust. "Oh, very well! I suppose even Miss Quinn is preferable to an old bag who plunges one into cold baths."

Mary reduced a triumphant grin to a demure smile. "Why, thank you."

The speed of her installation at Cheyne Walk was breathtaking, even by Anne's standards. Within a quarter of an hour, Mary's salary was negotiated, her duties reaffirmed, and the delivery of her small trunk arranged for later that evening. She would begin on the spot. As Anne took her leave, Mary felt a wave of sheer panic. Although her assignment was clear in her mind, she would have given much for five minutes' private conversation with Anne. Instead, she dredged up a shaky smile and made a modest bow. It wasn't as though she was completely adrift, Mary reminded herself. There was a simple letter-writing code by which she and Anne could exchange information. And above all, she had asked—pleaded, even—for this new task. This new challenge. This new life.

Before the drawing-room doors had closed on her so-called former employer, Mrs. and Miss Thorold had relapsed into what seemed their normal state: Mrs. Thorold dozed in her chair while Angelica practiced the pianoforte.

The music ended only with the appearance of the men. The sound of footsteps on the staircase made Angelica put away her sheet music, and even Mrs. Thorold appeared to wake up when the drawing-room door clicked open.

"Here you are, my dears, hallo, hallo . . ." A small, moonfaced, great-bellied man bustled into the room, dropping his hat on one side table, his gloves on another, and smoothing down a few wisps of combed-over hair that had come unstuck from his bald crown.

"You're rather early this evening, Papa," said Angelica sweetly, coming forward to have her forehead kissed.

"Hope I'm not interrupting your feminine chitchat," Thorold said, patting her cheek. He bowed respectfully to Mrs. Thorold and continued talking to Angelica. "Had a good day?"

"Yes, Papa. Shall I ring for your whiskey?"

"That's my girl." He turned to Mary politely. "I don't believe we've met, Miss . . . ?"

"Quinn. Mary Quinn." She bowed. "I've just been engaged as companion to Miss Thorold."

"Bless me, of course you have. I'm Henry Thorold, of course, and this is my secretary, Michael Gray."

Mary bowed again to the young man who trailed in Thorold's wake. "A pleasure to meet you, sirs." The secretary was good-looking in a pretty way, but it was to Mr.

Thorold that Mary's gaze returned. The man was instantly recognizable from the portrait on the stairs, of course. But his undignified energy and good humor came as a shock. She must learn to avoid stereotypes: there was no reason on earth why a ruthless merchant who evaded taxation and smuggled Hindu artifacts could not also be a jolly paterfamilias.

Drink in hand, Thorold lowered himself into the armchair beside Angelica's with a deep sigh. Michael chose a place on the sofa while Mrs. Thorold remained in her chair, rather outside the conversational triangle made by the other three. There was a silence. Finally, Thorold stirred himself to ask, "Anything to report, then? What has my darling been up to today?"

A short silence followed the question.

"Conversation and music, Papa." Angelica's voice was mild. So she behaved nicely in her father's presence, only letting loose with her mother.

Michael Gray smiled politely. "My congratulations, Miss Quinn. You must be exceptionally well qualified, if Miss Thorold has taken a liking to you."

Mrs. Thorold cut in unexpectedly. "Angelica and Miss Quinn will get on charmingly." It was definitely a command, despite her quavering voice. "And Miss Quinn will be useful at the party this Saturday."

"Party?" Thorold looked perplexed for a minute. Then he slapped one hand to his forehead. "But of course! The party!"

Angelica made a face. "About that party, Papa . . . Don't you think it's rather poor weather for a garden party? This—this—" Her voice trailed off as she searched for a polite word for *stink*.

"Miasma?" suggested Michael.

She ignored him. "This unseasonable heat is too much. Our guests will be most uncomfortable."

Mary looked at Angelica curiously. Why would a rich, bored young lady want to cancel a party?

"It is impossible to cancel now, Mr. Thorold," said Mrs. Thorold firmly. "The invitations went out three weeks ago."

"Our guests will understand our reasons for postponing," insisted Angelica. "They can hardly be eager to crowd into a drawing room twenty feet from the Thames."

"Then there are the preparations to think of," continued Mrs. Thorold as though Angelica had not spoken. "All that food ordered and the band booked and all those extra footmen and maids engaged. Not to mention the tent for the garden."

Thorold was looking from wife to daughter, as though at a tennis match. "You have a point," he said, vaguely addressing both.

"We cannot possibly cancel now; it's far too late," said Mrs. Thorold firmly.

"What about your health, Mama? It's so delicate," said Angelica simultaneously.

Both women turned to Thorold, awaiting a judgment. The silence stretched out for several long seconds. It was so quiet in the room that Mary heard him gulp. After what seemed like an age, he delicately cleared his throat. "Er . . . well, the thing is . . . we did—er—hum. There's the matter of . . ."

"Mr. Easton," said Mrs. Thorold crisply. All heads swung to look at her, and she slumped a little in her chair. "He's an excellent prospect for Angelica," she continued in a weaker voice, "and very much taken with her."

Thorold frowned. "It would be a shame to disappoint Easton. I saw him just today, and he told me how much he looked forward to the party."

"A suitor with money," pronounced Mrs. Thorold, "will make a pleasant change from the packs of fortune hunters swarming the house."

Thorold looked agreeable. "Told me he was after a contract in India! Clever chap . . . land of opportunity at the moment."

Mary leaned forward slightly, but that was all he said.

Angelica sighed heavily.

Michael looked at the ceiling.

Thorold nodded once. "Very well, then. The party must go on!"

Three

Saturday, 8 May

By midnight, all the Thorolds' guests had arrived with their ladies' maids in tow. Due to the weather, they avoided the tent in the beautifully lit but foul-smelling gardens, and the house was consequently a crush. Despite the extra footmen posted with large fans in the corners of every room, the air was thick and stale. The bouquets of hothouse flowers massed around the room already looked wilted, as did the footmen.

The heat aside, however, it was a beautiful gathering. Dozens of tall wax candles combined with the gaslights to make the room midday-bright. The young ladies wore frothy white dresses, lavishly trimmed with ribbons and flowers. Married and older women wore more colors, but for all ladies it was a season for dramatic décolletage, and showy gemstones glittered from a few dozen bare breast-bones. In their black dinner jackets and white ties, the gentlemen provided a dramatic contrast.

Gazing about the laughing, chattering, flirting, tipsy throng, Mary found it difficult to believe this polished luxury was built on creaking wooden ships and the backs of merchant sailors. International trade and dangerous labor had no place here, except as an unacknowledged, invisible source of wealth.

A fierce impatience knotted her gut. She'd spent four days living with the Thorolds. Four days keeping Angelica company. Four days absorbing hostile remarks and pretending not to notice sulks. Four days trapped in this dark, airless house while Mrs. Thorold went out in the carriage each afternoon. And all for what? The only bits of information she'd heard were sadly common-place. For example, Thorold had no obvious heir. His only son, Henry Jr. — the sickly boy in the portrait — had died several years ago, transforming the ambitious com-pany of Thorold & Son into the more subdued Thorold & Company. And last month, the parlor maid had been sacked for "immorality." She'd been six months' preg-nant at the time, and word in the kitchen was that Tho-rold was the father.

It was becoming clearer and clearer that Thorold and Gray never discussed business at home — at least not before the women. And there was so little time remain-ing: Anne and Felicity expected the assignment to end in just over one week. They'd sent her no additional instructions or information, which meant that they had no news — at least nothing that concerned her. She'd had no contact from the primary agent, which meant that her assistance was not required there. She was not to communicate with either the primary agent or the Agency unless she learned something concrete. And—completing the circle—the only way she'd discover anything would be actively to look for evidence of smuggling, and such. And—oh dear—it would be so much more interesting than wearing itchy dresses and fetching fruit ices for rude matrons.

She wouldn't. She should carry out her instructions to the letter.

And yet . . . what was the harm? There were, after all, only nine days left on the case.

She didn't know where to begin.

Oh, yes, she did.

The party was at its peak. No one would miss her for a mere quarter of an hour. She slipped past a knot of men near the entrance of the drawing room. Dressed as she was in a modest gray gown, most of the guests looked straight through her. Except—

A white shirtfront, rather wilted from the heat, suddenly loomed in front of her. "Where's the fire?"

She looked straight up into Michael's eyes. Green eyes. "I beg your pardon?" She sounded startled, breathless.

"You've been dashing about all evening. Avoiding someone?"

She laughed at that. "I don't know anybody to avoid."

"You know me."

"I suppose I do, slightly," she said, sounding a little surprised.

He made a comical face. " 'Slightly.' How very humbling, when I've been lying in wait for you all evening."

Was he flirting with her? Surely not. And how did one go about flirting back? Assuming one wanted to flirt back . . .

He seemed to enjoy the confusion written on her face. "Speechless?"

"I suspect you of trying to make me speechless."

He was really very handsome when he smiled like that. "Perhaps. But I'd like to try conversing with you as well. Will you grant me the next waltz?"

"Oh, I couldn't. . . ."

"Don't tell me your card is full."

"Of course not." She didn't even have a dance card. "But I shouldn't dance."

He looked amused. "Is it forbidden?"

"Of course not. It's only that—I'm not . . ." Mary gestured helplessly.

Michael's gaze traveled over her lightly, admiringly. "You look well equipped for dancing: female, two arms, two feet . . . that I can see, at any rate."

She had to laugh at that. "You are being difficult on purpose. I mean that I am not one of the young ladies. You ought to dance with someone else."

"I'm not an eligible bachelor. It's practically your responsibility to dance with me, you know."

"On the contrary . . . there seems to be a shortage of male partners. If you're so intent on dancing, you'd better ask one of the younger girls. That should be perfectly safe."

"I say, Gray!" commanded one of the men in the doorway.

"Coming!" Michael called. "This conversation is not finished," he warned her smilingly. "I'll be waiting for that dance."

She flashed him a cheeky look as she stepped around him. "You may wait all you like." Rounding the corner, she slipped down the corridor with a smile lingering on her lips. Perhaps flirting wasn't as difficult as she'd thought.

Both the noise level and the temperature fell somewhat as she neared the back of the house. The only room at this deserted end of the corridor was Thorold's office. The servants were below, feverishly producing more iced drinks, more food, opening more champagne.

Mary tried the door handle. Locked, naturally. She extracted a sturdy hairpin from her bun and crimped it deftly. Picking locks had always been one of her favorite parts of her old job: looking out for intruders while simultaneously listening to the tumblers of the lock required immense focus. During her training sessions at the Agency last month, she'd been pleased and surprised to find the old knowledge flooding back. Perhaps unsurprisingly, the talents she'd acquired as a young thief were all still there. She had struggled more with new skills, like code cracking. Now, however, she found that her nerves were unused to the pressure after all these years of ladylike respectability, and her hands shook in an alarming fashion. She stopped and forced herself to draw five deep breaths in succession. If she didn't calm herself, she'd only scratch the lock, lose her hairpin, and have to go back to the drawing room empty-handed. It was a sobering thought that helped to steady her fingers.

Her second attempt was much better. Almost immediately, she could feel the inside of the mortise lock— visualize the tenons revolving in their neat patterns. A brief burble of laughter from down the hall made her freeze, but its source didn't appear, and she continued her work. The last lever clicked into place, and she grinned. So satisfying.

The handle was well oiled. A glance inside confirmed that the room was empty, and she slipped inside, closing the door silently behind her. The heavy velvet curtains were open, and a blend of moonlight and garden torches half lit the room. She wouldn't need the stub of candle tucked in her pocket.

She turned to survey the office. To her right was Thorold's desk, square and massive and completely bare. Behind the desk sat a pair of filing cabinets, a tall wardrobe, and a drinks table with several well-filled decanters and a set of glasses. To her left was a series of glass-fronted bookcases filled with leather-bound books with gold-embossed spines. The windows were against the back wall.

She frowned and chewed her lip. She couldn't expect a miraculous discovery. Indeed, she told herself sternly, it was quite likely that Thorold kept all his trade-related documents at his warehouses. But she had to begin here in order to rule out the obvious.

She began on the left, with the bookcases. They had been recently dusted, so there was no way to tell if some volumes were more frequently used than others. Indeed, although the names were venerable—Milton, Shakespeare, Johnson—the books looked perfectly new. She pulled out a volume of Donne's sermons and smiled to herself: the pages were still uncut. Clearly, this library was purely for show. The rows upon rows of books were all like that—immaculate, respectable, untouched.

Until . . . as soon as she opened the door of the last bookcase, the one closest to the windows, she knew something was different. The pleasant odors of new leather and paper gave way to dust and . . . cigar smoke? She ran her eyes over the rows of books and began to realize that despite their elegant bindings, these were a very different type of book: *Aretine's Postures, The House of the Rod, Fanny Hill.* She selected one of the most worn and opened it: a tangle of naked bodies, some pink and white, some brown-skinned . . . some smiling, others—

Mary slammed the book closed, shaken. She wasn't an innocent. Growing up on the streets, she had seen obscene pictures before. But she'd never seen anything like this.

The women in these pictures were African slaves, and the white-skinned men their owners.

She fought a wave of nausea. Put the book back in its place. Swallowed a surge of bile that left a bitter taste in her mouth. She longed to wrench open the window and fill her lungs with the night air. Filthy as it was, it couldn't be worse than what she'd just seen.

Instead, she gave herself a sharp mental shake. Playing the delicate young lady was not an option. She was here to find information. Mary closed the bookcase firmly and turned to the rest of the room. The lock on the first filing cabinet was very simple. With a couple of twists of the hairpin, the catch released and she felt that tingle of excitement again as she eased the top drawer open. It slid quietly, revealing rows of neatly tied dockets, each clearly labeled by year and subject. *1836: The Americas; 1836: Bermuda and the West Indies; 1836: India.*

What was that sound? Mary glanced around the room. She distinctly heard something . . . but, straining her ears, she could hear only the distant voices of guests, punctuated by rumbles of laughter.

She returned to the filing cabinet. It didn't take long to learn that the files were old ones, ending in the year 1845. The second cabinet contained files from 1846 to 1855, but nothing more recent. Mary chewed her lip. The active files must be elsewhere. She peeked inside a few files at random just to be certain, but things seemed to be in order:

filed by docket number and date, without large gaps or other irregularities. Barring some sort of elaborate secret code, the files looked harmless. It seemed she would have to try the warehouse.

Again, that noise—like a small scraping. She paused to listen. Again, nothing but remote party noises.

Then, suddenly, something—footsteps clicking down the corridor and drawing closer. She slid the drawer closed—no time to lock it—and glanced about. Thought wildly about crawling under the desk, but as the footsteps neared, changed her mind. The wardrobe was nearby and—thank God—unlocked! She bundled herself inside, grateful for a narrow crinoline that allowed such freedom of movement. Pulled the door closed just as she heard the office doorknob click and rotate.

For several moments, Mary couldn't hear anything over the violent pounding of her pulse. She tried to draw a slow, deep breath. Then a second. A degree of calm returned with the third breath, and she blinked in the warm dark of the wardrobe. Her cheek brushed against a rough woolen garment—a coat?—and she could smell something like the blend of tobacco and male cologne that scented the bookcases.

Her mouth was dry. What was that sound in the room? Oh, why hadn't she taken the time to lock the door properly behind her? *Impatient*, she chided herself.

Slowly, a new noise entered her awareness, so gradually that at first she thought she'd dreamed it. It sounded almost like . . . quiet breathing. Yes, breathing. Not her own. And it was . . . behind her?

Preposterous.

Wasn't it?

Instinctively she caught her breath—and the other breath stopped half a moment later. After counting to five, she exhaled very quietly—and heard a faint echo a fraction behind hers.

Poppycock. She could not afford to indulge in this sort of panic. If she began now, where would it end? Right. She would have to demonstrate to herself, once and for all, that her imagination was getting the better of her.

Calmly, slowly, she reached behind with her left hand and came up against—yes, fabric. Fine linen, to be precise. So far, so good: she was inside a wardrobe, after all. The only problem was that this linen was oddly warm. Body warm. Beneath the tentative pressure of her palm, it seemed to be moving. . . .

With terrifying suddenness, an ungloved hand clamped roughly over her nose and mouth. A long arm pinned her arms against her sides. She was held tightly against a hard, warm surface.

"Hush," whispered a pair of lips pressed to her left ear. "If you scream, we are both lost."

She couldn't have screamed even if she'd chosen to. The sound was lodged at the back of her throat.

Her captor tightened the seal over her mouth and nose. "Understand?" His tone was level, his hand warm and dry. He could have been asking if she took sugar in her tea.

She managed, with difficulty, to nod once.

Long seconds slid by. The footsteps in the office came closer, then receded. The swish of metal on metal—once, twice—suggested that the curtains were being drawn.

Tears pricked at Mary's eyes and she forced them back, her jaw tightening with the effort. She would not, would not, *would not* give him the satisfaction of knowing she was frightened. Instead, she tried to evaluate what she knew about this man in the wardrobe. The voice was educated. Michael Gray? No. This man's scent was different—cedar soap and a trace of whiskey instead of the faint aura of macassar oil and pipe tobacco that clung to Michael. She surprised herself with her certainty on that subject.

The footsteps made another circuit of the room. Their owner emitted a dissatisfied "humph." Then, at long last, the door reopened, reclosed, and a key turned firmly in the lock.

Mary and her captor waited. She could feel his heartbeat, steady and slow, at her back. She counted to ten. Twenty. And then to thirty. Was he never going to let her go? She considered biting his hand.

Then his voice again, in her ear. "You will not scream or cry."

She shook her head weakly.

He waited several seconds before slowly uncovering her mouth.

She drew a long, shaky breath. Tried not to gasp as she did. She tried to move her arms, but his left arm was still locked round her.

After another pause, he released her arms, again slowly.

With trembling hands, she pushed open the wardrobe door and all but fell out. Strong hands caught her and set her upright—not harshly.

Slapping them away, she whirled round to face him. The room was almost completely dark with the curtains drawn, but she could make out a tall, lean figure.

A match flared brightly in his hand, giving her a glimpse of dark eyes and a harsh, uncompromising mouth. He produced a short candle and lit it, holding the light closer to her face. Its glare was almost painful after such prolonged blackness. They inspected each other for a long moment, then the corners of his mouth twitched. Did he find this *funny*? He looked as though he wanted to ask her a question, but seemed to think better of it.

She glared at him defiantly. Her own questions crowded her mouth, but she was determined not to speak until he did. After the heat of his body, her back felt cold.

He strode to the door, produced a key from his pocket, and unlocked it. Seeing that the corridor was unoccupied, he turned back to her and made a courtly gesture with his other hand. "After you." It was that same damned conversational tone.

Mary stared at him. *What the devil . . . ?*

He glanced into the hall again, then back at her impatiently. "Quickly, now."

Standing her ground, she shook her head slowly. "No. After you."

"Come, now—are we really going to squabble?" His tone was distinctly patronizing.

"I have no intention of squabbling," she said loftily. Now that he was talking, she felt more certain about holding her ground. "If you wish to leave, I wouldn't dream of stopping you."

He closed the door again and glared at her. "My dear girl, just what are you playing at?"

She looked at him haughtily. "You are hardly in a position to ask such a question."

The corners of his mouth twitched again. What an odd gentleman. *"Touché."* He paused and stared at the ceiling, as though for inspiration. "Very well, then. Might I propose that we leave the room simultaneously?"

Mary considered this. They could hardly remain. Apart from the risk of someone returning to the office, she would soon be missed at the party. He might be as well—assuming he was actually a guest. She inclined her head graciously. "An excellent idea," she murmured, mimicking his polite tone.

She glided toward the door, which he held open for her. They slipped into the corridor, and she watched while he locked the door again, then pocketed the key. It was a proper house key. How had he pinched that?

He glanced down at her, eyebrows rising arrogantly. "Well? Hadn't you better run along to the drawing room?"

Mary suppressed a powerful urge to hit him. With as much dignity as she could muster, she turned on her heel and walked quickly down the hall.

Four

Why hadn't she screamed bloody murder in that closet? As he stalked through the crowds in the drawing room, considering his next move, James Easton spotted his mystery lady assisting Angelica Thorold in the pouring of tea. They made a lovely contrast: Miss Thorold, with her blond ringlets and pink-and-white complexion, and Miss Closet (as he'd come to think of her), with her black hair and fierce eyes. What color were those eyes—hazelnut brown? It had been difficult to tell by candlelight. It was a distinctly un-English look that set off Miss Thorold's doll-like beauty to great advantage. Which was almost certainly the point.

Miss Closet must have paused to repin that hair. It was scraped back severely now, when a few minutes ago it had been tumbling round her shoulders. Her scent came back to him—clean laundry, lemony soap, girl. He'd been surprised by the absence of perfume and then grateful for it in that small space.

He considered her from the opposite end of the room. Her gown, plain and high-necked, made it clear that she was not a debutante. And her hair was wrong, too: the fashion for young ladies this season was a cascade of ringlets pinned high over each ear. Her role at the tea table seemed to confirm all that. Miss Closet kept back slightly, her gaze lowered, and poured cup after cup of tea. Miss Thorold, in contrast, stood forward, daintily adding cream and sugar to the cups and passing them to a string of guests—mainly admiring bachelors. James's elder brother, George, was part of the pack.

As though she could feel his open stare, Miss Closet suddenly raised her head and met his gaze. A prickle of energy, both pleasant and startling, rippled up and down his body. He had to force himself to remain still and expressionless. Her look was defiant when it should have been ashamed. She gazed at him a moment longer—taking his measure?—and then looked away haughtily, as though she had seen all she required. He bit back a grin. Arrogant brat.

The girl was rather attractive for a governess. She was no fool, either—her behavior in the closet suggested as much. A lesser woman would have screamed or struggled, or at least begun to cry silently. But her reaction had been quick, disciplined, and pragmatic. Not an ordinary young lady, then. Perhaps she was a poor relation? Finally, there was the question of what the devil she'd been doing poking around that office. Alone. In the dark.

James edged his way round the room, toward the open balcony doors. At this point, he'd take stench over stifling.

"Young Mashter Jamesh—what a shurprishe!"

He blinked and focused on the man who'd popped up beside him. "Mr. Standish. Evening." Warner Standish was an old family friend, a pompous fool, and a shameless gossip.

Standish's pointy reddish beard parted to reveal the cause of the lisp: a magnificent set of new wooden dentures. "Didn't think I'd run into you here, young fellow. Nearly time for your beddy-byesh!"

James shrugged. Was it worth pointing out that he was nearly twenty? Probably not.

"Are you at Eton or Harrow? I forget."

Neither. "I left school a few years ago, Mr. Standish."

"Ah. Then you're up at Oxford."

"No; working with my brother." James gritted his teeth.

"At that bridge-making thingy? How very peculiar!"

"Civil engineering is the family business." *As you perfectly well know, you old sot,* he added mentally.

"Where'sh your brother, then?" demanded Standish. "Not sheen him tonight."

"You must be the only one," said James through gritted teeth. Good Lord, George was embarrassing. Tonight he'd made a complete fool of himself over Miss Thorold, monopolizing her conversation, following her about with glasses of punch and plates of cakes, and trying to dance every waltz with her even though her dance card was full. Everyone had been laughing at George.

"Eh? Whashat?" hollered Standish.

James indicated with his chin. "Tea table."

"Ah. Awaiting hish audiensh with Mish Thorold, eh?"

"He's likely on his fourth cup by now. By the way," he added casually, "who's that pouring tea with Miss Thorold?"

"I think it'sh rather a queshtion of what, not who, dear boy."

James raised an eyebrow. "Oh?"

"I ashked about her earlier. Thorold *shays* she'sh hish daughter'sh new lady companion . . . name of Quinn. *Mish* Quinn."

"'Says' . . . ?"

"Given what jusht happened, it'sh hardly shurprishing, ish it?"

James shook his head. He was generally ignorant of gossip. "You'll have to explain it to me, I'm afraid."

Standish smirked. "One of the parlor maidsh ish on leave . . . for about nine monthsh, if you follow my meaning. Replashement's got a face like a horshe'sh arsh. Thish one turned up a month later."

James's jaw tightened.

"Thorold'sh a clever devil. Although I shouldn't have tried to pash her off ash a paid companion, m'shelf . . . rather obvioush, don't you think?"

"In his own house?"

Standish sniggered. "What could be more convenient?" He turned and looked across the room at Miss Quinn, still pouring cups of tea. "Tashty morshel, if you ashk me. Shomething exshotic about her . . . remindsh me of a Shpanish danshing girl I once knew. Or wash she Egyptian? Mmm—p'rapsh even shome short of half-cashte?" He sighed happily. "Damned if I can recall, but quite a houri, she wash."

James tried hard not to picture this. But the rest of Standish's argument made perfect sense. The girl was attractive, well spoken, unmarried. And she was young: sixteen or seventeen at a guess. It explained her low profile in this gathering. It also explained her unusual composure in the wardrobe and why she chose to remain silent and hidden with a stranger over being discovered with him and rescued. Yes, it was by far the most logical explanation for the mystery of Miss Closet.

"Is this generally known?" He kept his voice casual. "Or is it your theory?"

"Not pershuaded?"

James shrugged. "If there's no proof . . ."

Standish lowered his voice. "Don't you shee the ice between her and Mish Thorold? The young lady doeshn't like having her in the houshe."

James had, in fact, noticed the strain between the two young women. "Hmm."

Standish grinned at him broadly. "You're quite taken with her, aren't you?"

Tearing his eyes from Miss Quinn, James fixed him with a cold look. "I'm merely surprised that Thorold would introduce his mistress to his wife and daughter."

"Gone all high-minded and moralishtic, have you?"

"Merely wondering why they haven't clawed each other's eyes out by now."

"Perhapsh they've already had a go. I shay, if you're going to the bar, get me a whishkey and shoda, will you, young Jamesh?"

But James was already out of earshot.

Who could have guessed that so many guests would require tea on such a hot night? Mary discreetly wiped a trickle of perspiration from her forehead and hefted the steaming kettle. Pouring tea was an excellent opportunity for Angelica Thorold to display her charms—a soft voice, dainty fingers stripped of gloves, a glittering web of diamonds at her breast. And it worked: the table was thronged with men, many of whom were either bachelors or widowers. It wasn't that Mary begrudged the girl her social triumph, but after nearly an hour, this tea business was getting distinctly monotonous.

It was also embarrassing. Although Mary tried to keep her head down and stand behind Angelica, she was still the target of lingering looks and invasive stares. She had always hated being stared at. While most of it was harmless, there was always the danger that someone might look at her and guess the truth . . . and she couldn't afford to be spotted for what she really was.

She overheard odd snippets of conversations in which guests inquired about her. One or two of these had been deliberately loud in their speculations, making the blood rush to her cheeks and her hands clench round the teapot. She forced herself to calm down; temper and bone china were a poor mix. Mechanically, she poured another cup of Darjeeling.

"Hello again, Miss Thorold!" said a stocky, pink-cheeked man. He was about thirty, with light brown hair, a fulsome beard, and a bright sheen of perspiration coating his face.

Angelica laughed in disbelief. "Mr. George Easton! This must be your sixth cup of tea this evening!"

"Indeed, Miss Thorold, but I find I'm terribly thirsty this evening! It must be the heat!"

"Indeed?"

"Or the smashing tea! Or"—he leaned close— "perhaps it's the lovely lady who—ouch!" He yelped, pivoted, and scowled at the man behind him. "Stop elbowing me!" Then his voice flattened. "Oh. It's you, James."

James ignored him. "As my brother was trying to say, Miss Thorold, it's a lovely party."

In the act of handing a cup and saucer to Angelica, Mary's hand jerked with surprise and her head snapped up: the second voice. It was that man from the wardrobe! The cup wobbled in its saucer, then recovered. A moment later, however, one of George's more extravagant gestures tipped it again, sending a flood of scalding tea over Mary's left hand. At least her gasp of recognition was covered by a louder hiss of pain. She managed to lower the cup to the table without breaking it, although she did spill tea all over the table and floor.

Angelica jumped back with a little shriek. "You clumsy thing!" she cried, inspecting her dress for damage.

"I beg your pardon," muttered Mary through clenched teeth. "It was an accident." She fumbled about for a napkin with which to mop up the mess.

James was more efficient. Beckoning a passing footman, he said, "Clean up this spill." Glancing at Angelica, who was still fussing about her dress, he added dryly, "And fetch Miss Thorold's maid. Quickly."

"Miss Thorold, are you quite all right?" asked George. He took the opportunity to seize Angelica's hand. "What a nasty accident." He looked at Mary in accusation.

Angelica's shriek created a scrum of fussing guests: sympathetic young ladies, openly relieved that their own dresses were unstained, and gallant young gentlemen who continually reassured Angelica that she looked perfectly lovely, really she did. A clutch of middle-aged matrons bustled through and, in their rush toward Angelica, pushed Mary out of the way and toward the balcony doors. She didn't mind. Better to be ignored than scolded.

"Show me that burn."

The quiet voice made Mary start once again. She tilted her head back and looked up into James's dark eyes, expecting mockery or contempt. What she saw instead was . . . concern? She held out her hand. "It is not very painful."

He frowned. The back of her hand was covered in angry red blotches. "Scalds are always painful." He lifted a glass of punch out of a surprised guest's hand and scooped the bits of crushed ice into his handkerchief. "Here." His voice was brusque but his fingers careful as he folded a makeshift ice pack and placed it gently on Mary's hand.

"Thank you." Mary stole another look at him. He behaved like an older man, but in the bright lights of the drawing room, she could see that he was clearly much younger than she'd first thought. Why, he couldn't have been more than twenty!

"I apologize for my brother's clumsiness." James was tall and angular, George stocky and broad-faced. There was absolutely no family resemblance, unless one counted pushy behavior.

"No apology is necessary."

There was a lengthy pause. Then he said, "A physician ought to look at that."

"It's nothing," she insisted.

"Will the Thorolds think to call one for you?"

"My hand is fine." Her burned skin throbbed at the lie.

"Very well, then," he said after a pause. "If it's fine, dance the next waltz with me."

She gaped at him. A long second passed. And then another. "I beg your pardon?"

"The next waltz. Dance it with me." He sounded impatient. "You *do* waltz, don't you?"

"I can't—" Mary choked, and tried again. "I can't dance with you!"

He leaned in, slightly menacing. "Why not?"

Glaring at him, she stood to her full height—not that it counted for much—and enunciated clearly. "A gentleman does not command a lady to dance; he asks. If rejected, he leaves her presence."

The corners of his mouth definitely crooked upward this time. "That's all very well, but I believe you gave up your status as a lady when you climbed into that wardrobe with me."

"Hush!" Mary blushed and looked around guiltily. "You make it sound as though . . ." Her voice trailed off.

He raised one dark eyebrow. "Didn't you?"

They locked gazes for a long moment. James's expression was unreadable, Mary's openly hostile. Then she took a deep breath. "I can't dance with a guest. It would be inappropriate."

"Not as inappropriate as being rude to a guest," he said smoothly. "Isn't it your job to do as you're told?"

"You ought to dance with Miss Thorold," said Mary through gritted teeth.

"Her card's full." Then, as though a new thought had just occurred to him, he added, "It's not that I long to dance with you for your own charming self, you know. But we must discuss the incident in the office, and that is the easiest way."

Mary didn't want to dance with James Easton. She didn't like James Easton, not even a little. But her pride stung, all the same. "I never imagined that your interest was personal," she said stiffly. "And there is nothing to discuss. Now, if you will be so kind as to excuse me. . . ." She took a dignified step to the right and nearly walked into Michael Gray.

"My dear girl!" He caught her gently, his hands folding round her elbows to steady her. "What on earth has happened? I could hear the uproar from the billiards room."

He was heaven-sent. Mary resisted the impulse to stick out her tongue at James Easton. "I spilled some tea. By accident," she added hastily. "I think I splashed Miss Thorold's dress in the process. Her, ah, friends are rather concerned about her."

Michael glanced at Angelica, who was now being led from the room, bravely blinking back tears. "Good Lord, is that all? It sounded as though someone was being murdered."

He was still holding her arms. Mary shifted slightly and he released her with a teasing smile. "I am glad to see that you are unharmed and unhysterical." Then he caught a glimpse of her left hand and let out a sharp exclamation. "But you didn't mention seriously burning yourself!"

He seized her fingertips and, ignoring her protests, lifted away the improvised ice pack. The burns, which covered the back of her hand and wrist, did look violent: bright red and swollen from both the scalding tea and now the ice.

"It looks much worse than it feels," Mary said, squirming under his scrutiny. She could feel James watching the two of them. "Truly, Mr. Gray, it'll be fine."

Michael shook his head. "That's a shocking falsehood, my girl. Come. Let's go to the kitchen to get some salve for this burn. And call me Michael."

She hesitated. She didn't want salve. She wanted to be left alone to think about what this evening's events meant. And she ought to check on Angelica. Yet going with Michael would at least get her out of the drawing room and away from the scrutiny of James Easton.

Michael smiled—pure flirtation. "First you won't dance with me, and now you won't accept assistance from me. I assure you, Mary—may I call you Mary?—I don't bite."

Risking a glance at James from under her lashes, she saw his frown deepen. He had one of the most forbidding faces she'd seen in some time, better suited to an inquisition than a party.

"Salve?" she said sweetly. "What a clever idea, Michael." Placing her uninjured hand in the crook of his arm, she permitted him to lead her away.

Five

Sunday, 9 May

Throughout the morning, a steady parade of foot-men delivered a series of bouquets to the house. They were for Angelica, tokens of her status as a rich and attractive potential bride. There were so many that the drawing room looked like a greenhouse or a flo-rist's shop, with vases balanced precariously on every possible surface. Instead of being pleased, though, Angelica seemed bored and even unhappy. When the ladies gathered in the drawing room after luncheon, she curled herself into an armchair and stared out the window. Even after Mary encouraged her to play something on the pianoforte, she only got as far as riffling through her music books before slumping back into her seat.

"Where is Mr. Easton's bouquet, my dear?" asked Mrs. Thorold.

"I've no idea, Mama."

This was Mary's cue to seek it out and bring it to a position of prominence.

"Very nice," was Mrs. Thorold's verdict. "China roses and yellow jasmine against a background of ferns."

Angelica sighed and rolled over in her chair. "Delightful." Her sarcasm was unmistakable.

Mrs. Thorold blinked slowly. "What does it signify, darling?"

Angelica rolled her eyes and recited mechanically. "Roses represent beauty. Yellow jasmine signifies grace and elegance. Ferns speak of the gentleman's fascination. Therefore, the blossoms represent me, surrounded by the dark greenery of his admiration."

Mary bit her lip to keep from grinning. At the Academy, she'd heard of the language of flowers. Somehow, though, she'd never imagined it being taken so literally.

"A very delicate compliment," said Mrs. Thorold. "Mr. Easton is a fine prospect, my dear. Ambitious, of a good family, and it's obvious he's quite taken with you."

Angelica appeared to wake up slightly. "He is rather attractive, in spite of those fierce features." She seemed to consider. "I would have thought he was too young, Mama."

"He is one and thirty, my dear, and a good match for you in every sense."

"Oh. *George* Easton."

Mrs. Thorold's eyes widened. "You can't think I meant—really, Angelica!" She seemed genuinely annoyed. "A *younger* son? Have you learned nothing?"

Angelica made a sour face. "I don't see that it matters,

Mama. They're businessmen, not aristocrats with inherited titles."

Mrs. Thorold ignored this piece of logic. "You will forget about other candidates. This afternoon, you will encourage *George* Easton. Miss Quinn, you will ensure she does so."

"I take it you'll be in your room resting, Mama?" Angelica's jaw was tense.

"I'm going now, dear." She paused in the doorway and fixed Angelica with a sharp look. "Sit up straight and behave prettily. Or else . . ."

The moment the door closed behind Mrs. Thorold, Angelica sprang from her chair. "Behave prettily!" she snarled. "I suppose you'll be taking notes, Miss Quinn?"

Mary blinked. "I—well, no."

"And reporting every word to your kind employer?"

"What?" Mary asked faintly. Angelica couldn't be referring to the Agency. . . .

"Permit me to teach you a lesson, Miss Quinn." Angelica leaned over Mary's chair, her scarlet face just inches from Mary's. The effect was rather grotesque.

Mary tried to sound calm. "What is that, Miss Thorold?"

"My mother may pay your salary, but I'll make your life a living hell if you cross me!"

Angelica was very convincing. However, Mary was mainly relieved that her "kind employer" meant Mrs. Thorold, and not Anne Treleaven.

There must have been something in Mary's expression

that Angelica didn't like. She glared at Mary for a moment longer. Then, without warning, she seized Mary's burned hand, her sharp fingernails digging deep into the pink, blistered skin.

Mary sucked in a sharp breath. Her eyes watered with pain, but she managed not to scream.

Angelica stared into her eyes, daring her to move.

Mary remained perfectly still, choking down the urge to fight back.

After several seconds, Angelica let go. Her fingernails glistened red at the tips. "You've been warned."

The bloodletting seemed to improve Angelica's mood. When her callers began to arrive a few minutes later—there was one for each bouquet sent—she had achieved a reasonable degree of good humor, and there was still a faint pink flush on her cheeks. Mary returned to the drawing room, hand bandaged, in time to hear the footman announce, "Mr. George Easton. Mr. James Easton."

George led the way with quick, eager steps. He was immaculately turned out in a silk waistcoat and patterned cravat, his boots were brightly polished, and his watch chain gleamed as brilliantly as his smile. He'd even waxed the ends of his moustache. James, a few steps behind, was very soberly dressed: gray waistcoat, plain cravat. His mouth had a slightly cynical twist to it, visible because he was clean shaven.

Very properly, Angelica greeted the elder brother first.

"Mr. Easton! I must thank you for that exquisite bouquet. How did you know that I adore China roses?"

George bowed ceremoniously over her hand, then straightened and glanced around the room. "I am impressed that you remember which bouquet is mine, Miss Thorold."

She gave a tinkling laugh and presented her hand to James. "I must confess that I remember only my favorites." Settling herself in the middle of an unoccupied sofa, she glanced over her shoulder and said carelessly, "Ring for tea, Miss Quinn." With a graceful gesture, she invited the brothers to join her.

They sat.

Mary rang the bellpull.

Tea arrived.

From her place in a straight-backed chair near the window, Mary was in a good position to watch them maneuver and flirt. Angelica's manner was girlish and playful and focused very much on James. She tossed an occasional remark to George to prevent him from wandering away, but her preference was obvious. Mary couldn't be certain whether this was to spite her mother or because she genuinely preferred James.

Mary kept her mouth shut and pretended to knit. Her hand throbbed. For someone who played the pianoforte, Angelica had very sharp fingernails. After a little while, though, the conversation took an interesting turn.

"What I object to," said James, "is the way Florence

Nightingale has become a sort of modern-day saint. Nursing soldiers was one thing, but she's now the center of a ridiculous cult. When you think of those foolish young ladies leaping onto the first train bound for the Crimea . . . it was dangerous and utterly irresponsible."

Angelica tinkled with appreciative laughter. "Oh, how true!"

"Every bored old maid in England now thinks herself fit to play battlefield surgeon," he continued with lazy disdain.

"Without those 'bored old maids' in the Crimea, English losses would have been much greater." Mary managed to surprise herself: that clear, caustic voice was hers. Was she mad, intruding into their private conversation?

All three pivoted toward her.

James merely elevated his eyebrows. "True. But I am speaking of the tendency to romanticize the nursing profession. . . . It is a messy, ugly business, and so very few young ladies seem to understand that."

Mary raised her eyebrows back at him. "Certainly, the newspapers made Miss Nightingale and her nurses into heroines. They also romanticized the soldiers, and plenty of foolish young gentlemen still manage to buy commissions."

He sighed patronizingly. "When men enlist, they know they are risking their lives. When gently bred young women flock to a military encampment, they not only endanger themselves; they also distract those who must look after them and who ought to be thinking of other things."

"And males are only too eager to blame all their short-comings on the distraction represented by females," Mary retorted. "As though nurses are the only women in an encampment!"

George's jaw dropped at her rather obvious reference to prostitutes.

James grinned.

"I had no idea you two were so well acquainted," snapped Angelica, her eyes small and hard.

James seemed not to notice her tone. "Indeed," he said blandly, "I have not had the pleasure of a proper introduction."

George's face was rigid with disapproval.

Angelica could hardly refuse, although her voice was icy. "May I present to you Miss Mary Quinn. Miss Quinn, George and James Easton."

George shook her hand as briefly as possible. "A pleasure," he mumbled, his face suggesting anything but.

James bowed deeply over her hand, his lips not quite touching her fingertips. "*Enchanté,* Miss Quinn. I delight in meeting dangerous radicals."

She muttered something and snatched back her hand.

"Speaking of nursing . . . I hope your hand is beginning to heal nicely."

Her right hand was on fire. "Yes, thank you."

"Did the special salve help at all?" His tone was vaguely . . . insolent, she'd have said, except that he was her social superior.

Mary's chin lifted a fraction. "Indeed it did." If anything, the greasy ointment seemed to make everything worse.

"Such a relief to hear that," he murmured. "And how very kind of that gentleman to assist you so promptly. . . . One of the family, is he?"

What was he driving at? "Mr. Gray is secretary to Mr. Thorold," she explained in her starchiest voice.

"Ah. I thought I'd seen him before. Have you known him long?"

"Only for a few days, since I was engaged by Mrs. Thorold."

He raised one eyebrow. "I'd no idea you were so recently engaged. You seem so very familiar with the house."

Mary gritted her teeth. "You, too, seem to know the house—and the family—quite intimately."

His lips twitched in a familiar way. "Intimacies can spring up so quickly, can't they? That between you and Mr. Gray, for example . . ."

Angelica's expression underwent a sudden change from bored irritation to avid interest.

Mary frowned at him repressively. "I'm afraid *intimacy* is entirely the wrong word, Mr. Easton. Mr. Gray merely showed polite concern for my injury."

"Mr. Gray's 'polite concern' was extreme," James persisted. His mouth curved in a mocking smile. "Few husbands show such tender care to their wives."

Angelica's smile was hard and brittle. "Michael Gray fawns over all young females," she snapped. "It is his greatest fault. Papa says so," she added, as though that settled the matter.

George turned to her immediately. "I hope he does not tire you with such cloying attentions, Miss Thorold."

"He wouldn't dare!" Angelica tossed her head like a rebellious heroine in a novel. "He knows his place."

"I'm relieved to hear it."

"I hope you, too, know your place, Miss Quinn," drawled James.

Her face flushed with anger. "Are you lecturing me, Mr. Easton?"

"No, I am merely observing that young women in your . . . position . . . sometimes find themselves in rather awkward situations." He managed to make the word "position" sound particularly offensive.

Mary drew herself up in her chair, spine like a plumb line. He was alluding to more than the wardrobe incident. Fragments of last night's conversations came back to her: he was accusing her of being someone's mistress. But whose? Thorold's? Michael's?

James lounged back in his chair, crossing one ankle over the other knee. "Merely that governesses and paid companions occupy such a delicate place in the social hierarchy. . . . If a secretary—or another male—behaves inappropriately toward them, what recourse do the poor things have?"

Mary was livid. "You have a distinct interest in the powerlessness of women and strong ideas of where they do and do not belong."

Angelica suddenly spoke, her cheeks scarlet. "Are you—are you casting aspersions on my family, sir?" From the quaver in her voice, it seemed that she, too, had heard something about the former parlor maid.

The cursed man looked amused at the reaction he'd created. "Oh dear, I seem accidentally to have offended both of you. I beg your pardon, Miss Thorold."

Once again, Mary fought the urge to punch him.

Angelica still looked vexed.

George jumped in anxiously. "My dear Miss Thorold, my brother was speaking generally; no reflection upon you or your household was intended." He turned to his brother ominously. "Isn't that right, James?"

"That's right, George." James's tone was mild and suggested that all this fuss was someone else's doing.

Angelica's neck remained stiff, but in a few moments she relented. "I suppose it is a compliment that you respect my intelligence enough to discuss such matters with me."

"Naturally, my dear Miss Thorold." James's voice held a suspicion of laughter, but Angelica seemed to enjoy his use of "my dear." He turned that dark, persuasive gaze onto Mary. "Miss Quinn, I do hope we understand each other?"

She widened her eyes in mock innocence. "I believe we do, Mr. Easton."

"I am so relieved." Quite suddenly, James stood up. "I've been enjoying myself so much that I nearly forgot my next appointment. Thank you for the tea and the delightful conversation."

George looked startled. "What appointment?"

James smiled. "No need for you to rush off, Brother. I'll see you this evening."

Angelica blinked, her little pink mouth agape. It may well have been the first time a gentleman had left her company before she dismissed him. "Oh. I see." She blinked again, then rallied. "Good-bye, then. Until next time?"

"Until then. I'll see myself out. Good afternoon, Miss Thorold." He was at the drawing-room door when he turned to glance over his shoulder. "And Miss Quinn . . ."

She arched one eyebrow.

"Dare I fear you'll say 'good riddance'?"

Six

Monday, 10 May

The letter was addressed to G. Easton, Esquire, but when James saw the postmark, he opened it anyway. A brilliant grin lit up his face, and he went tearing across the main office to his brother's private room.

"We got it!" he bellowed, bursting through the door. "We're in!"

George jerked upright and scowled. "Bloody hell, James, can't you learn to knock?"

James thrust the letter in his brother's face. "Look! The railway contract. In India. We're going to build railways in India. We break ground in September, which means— my God—you'll have to leave by the end of the month! Earlier, if possible." He began to babble on about booking passage and quinine tablets but soon ground to a halt. "George? Are you listening?"

George looked up from his blotter. "Mm?"

"This is the biggest contract Easton Engineering has ever won, and you're going to go to India, and you look like someone's just stolen your accordion. What's wrong with you?"

George heaved an enormous sigh. "She has, in a way."

"I don't follow. Who's 'she'?"

"Miss Thorold, of course. At the party, I told her that I was a musician, too, and she seemed interested, but when I said I played the accordion, she—she *laughed!*"

James hid a smile. "Well, perhaps she was laughing sympathetically."

"It's no use. She thinks I'm a clown."

"That's not true," lied James valiantly. He noticed, for the first time, that George's desk blotter was covered in doodles: *Mrs. George Easton. Angelica Easton. George & Angelica.* The most popular was simply *Angelica*, surrounded by curlicues and hearts and arrows.

George rubbed his face. "The poets are right: it's a disease. I can't sleep, I can't eat, I can't work. . . . She's all I can think about."

"You ate a big dinner last night."

"That was different."

"Because it was roast chicken?" James tried not to laugh. "Come on, George. There are dozens of girls who'd marry you. Why Miss Thorold?"

George glared at him. "That question shows how tragically little you know about love."

"I'm rather relieved, if this is the other choice." James indicated the blotter. "You'll be writing poetry next."

George flushed from his hairline to his collar, and James began to laugh again. "No! Really? Oh dear."

"Are you quite finished mocking me?"

"Never, old chap. But let's talk about this new railway in Calcutta."

"What about it?" George sounded miffed.

"What do you mean, 'what about it'? You're going to be building it in a couple of months' time! In fact, it's just what you need. It's been too long since you've taken the lead role on a job, and it'll take your mind off Little Miss Whosit." James was genuinely enthusiastic. "In a fortnight's time you'll be on a boat, bound for the beautiful, spice-laden East, and all thoughts of Miss What's-her-name will have vanished from your thick skull."

George sat up straight. "Two weeks?"

"Well, you'll want to —"

"But that's plenty of time!" His eyes brightened and he smiled at James for the first time. "I can easily manage it in a fortnight!"

"Of course you can," said James, relieved. This was more like the old George.

George looked him straight in the eye. "Do you really think so?"

"Yes."

He sprang over the desk and shook James's hand enthusiastically. "Thank you! Your confidence means a great deal to me. I know you're not terribly interested in the matter yourself, and for a while you were downright dismissive of the whole thing, but it's smashing to know that my baby brother supports me—"

Not interested? Downright dismissive? Of the India job? James suddenly had the uncomfortable sensation that they were talking at cross-purposes. "Er—my confidence in what respect, George?"

"Why, for my marrying Miss Thorold and taking her to India with me!"

Oh, no. Oh, no. *"That's* what you meant?"

But George had stopped listening. "She's a healthy girl, not like her mother. The climate will pose no threat to her. And the romance of India—the beauty of it, as you said—will help me to win her!"

James sighed inwardly. Worse and worse. He'd been quietly opposed to the Thorold connection from the start, having heard some unsavory rumors concerning Thorold's business. However, he'd also been confident of ferreting out the truth before George got as far as a proposal—hence that search of Thorold's study. But a whirlwind courtship was a different matter. Even if Angelica seemed lukewarm, her parents were enthusiastic. They could force her to accept George's offer. James had very little time in which to act. And so far—thanks to Miss Quinn—he'd learned nothing.

"Here, before you go, tell me what you think of this!" George scrabbled about in a desk drawer and pulled out a sheet of lavender notepaper decorated with flowers.

James took the page and scanned it. "Would you like my honest opinion?"

George's face dimmed. "That bad, eh? It's bloody hard work rhyming the name Angelica, you know."

James took pity on him. "I'll write you a better poem." *But poem or no poem,* he added mentally, *you're not marrying into a family of crooks.*

Tuesday, 11 May

"Hoy!"

James didn't react to the first bellow. Adams, the foreman, tended to be excitable.

"M'sr Eas'n!"

That, however, he couldn't really ignore. James mopped his forehead and the back of his neck and turned reluctantly to investigate the most recent catastrophe that had befallen the building site. This job—the construction of a new tunnel beneath the Thames—had been a headache from the day they'd begun. It should already have been completed. Now the blinding stench of the river threatened to prolong it even more, as many of his best workers were fearful of catching disease from the evil smell. James wasn't convinced that the stink itself made one ill, but he'd still sent the workers home yesterday because they were retching too violently to work safely. If this weather continued, they'd have to work by night. It was either that or postpone the project until the autumn.

"I dream of the day," said James as he located the senior foreman, "that you address me as something other than 'Hoy.'"

Adams grinned and shoved his cap back on his head. "I b'lieve I called you 'oi' the other day, sir."

"And what is this?" He motioned to the scrawny little boy Adams held by the throat, muddy boots dangling in midair.

"This here lad—"

"Is strangling. Set him down."

Adams dropped the boy abruptly but kept a firm grip on his shoulder. "He's trespassing. He won't go away! I turned the little bugger out not ten minutes ago, and now it's back. Shall I chuck it in the river, sir?"

The boy drew breath to defend himself and immediately launched into a coughing fit that doubled him over. When he straightened, eyes watering, he turned to James. "Message for Mr. Easton, sir."

"That's what he keeps saying, but he won't give anyone the message! Says he has to speak with you, personal." Adams sounded irritated.

James sighed. "Go on, then."

The boy had regained some of his breath. "It's about—" he hesitated and looked at Adams suspiciously—"about that job in *Chelsea*, sir."

There was no job in Chelsea. James narrowed his eyes. "Chelsea."

"The *house*, sir."

Oh, good God. This was what came of hiring off-duty coppers to watch the Thorold house: they farmed the work out to little boys for a pittance of the fee he'd paid them to do the job properly. He should have known.

"Oh—that job." James nodded to Adams and beckoned the boy to follow him. As they strolled round the perimeter of the site, he looked sharply at the lad. "How old are you?"

"Ten, sir."

Old enough to be working, then. "How did you find me?"

"Didn't think I would, sir. Inspector Furley said something about a tunnel under the river, but he's dead drunk, and I thought he was talking rubbish again," the lad said, rubbing his nose energetically. "I wouldn't have come to you direct, but it's a matter of urgency. I take full responsibility, sir."

Despite his irritation with Furley, James was tickled by the boy's manner. "Well, then—give me your news."

The boy's narrative was clear and swift. The young lady he was assigned to watch had left the house at half past nine and taken a hackney cab to the customs house, where she sat watching its doors. After a quarter of an hour, Mr. Thorold emerged and melted away into the crowds. Instead of following him, however, she dismissed the cab and entered the building.

James frowned. "How did you follow her?"

"On the back of her cab, sir."

A grubby boy hitching a ride on the back of a cab — it was a common sight. "Good. What time was this?"

"Quarter of an hour ago, sir, p'raps a touch more. I watched the door for a few minutes, but she didn't come out. Since it's so close by, and p'raps a longish visit, since she paid off the driver, I thought you'd like to know."

James blinked in surprise. "Good thinking, er . . ."

"Quigley, sir. Alfred Quigley."

"Right. A sound morning's work." James tossed the boy a crown and turned on his heel. Then he paused and looked back at the boy. "Er — Quigley."

"Sir?"

"I won't be able to observe the lady all day. Follow me, and continue to watch her."

"Yes, sir."

"And from now on, you report directly to me."

The boy's eyes widened slightly. "What about Inspector Furley, sir?"

"I'll sort things with him. From now on, you're on my team."

James's timing — or rather, Alfred Quigley's timing — was excellent: his hackney cab drew up outside the gates of the customs house just in time to see a familiar figure emerge from the heavy double-fronted doors. She was heavily veiled and dressed even more plainly than usual, but he recognized her by the brisk certainty of her movements. With a light step, she let herself out through the gate and hailed a passing cab.

Feeling rather foolish, James muttered to his driver, "Follow that cab."

The cabman guffawed. "I've heard that one before, guv."

The roads were choked with people, animals, and rubbish of every sort, and it took a full quarter of an hour just to reach the end of the street. But the driver followed her through the chaos and finally over the Thames at London Bridge into Southwark.

The cabs drew up near the West India Dock, and James watched her emerge, glance around, then step down to complete her journey on foot. He watched from the privacy of his vehicle for a minute or two as her progress was slowed by her obvious desire to keep her skirts out of the muck. She kept them raised as high as decency permitted, to the tops of her narrow buttoned boots. Although it was midday, a moderate layer of fog blanketed the streets. As she disappeared into its depths, James calmly paid his driver, tilted the brim of his hat low over the eyes, and stepped down. There was no need to rush; he knew precisely where she was going.

Just round the corner, the warehouses of the merchant

trading company Thorold & Company occupied half an acre of reclaimed marshland on the south bank of the Thames. The red brick buildings were squat and square, with tall, narrow windows. They were likely only a couple of decades old but were already clad in a thick layer of dark grime.

Keeping back a bit, James leaned against a streetlamp—burning in a futile attempt to light the fog—and watched her pace slow even more as she neared the main entrance to the warehouses. She kept her veil down, but her head was turned toward the buildings.

What the devil was she after?

The area was busy enough—the movements and cries of errand boys, vagrants, a match girl, dock laborers, sailors ashore, men in tweed suits, and the odd early prostitute made it easy for him to watch her—but it was hardly a place for a lady. Especially one without a servant hovering two steps behind. Even with her veil lowered, she was attracting looks and the occasional remark. If she came to a halt, she would be harassed. James might be forced to go to her rescue. He wondered whether he would oblige.

Immediately after their encounter in Thorold's study, he'd begun inquiries about her. Although he was new to this cloak and dagger business, he did have some contacts. All he'd learned was that she had previously been a junior teacher in a girl's school, and before that, a student there. The school apparently took a lot of charity girls, and she seemed to have been one of them. At least he had not been able to discover family members or someone who'd paid her fees. The trail ended there. Miss Quinn had no friends outside the school, no one she visited regularly, and no other connections.

If anything, those few details were more perplexing than ever. Last night, he'd stayed up late, unable to sleep, staring at the meager details of her life: Mary Quinn, schoolteacher and paid companion. Date of birth: unknown. Birthplace: unknown. Parentage: unknown. Childhood: unknown. It was preposterous. According to his source, more information ought to be available, even concerning orphans raised by the parish. Either the girl was a spectacularly neglected orphan or she was living under a false name. Neither possibility made much sense.

James studied her as she inspected the warehouses. Her prim garments and graceful movements didn't suggest criminality or guilt. Yes, he knew that appearances were sometimes deceiving and that the mildest features could mask cruelty or vice. But he found it difficult to believe that she was an ordinary thief or an aspiring blackmailer—or Thorold's mistress. Lying awake in bed last night, he'd considered one preposterous scenario after another: she was Thorold's illegitimate child, searching for evidence of the inheritance Thorold had stolen from her, or an innocent girl forced (by whom? Gray?) into searching the office or . . .

Mary crossed the street and continued to walk slowly near the Thorold compound. She seemed to be examining the high iron fence, topped with spikes, which ran round the perimeter of the property. Her innocence was looking more improbable by the minute. James knew that his own actions were suspicious, of course. But his motives were straightforward enough.

He knew full well what he ought to do: forget about her, except when her actions affected his own quest. He knew, equally well, what he ought *not* do: he ought not waste his time—and lose sleep—wondering about her motives. He ought not worry about the dangers to which she might expose herself. He ought not waste time bandying words with her when he called on Angelica. And he most certainly ought *not* admire the slim elegance of her figure just a hundred yards ahead of him.

Certainly not the last.

And speaking of wasting time . . . he consulted his pocket watch. He'd now seen what Mary was up to, if not why, and he had to meet with a client in half an hour. James inclined his head slightly and stopped at a quiet street corner.

Mary drifted slowly from view.

"Sir?" Alfred Quigley popped up.

"Report to me this evening at my office. I shall be there until eight o'clock." He murmured the address.

Quigley nodded once and skipped off, immediately losing himself in the throng.

At seven o'clock the same evening, James was the last man at work at his offices in Great George Street. He generally was, although this evening he was distracted and unproductive. He had just resolved for the ninth time to stop thinking about Mary Quinn when a light scratching at the door made his head snap up. "Enter."

Alfred Quigley slid noiselessly into the room. "Evening, Mr. Easton."

"Well, Quigley?"

The lad's report was straightforward enough. Miss Quinn spent another ten minutes casing the warehouse grounds, then took an omnibus back toward town. She stopped on the way in Clerkenwell and purchased a number of items, including several yards of strong rope and some boys' clothing, paying cash for these items. Alighting again in Bond Street, she bought some ribbons and silk thread, which were charged to the Thorolds' account. The rest of her day was spent indoors.

James's expression darkened as he listened to Quigley's report. "What do you suppose she intends doing with this rope and costume?"

"Seems like she wants to get into the warehouse, sir. Although it's an unusual lady who can tie knots and things."

"Indeed."

He brooded for a few minutes longer. The silence was broken only by Quigley's attempt to stifle a yawn.

"I'm keeping you," James said abruptly. "You'd best get home and to sleep."

"D'you need me to watch the lady tonight, sir?" It was a heroic offer: his eyes were nearly crossed with fatigue.

"No. I'll go." James paused. The boy was only ten. "Do you have far to go home?"

"No, sir. I live with my mother nearby, in Church Street."

"Good. We'll speak tomorrow."

As Quigley disappeared, James's conscience jabbed him again.

"Quigley!"

"Sir?"

"Have you eaten?" Good Lord, he was turning into a nursemaid.

A broad grin appeared on Quigley's small, freckled face. It was the first truly boyish expression he'd displayed. "Eel pie and mash. They was beautiful, sir."

Seven

It was a quarter to one when Mary arrived at the warehouses of Thorold & Company for the second time that day. The street seemed still and vacant except for a couple of vagrants she'd passed curled up in doorways for a fitful night's sleep. Proper darkness never really fell on this part of London. The river reflected a great deal of light from the moon, domestic fires, and street lanterns, although this in turn was smothered by the dense fog. Tonight, Southwark was in the clutches of a pea-souper so thick it was like a physical presence. When, as an experiment, Mary held out her hand at arm's length, her fingers looked ghostly and not quite solid.

It was more than five years since she'd worn boys' clothing. She'd almost forgotten how comfortable and practical trousers were. And with her cap pulled low over her eyes, the cabman hadn't betrayed a flicker of interest in her destination or her purpose. He'd been more worried about whether she could afford the fare. Once the investigation was finished, she would have to do this again just for fun—although she could do without the trespassing and the stinking river.

For now, though, she needed to stay focused on finding the evidence. Thus far, she'd spent exactly one week with the Thorolds and had absolutely nothing to show for it. With the case closing in six days' time, she had to come up with something to help the Agency solve the case— didn't she? She'd debated the point with herself all day. Her original orders were only to watch and listen. Technically. But Anne and Felicity had good reasons for posting her within the household. It wasn't as though she was acting from personal nosiness or a desire to compete with the primary agent; she had the Agency's interests in mind. And she couldn't contribute if she didn't act. After all, what good was an agent who knew nothing, heard nothing, did nothing, and failed to use her brains?

That, at least, was what she'd been telling her conscience all day. Now it was too late to dither.

Shrugging off a lingering sense of being watched, she sidled up to the iron fence and experimentally inserted her head between the bars. It was a tight fit, but just about possible. In her days as a housebreaker, one of her mottoes had been, "Where the head will go, the body will follow." She dropped her bag of equipment through the bars and waited. If a guard dog was on the prowl, it would shortly make itself known.

A minute passed. Nothing . . . except that nagging

suspicion that she was not quite alone. She spun round: still nothing, of course. Ninny. With a swipe at her perspiring forehead, Mary squeezed through the bars with a slight grunt of discomfort. "Where the head will go . . ." In those days, she'd been flat-chested.

The cobblestones in the courtyard were slick. She found her equipment and picked her way carefully through the yard, alert for voices and footsteps. At the main building, someone had left the door near the loading bay unlocked. Honestly! Thorold needed better security. Mary realized that her uneasiness had vanished; if anything, she was enjoying herself. Her senses were heightened. A surge of exhilaration sped through her veins that had nothing to do with the justice or value of her enterprise and everything to do with being on the prowl once more. She'd lost sight of the pure, concentrated thrill of danger until now.

She eased inside, into tarry blackness. Bereft of vision, other senses slowly took its place. The quality of the silence was cavernous—even without a sound to create an echo, she knew the room was vast. It smelled of sawdust and salt, of pitch and resin. The floorboards were rough planks, gritty with sand and grime.

In the dark, it was easier to crawl than to walk. On all fours, she crossed that enormous floor, moving slowly and cautiously from pallet to pallet, all stacked high with crates. The gargantuan proportions of the room were confusing: when she reached the standard-size door at the other end, it felt oddly miniaturized. This one was locked, but with a lock so simple Mary had to smile. Why bother?

She eased the door open a crack and listened again. A faint shuffling sound resolved itself into footsteps. Pressing the door closed again, Mary flattened herself against the wall, keeping her ear by the keyhole, her breathing slow and shallow.

A sentry, trudging.

Coming to a halt just outside her door. The bright glow of his lantern cast a little beam of yellow light through the keyhole.

A sigh.

A pause.

A fart.

And then the footsteps receded.

She waited an additional three minutes, then slowly opened the door a fraction. Pale illumination came from a series of skylights cut into the roof of the building, revealing a broad flight of stairs. The moon was asserting itself, even through the fog.

Mary stayed close to the walls, testing each tread for creaks before placing her full weight on it. It was slow going. When she finally reached the top floor, she glided past the smaller doors toward the end of the hall. The imposing mahogany door at the end was obviously what she wanted. The brass nameplate confirmed it: H. Thorold, Esq. With a smile, she gently touched the doorknob. Locked, of course.

As she fitted a skeleton key to the lock, a faint growling sound seemed to emerge from the door. She paused, peered into the corridor behind her. Nothing. But the growl began to rise, from a faint rumble to a distinctly animal sound.

A dog. She nearly fumbled the key. A guard dog.

"Shhh . . ." she began hesitantly.

The growling continued, ending in a snarl. It couldn't be long before the beast exploded into full-fledged barking.

"Be quiet," she said with as much authority as she could muster. "I need you to be silent, dog."

There was a momentary lull in the rumbling.

"That's a good boy," Mary continued, wiping her perspiring palms on her trousers. "Very nice," she murmured encouragingly as the growling slowly subsided.

When all she could hear was its steady panting, she began to turn the key in the lock, speaking quietly and soothingly the whole time to the animal inside. The lock opened with a distinct clicking noise. As Mary tentatively pushed the door ajar, she continued to croon nonsense to the dog.

A pair of eyes gleamed at her from the darkness. Wolf eyes.

Her breath hitched in her throat. "Good evening, my dear," she managed to croak. "You've been a very good dog so far."

The eyes seemed to glow eerily. They didn't blink.

"I'd like to come into your office," Mary murmured, hoping she sounded calmer than she felt. "I'll begin very slowly, all right?" Crouching low to the floor, she inched across the threshold.

The animal actually seemed to pause and consider what to do.

A sudden recollection flashed through Mary's mind. With slow, careful movements, she groped in her satchel. When her fingers closed round the cloth-wrapped object, she heard the animal snuffle with curiosity. She unwrapped the item under its shining gaze: a chunk of cold boiled mutton. She'd taken it from the larder earlier this evening, anticipating just such a moment. She simply hadn't expected to meet the guard dog *inside* Thorold's office.

The animal sniffed once, then lunged at her. She felt a blast of hot, doggy breath, a cool paw. And then the dog retreated with its prize, gnawing at it with eager greed.

Mary slithered into the office, closed the door, and went limp with relief. Her back was damp with perspiration again, and when the dog came back to inspect her prone figure, sniffing at her with open curiosity, it was all she could do not to laugh aloud.

She struck a match and lit her candle. Girl and dog surveyed each other curiously. It—no, he—was a massive black mongrel. Short-haired, with big, floppy ears and an alert expression. Not at all the usual sort of guard dog, but she liked his ungainly looks.

"What's a man like Thorold doing with a lovely dog like you?" she murmured.

The dog seemed to shrug in reply.

They spent a few minutes getting to know each other before Mary reluctantly pushed her new friend aside. The clock on Thorold's mantel showed twenty-five minutes past one o'clock. "I must ask you to excuse me," she said apologetically, locking the office door. "I have a great deal of work to do."

Thorold's office at work was much like his study at home—no stray papers lying about, plenty of massive filing cabinets. Probably no obscene pictures, although one could never be certain. The procedure was simple enough: skim through the files, check randomly to ensure that they were correctly labeled, and replace as found. It was also quick work.

As quarter hours and then half hours slipped away, however, Mary grew frustrated. Once again, she hadn't expected to find stacks of incriminating information in the first file. Yet all these files were neatly numbered and docketed, and they correlated with other documents she'd noticed. There was no sign of the scrappy, informal type of documentation she associated with illegal trade. Then again, what did she know? Perhaps there wasn't any written evidence whatsoever. What then?

"What am I doing here, dog?" she asked ruefully. "It could take me weeks of nights to sift through all this."

The clock on the desk made a clicking sound, drawing her attention to it. Four o'clock! At Cheyne Walk, the servants would soon rise. She replaced the furniture as she'd found it and said a regretful good-bye to the dog. Any worries she had about his creating a fuss vanished when she unlocked the door. He seemed to understand the need for silence. After licking her hand affectionately, he crept back under the desk and lay there quietly.

Retracing her steps, Mary nearly ran into one of the night watchmen in the stairwell. Fortunately, he was so sleepy that he failed to notice the slight bulge in the shadows on the third floor landing. In fact, she'd had uncommon good luck all night, apart from the matter of the files themselves. As she slid through the bars of the iron fence, once again mashing her breasts in the process, it was still grayish dark outside. She would make it, she thought happily. She hadn't yet found what she was looking for, but she would—

Damn.

Absorbed in self-congratulation, she had forgotten the cardinal rule of housebreaking: stay alert and don't let your mind wander.

"Hail, fellow, well met," drawled a voice from the fog.

Large hands clamped around her upper arms. She sucked in a breath so sharp it hurt. She could discern only the general outline of her captor: tall, lean, male.

Instinct took over when fear might have paralyzed.

Mary struck out, stamping on the man's instep, using her elbows as weapons, twisting hard and fast out of his grasp. His face loomed indistinctly in the gray mist, and she attacked again, landing a hard punch on his nose.

He grunted, cursed, and stumbled back a step.

She took that as her cue to run. Sprinting toward the nearest bridge, she could hear his footsteps pounding after her. He had a significant size advantage; unless he was quite injured, he would catch her. She dropped her satchel in favor of speed.

Even as she fled, wisps of fog brushing her face like so many cobwebs, something tugged at her memory. Her assailant seemed vaguely familiar. Not that she was tempted to turn round to check.

The voice?

The shape of his head?

Something tugged hard at the back of her jacket—his hand, perhaps. She let the jacket slide off her shoulders without breaking stride.

Just before he caught her, she had a moment of sick premonition. It had been the same way the first time—the last time—she'd been caught. A flash of dread, of knowing. And then it happened.

A hand seized the back of her shirt, hauling her up short with a ripping sound. The seams cut into her underarms, and she went flying backward, landing with a thud against a hard, angular body.

"You damned fool!" snarled a familiar voice. "Stop fighting and I won't hurt you."

Mary froze, elbow poised in mid-jab. She couldn't decide whether to be grateful or appalled. "Let me guess," she said weakly. "You'd like to waltz?"

Eight

James Easton had never before experienced the urge to wring a girl's neck. It was a powerful one, however, and he kept his fist clenched round her coarse cotton shirt in order to avoid acting on it.

"You and I," he growled, swinging her round to face him, "are going to talk."

"Perhaps later," she suggested. "After supper and the charity raffle."

For all her flippant words, her eyes were wide with fear. Good. At this moment, he wanted her to be *terrified*. He kept a firm grip on her shirt—she could hardly run off without it, could she?—and marched her alongside as he retraced their steps and retrieved her scattered belongings. Jacket. Bag.

They kept marching back toward the warehouse until they saw, looming in the mist, a large black carriage.

She stiffened as soon as she saw it. "Oh, no."

"Oh, yes."

"I am not getting in that with you."

"Why not?"

She squirmed against his grip. "It's . . . not proper."

He would have laughed, except that she'd knocked his sense of humor sorely out of joint along with his nose. "But running around London in the middle of the night, dressed as a boy, is."

She had no reply to that. A minor miracle.

He opened the door and tossed her inside like a bundle of laundry, then climbed in and barred the door.

She moved immediately toward the door on the other side.

Lunging forward, he pinned her to the bench, one hand clenched on each narrow shoulder. "Don't bother trying. You'll not get out until I tell you to." Glaring at her, he rapped the ceiling of the carriage twice. The vehicle lurched into motion.

Her hair had come loose during her flight. She looked ridiculously young. And she'd lost most of the buttons on her shirt—they must have popped off when he'd grabbed it. Color flooded her cheeks, and she clutched the shirt closed with a sudden movement, making him blush and avert his eyes. "May I have my jacket?" she whispered.

He passed it to her but couldn't manage an apology. His tongue lay like a stone in his mouth. Instead, he busied himself with drawing the curtains on both windows.

An awkward silence ensued. It was Mary who broke it. "Your nose is bleeding."

James blinked and touched it experimentally. "So it is." He fumbled for his handkerchief.

"Is it . . . broken?"

He couldn't help it: the corners of his mouth turned up. "You sound hopeful."

She began to laugh, then quickly stifled it. "Not at all," she said hurriedly. "I didn't intend to—that is, I meant to punch you that hard; only I didn't know that it was you. . . ." Her voice trailed off.

"Does it look broken?" He lifted the handkerchief and leaned toward her.

Slender fingers traced the bridge of his nose, so lightly he could scarcely tell she was touching him. "Possibly . . . At the very least, you'll have a bruise."

"As long as it's not pointing to one side, I'm not worried."

She drew back her hand uncertainly. "You ought to see a physician."

He grinned suddenly, then winced. "That's what I said to you. Did you?"

She waved dismissively. "It's healing."

James was startled to find that he was enjoying her company. The glint in her eyes, her saucy attitude, the intimacy of the carriage . . . It was high time to return to the matter at hand. "So, Miss Quinn, what is your interest in Henry Thorold's private affairs?"

All warmth drained from her face as she straightened her spine. "That is none of your concern."

"Ah, but it is," he insisted. "My family might soon be linked with the Thorolds. As such, I must know why you broke into his warehouses tonight and what you found."

"Is that why you're sneaking about? Spying on your future relations?"

He tried to look ashamed but failed utterly. "A sad commentary on our modern times, isn't it?"

"Tragic," she snapped. "I'll leave you to mourn in private." She banged the roof twice, sharply, and reached for the door latch.

James leaned back and crossed his arms. "I don't recommend leaping from a moving carriage, Miss Quinn."

He was right. The carriage continued to bowl along at a fast trot. She glared at him. "Why aren't we stopping?"

He couldn't repress a small smile. "Because my coachman is well trained. He knows my knock."

She stared at him for a second, then pulled the curtain aside. "Where are we, anyway?" Because the inside of the carriage was lit, all she saw was her own face in the window.

He shrugged. "Twickenham perhaps?" What would it feel like to touch hair that silken straight? He pushed away the thought the moment it formed.

Her entire body stiffened. "This is kidnapping!"

"No, it's not. Don't flatter yourself, Miss Quinn."

She narrowed her eyes. "Then what do you want?"

"Merely a brief conversation. I'll return you to Cheyne Walk once we've had our talk."

"Do you really expect me to believe that?"

His lip curled. "My dear Miss Quinn, if I wanted melodrama and cliché, I would go to the theater. I am not kidnapping you. I have no ulterior motive. And yes, I expect you to believe me. Now let us talk. It will be to our benefit to share information, and possibly even work together. Or at least, not against each other."

He expected more indignation. Instead, she folded her arms and eyed him coldly. "Fair enough, I suppose. You first."

"I recently learned that some private investors lost heavily in several of Thorold's trade expeditions over the past few years. Apparently, Thorold claimed that the ships were either wrecked or lost at sea. However, these investors have since come to believe that, contrary to his claims, the ships were not actually lost. They think that Thorold has kept the profits for himself instead."

She looked skeptical, and he hurried on, anticipating her questions. "Normally, it is difficult to dispute these sorts of events: each ship is registered and its progress charted. It is quite a public event when ships are lost or capsized, and it does happen. However, the goods on these particular passages were smuggled and the investors expected to receive a high return on their investments by avoiding duties and taxes. For the same reasons, Thorold was able to be vague about the details. It would have been easy for him to lie about the shipments."

James noted with satisfaction that she was listening

in earnest now. The girl was infuriating, but at least she wasn't a ninny. "You appreciate, of course, the position I am in: it's potentially very embarrassing."

"Is it the smuggling itself that bothers you or merely the double-crossing? Honor among thieves and all that."

"There's no need to sneer. I object to both."

"And so you decided to investigate . . ."

"Yes."

"Why do so yourself?"

"Discretion isn't a good reason?"

"One can buy discretion."

He nodded. "It's also a matter of time. George wants to propose to Miss Thorold very soon, and I need evidence in hand if I'm to stop him."

That made sense. "What was the cargo?"

He paused reluctantly. "Opium mainly. But I'm told that Thorold is also interested in gemstones."

"And when was this?"

"Between two and seven years ago, according to my source."

She thought about that. "It's quite likely that all the records from those journeys have long been destroyed. If they existed in the first place."

He scrubbed his face with his hands wearily. "I know. This is also why I've not gone to the authorities."

"I take it you're interested mainly in the China route, then."

"I'm not sure. . . . Opium is also cultivated on the

Indian subcontinent, and the bulk of Thorold's trade lies there."

Mary stared at him in disbelief. "So you've no idea where the ships originated or what route they might have taken?"

"I've just begun my research," he said defensively.

"And you expect to learn all this . . . how?" She gestured incredulously. "By following me around London?"

His left eyebrow rose. "Melodrama again?"

She sighed. "I simply don't see why you think I might be useful to you."

"Frankly, I'm more concerned that you might be harmful to me. Now that I've explained myself, what's your interest?"

"It won't take long to tell. You'd better tell your coachman to drive for Chelsea; I need to be back before the servants are up and about."

"Not till you've explained yourself."

She fixed him with what she obviously thought was a withering look.

He shrugged amiably and glanced out the window again. "Then again, it's a lovely day for a long drive in the country."

"Oh, very well," she sighed. She paused, appearing to collect her thoughts. "I believe you know about the Thorolds' last parlor maid, Gladys."

He kept his face very still, his expression neutral. "Yes."

"Her sister hasn't heard from her since she was

dismissed, which is unlike Gladys. The sister is a friend of mine. She is extremely concerned and asked me to try to find out what's happened to her."

He waited for several seconds, but it seemed she was finished. He stared at her in disbelief. *"A vanished servant?"*

"Yes."

"And you expect me to believe that?"

"Now who's indulging in melodrama?"

He frowned. "It sounds like a task for the police."

"Rather like yours?"

He frowned but didn't pursue it. "What did you find tonight?"

She sighed. "Nothing."

He thought about rifling through her small satchel to be sure, but that was too rude. (A strange idea, considering how he'd manhandled her earlier.) "What were you looking for?"

"Everything, really. Letters. Instructions. Records of payment. Anything that refers to her or to homes for fallen women or brothels or workhouses or any of the places she might have ended up."

"But why would Thorold have those documents? Mrs. Thorold is in charge of the domestic staff."

"Mrs. Thorold doesn't appear to have any files; she dislikes putting pen to paper. And really—do you think that a man like Thorold could ask his invalid wife to deal with the fate of a maid whom he'd seduced?"

"But why would he keep records concerning her? Wouldn't he just kick her into the street?"

Mary looked scornful. "You would suggest that. And I admit, it's quite likely. However, Gladys was pregnant. Thorold lost his son a few years ago, and he has a sentimental streak. There's a slight chance he may have tried to help the girl, perhaps even maintain contact. He could never acknowledge the child publicly, but that doesn't seem to stop some men."

"I see." He was silent for a minute.

"Will that affect your brother's attitude toward Miss Thorold?"

"No. George has absolutely lost his mind over her. Besides, the old pregnant mistress plot won't affect us legally." He caught the look on her face. "No disrespect intended toward your friend Gladys, of course."

"Of course." Her voice was glacial.

He coughed awkwardly. "Er—I don't suppose you remember whether any of the documents you saw related to—"

"Your interests? There was nothing to do with opium, in any case. Everything I found was legal. Most frequently, Thorold's ships carry manufactured goods, like textiles and stainless steel, to India and transport back things like tea and rice. Occasionally the ships make a third stop in America or the West Indies but much less so these days."

"I see."

"Do you?"

It was impossible to read her expression. Her eyes—nut brown in some lights, greenish in others, he now knew—were steady, defiant. He didn't know how to reply. She had a dark smudge—coal? dirt?—on her cheek that was, for some reason, rather charming.

"What was all that nonsense the other day about my being Thorold's mistress?"

He hoped the dim light masked his blush. "It was merely a theory."

"It sounded like an accusation."

The heat under his collar intensified. "I apologize." He uttered the words with difficulty.

Amusement flickered in her eyes. "It's not often that you do, is it?"

He grinned despite himself. "No. You're in select company."

"Well, as long as we're being civil to each other, why don't you return me to Chelsea?"

Obediently, he thrust his head out the window and called instructions to the coachman. "It will only take a few minutes," he said, taking out his watch. "We're nearly at Battersea and it's just past five o'clock."

"Thank you." She looked faintly self-mocking as soon as she'd said it.

"Oh, it's been my pleasure entirely, Miss Quinn." He grinned. "We must do this again soon."

She couldn't quite repress a smile. "As soon as your nose heals, perhaps."

He ran one finger along the bridge. "It should be fine. Where on earth did you learn to fight like that?"

"Like what?"

"Like a man, I suppose. Most young ladies would have screamed and tried to claw at my face. Or perhaps simply fainted."

"I was a tomboy."

"A tomboy with a lot of brothers?" He could picture it: a slight, fierce girl surrounded by a pack of hulking boys.

"Something like that. And now you owe me an answer: how did you know I was at the warehouses tonight?"

He looked smug. "I saw you inspecting them earlier."

Her eyes widened. "This morning? But how did you know I'd be there?"

"I, er, was informed of your whereabouts."

"Who by?"

"By an employee."

"You were having me watched?"

"I suppose it wasn't very sporting of me. . . ."

She considered for a moment, then admitted, "I'd have done the same thing in your situation."

From the sound of the carriage wheels, they were crossing Battersea Bridge. In a minute, they would be at Cheyne Walk itself.

"Look—I think we ought to collaborate," he said, sitting forward.

A small frown appeared between her brows. "Why?"

"Because we can cover more ground that way," he

said impatiently. "And because we'll run less risk of interfering with each other's inquiries, not to mention putting Thorold on the alert."

"But we're looking at entirely different events and time periods."

"But for similar types of proof . . . assuming they exist. Look, you can't keep breaking into the warehouses to read Thorold's files night after night. You might have one or two more opportunities at most before a watchman catches you. If you still haven't found anything concrete at that point, what will you do?"

"Improvise, I suppose."

"Precisely. And that's where an associate would be useful."

She eyed him warily. "And you, naturally, would be the perfect associate."

"I found you tonight, didn't I?"

The carriage came to a halt. James glanced outside. "We're just around the corner. Lawrence Street," he said. "This do?"

"Perfect." She moved to get out, but his long fingers closed over hers on the door handle.

"Think about it, at least."

She froze, her face mere inches from his. "Why are you so certain you can trust me?" she asked softly, looking straight into his eyes.

His gaze was steady. "I'm not. But I'm willing to take that risk."

Nine

Wednesday, 12 May

Mary entered the house the same way she had left, through a window at the back. It was half past five in the morning and the servants had just begun their day's work. Her absence seemed to have gone unnoticed. She ought to have been able to sleep for a couple of hours, but she was too distracted. Instead, she lay in bed fretting while images of the night's adventures swarmed her brain. The eerie fog. The cavernous warehouses with their peculiar, shifting shadows. That charming dog. And, above all, the dark gaze of James Easton.

The way he looked at her was disconcerting: carefully, lingeringly, as though she were a puzzle to be deciphered. And she wasn't uncomfortable in his presence. That was odd. Normally, if someone—especially a man—stared at her for longer than a few seconds, she wanted to bolt. Yet with James, her desire was to stare back, to examine him as closely as he did her. It was an impulse that made her both elated and wary. She couldn't afford to find him intriguing . . . could she?

Then there was her new cover story about Gladys. She'd been polishing it for a while, making it believable and realistic. It had been the perfect opportunity to try it out. So why was she slightly disappointed that he'd swallowed it whole?

She finally achieved a restless half sleep but was awakened the next minute by a servant bearing a cup of tea and muttering about bath water. Her sheets were tangled round her legs as though she'd spent hours in the clutches of a nightmare. Even after she had bathed and dressed, her limbs felt rubbery. Her eyes were gritty with exhaustion. At moments, she felt positively dizzy from lack of sleep.

Mornings with the ladies were leisurely to the point of boredom. Mrs. Thorold and Angelica breakfasted in their bedrooms and appeared only after the men had gone out. During these hours Angelica was mute and sluggish, yawning as she and her mother took turns dictating little notes to Mary and dozing in armchairs. With luncheon, the mood shifted. Mrs. Thorold, with the single-minded dedication of the invalid, drove out most days to see one of her array of physicians. She was much addicted to these expeditions; although the family could easily afford to pay for house calls, there was something about the outings themselves she seemed to find compelling. And really, how different was her routine from the elaborate social visits most ladies conducted instead? With use of the carriage thus monopolized by her mother, Angelica either practiced the pianoforte or had a music lesson. The girl was a talented musician and it was tempting to stay and listen, but during this time, Mary could do some sleuthing while "taking a little stroll" or "running a few errands."

Today, however, even her bones felt hollow and she was oddly clumsy, dropping things and bumping into door frames. After luncheon, she briefly considered trying to interview the domestics about recent changes in the household routines or deliveries of items that could possibly be the looted Indian artifacts or gems. But the servants were still shy of her. Her position as lady's companion was a strange one. She was technically a servant herself, of course. Yet she dined with the family, and her bedroom was on the same floor. She called the servants by their given names, while they addressed her as "Miss Quinn." It would have been extremely odd for her to fraternize with them or to venture belowstairs. Even the sullen little skivvy who woke her each morning seemed wary of her.

Mary stifled another yawn. Perhaps a dull book would lull her to sleep. After a nap, she would feel more herself. The parlor connected to the drawing room was cool and dark, and she browsed the shelves with heavy eyes. The books here belonged mainly to Angelica, and the selection was slim: Gothic novels and albums of sentimental poetry, with the odd work of "improving" literature.

She chose, at random, a volume called *A Garland of Poetic Posies* and settled into a wing chair in the gloomiest corner of the room.

The house was quiet, apart from the emphatic chords of the pianoforte in the next room. Half an hour might have passed in drowsy stupor for Mary before the music halted abruptly, mid-phrase. This itself was not unusual, but then Angelica's sharp whisper caught Mary's attention. "Michael! What are you doing here?"

"Talking to you, of course."

"Do be serious!"

"I am perfectly serious. Mrs. Thorold is resting, I assume. Where's Miss Quinn?"

A pause. Then Angelica sneered, "Don't you mean Mary?"

A lady would make her presence known, thought Mary. Shuffle her feet, or cough discreetly, or something. But she continued to sit very still.

Michael's voice was tense. "Are you suggesting that I'm too friendly with Miss Quinn?"

"I don't need to suggest anything. I saw you flirting with her at the party and rushing to her rescue. Everybody saw!"

He sighed. "That was the point. I thought we decided it would be best if I distracted her. Showing interest was the easiest way to do so."

There it was: the unflattering truth behind Michael's flirtatious behavior. Mary wondered if her feelings ought to be hurt. Perhaps they were a little, but her curiosity was stronger than her pride. She was more interested in learning what she was being distracted from.

"There's 'showing interest,' and there's behaving like a besotted puppy!" snapped Angelica. "What a ridiculous performance!"

"I'm sorry you feel that way." Michael's voice was quiet, but it vibrated with restrained emotion.

"I'm not the only one. Miss Quinn thinks you're a fool, too, you know. She spilled that tea deliberately to attract attention. And it worked! You and James Easton came charging to her rescue, making spectacles of yourselves —"

"Enough," he interrupted. "Someone's going to hear you."

But Angelica continued, her voice rising and beginning to shake. "She's up to something, you know. She sits there looking as though butter wouldn't melt in her mouth, batting her eyelashes at you and Papa, and you fall for her act. You think I'm too stupid to see what's right before my eyes, but it's you who's blind!"

"Keep your voice down."

"Don't touch me! It's true, it's true. You don't believe me now, but you'll see!"

There was an extended silence. Was Michael hurting Angelica? No. It was too quiet for that. Mary counted to twenty before they spoke again.

"You didn't answer my question: where are Mrs. Thorold and Miss Quinn?"

118

"Why does it matter?"

"I need to speak with you. In confidence."

Another long pause. Then came Angelica's voice, sounding uncertain. "Mama's in her room. Miss Quinn is . . . God knows where. She often goes for a walk after luncheon."

"I hope 'God knows where' is far away."

"You're being very mysterious, Michael."

He sighed. "Your father is up to something."

Angelica tried for a careless laugh. "He's always up to something! Honestly, if I had a penny for each time he concocted a new scheme . . ."

"You'd be an heiress. Which you are." His voice was quite humorless. "Listen to me. Your father is planning to send you to Brighton for the summer."

She gasped. "What?"

"He's not going, of course. He's talking about letting a house for you, your mother, and Miss Quinn."

"What? He—why would he do such a thing?"

Another of those heavy silences.

When Michael spoke again, he sounded grim and tired. "He *says* it's due to the unusual heat—he's concerned about your health, and that of your mother."

"That's nonsense. Mama's health has been delicate for years; there's no reason for him to be concerned this year, above all others."

"Actually, there is. The weather's far too hot for the season, and the almanac calls for more of the same.

Everybody knows that the ghastly odor coming from the river causes infection and disease. All the best doctors are warning about the dangers of the miasma."

She sighed. "All the same . . . the timing is . . ."

"I know."

"Did he tell you about this?"

"He asked me to find the Brighton house. I'm meant to be with the estate agent now."

Another of those damnable silences. Mary dearly wished she could see their faces, their postures.

"Do you think this has anything to do with—"

"I don't see how. Yet it's the likeliest explanation."

"But who would suspect—"

"Let's not speak of it here. Can we meet privately?"

"Tomorrow. The usual . . ." The floorboards creaked. Their voices became fainter, until they were barely audible; they must have moved to the farthest end of the drawing room. For a few minutes, Mary could barely make out murmuring. Then, suddenly, there was more movement—rapid this time.

In a moment, the drawing-room door clicked open and Mary heard Mrs. Thorold's plaintive voice. "Who was that, darling?"

"Who was what?"

"I thought I heard voices."

"Er . . . mine, perhaps? I was humming a little."

"No, not that sort of voice. I thought I heard a man."

Angelica's laugh was forced. "As you can see, Mama, I'm perfectly alone. I can't imagine what you mean."

Mrs. Thorold grunted softly. Mary pictured the two women, staring each other down in the soft gloom. At last, she seemed to relent. "Perhaps I was mistaken, my dear."

"Perhaps you're feeling unwell!"

She sighed. "Where is Miss Quinn?"

"She's probably out walking somewhere." Angelica paused. "*Are* you feeling ill, Mama? You do look a bit . . . different. In fact, you look absolutely flushed!"

"Do I?"

"Mama, have you been exerting yourself? You really ought not move quickly or do anything difficult. Your own physicians tell you so."

"Yes, darling."

"And why are you dressed to go out?"

"I'm fine, darling"—The assurance was unconvincing—"only I rushed down the stairs a little because of those voices."

"Oh, poor Mama. Shall I help you back upstairs? You really ought to rest a little more."

"No, no. I must go out."

"So soon after luncheon?"

"My appointment is early today. Ring for the carriage, darling; I'm late as it is. And my hat . . . I must have my hat."

Even Mary knew that Mrs. Thorold wasn't the sort of woman who rushed for anyone.

Mother and daughter exited the drawing room with Angelica sounding kinder in that moment than Mary had ever heard her. And when, a minute later, she heard the drawing-room door click softly for a second time, she thought she knew why.

Ten

It was a little after midnight when James's carriage drew up in a narrow alley not far from Thorold's warehouses. He slid open a window and listened attentively. London was never quiet at night. Some areas, like the Haymarket, were only beginning their long nights of drinking and revelry, of course, and their streets would be thronged. But even industrial zones such as this one had their constant sound scape: the ring of horseshoes on cobblestones, the odd voice from a boat on the river, the lapping of the tide. An open fire burned somewhere by the Thames, its dull roar distorted by the water.

He got down from the carriage to stretch his legs. Barker, his coachman, gave him a look and tilted his hat even lower over his eyes. He found this sort of nocturnal prowling beneath his dignity but had accompanied James on both nights with a long-suffering air.

James ignored him. Instead, his attention was attracted by the manic barking of a dog. A rather large dog, from the sound of things. It was coming from . . . within the warehouse gates? He took a few steps closer, his body tightening, ready for action. A pair of male voices joined the dog's, their cries unintelligible, drowned out by the thumping of their boots against cobblestones.

He heard her footsteps, light and efficient, before he saw her. She was dressed in the same dark boys' clothes, a rough cap pulled low over her ears, sprinting with admirable speed. For a moment, only her face was visible in the shadows. It wore an expression of intense worry.

"This way." He stepped out of the alley, and she stumbled, barely regaining her balance and pulling up short. Alarm contorted her face, but the look quickly shifted to recognition, and she pelted toward him.

Ignoring his extended hand, she vaulted into the carriage unassisted. James sprang in after her. There was no need to thump the roof tonight; he was still closing the door as the carriage sprang into motion. He fell into his seat with an amused grunt. At least the girl wasn't dull.

Still ignoring him, Mary snuffed both candles inside the carriage and pressed her face against one of the windows. The night was dark and the streets narrow and rutted, but Barker was driving as fast as possible, the carriage was light and well sprung, the horses fresh.

James glanced out of his own window. The two men were still in pursuit, with the dog nearly at the carriage wheels. As Barker gained speed, however, the human figures quickly began to recede. A shrill whistle a few moments later called off the dog. For her part, Mary remained tense at the window for a minute longer before turning round and sprawling across the seat. Her breathing was rapid and shallow and her face flushed.

James grinned. Her current posture was more suited to a sailor than a lady's companion.

So was her speech. The first intelligible phrase he heard was "Damn the dog."

"You must prefer lapdogs."

"Hardly," she snarled. "I made friends with that bloody dog last night. That's why he came after me. He wanted to play!"

Was she glaring at him? It occurred to him to relight the candles.

The warm, yellow light seemed to prompt her. With a faint blush, she scrambled into a more ladylike position: knees together, hands clasped in her lap. "Er . . . thank you," she murmured faintly. "For . . . hm."

James ignored this. "Were you going in or coming out when they spotted you?"

"In," she mumbled. "I was just past the fence."

"You're damned lucky I happened to be in the alley."

She lifted her chin. "I'd have managed something."

"Hogwash," he said brusquely. "They'd have caught you in another minute." He fixed her with a fierce look. "They hang thieves, you know."

She caught her breath on a sharp inhale. Her cheeks flushed a deep pink. But all she said was "You were only in the alley because you want information from me."

"And I had to settle for saving your life."

"Well, you must be very pleased to have me in your debt." She was certainly glaring at him now. "Where are we going, anyway?"

He looked at her for a long moment, considering. "That depends."

Her eyes widened. "What on?"

"Are we going to work together?"

She shifted warily. "I haven't decided yet."

"Well, decide now."

"Why?"

Why? Was she being annoying just for the sake of it? "On second thought, never mind. I'll just dump you in the Thames instead."

She startled him by grinning—not sarcastically but with genuine amusement. "You'd like that, wouldn't you?"

"It's tempting," he admitted.

"I still don't see that working together will be of any use."

"We've each been grossly unproductive so far," he pointed out. "We can hardly get worse. At the very least, if we share information, we won't duplicate our labor."

"Hopefully."

"I could be helpful to you."

"That's a load of rubbish. You merely want to keep an eye on me."

"Do I?"

"Of course. You're not the collaborative type. Why don't you just say what you mean instead of attempting to manipulate me with specious arguments?"

He grinned. "Very well: I don't trust you, and I wish to keep an eye on your activities. Naturally, you feel the same way."

She pretended to mull it over for a little longer, but the slight relaxation in her posture told James she'd already decided. At last, she nodded grudgingly. "Very well. But this is to be an equal partnership—you will share all your information, and I mine."

"But of course."

Her eyes narrowed. "If I find that you've deceived me or kept information from me, I'll hurl you to the wolves."

"Likewise."

"And don't assume that because I'm female, I'm incompetent. I will not have you second-guessing me or protecting me."

"Naturally."

Their gazes locked for a long moment: testing, challenging, confirming. Then James abruptly held out his hand.

Mary merely blinked at it.

He raised an eyebrow. "Well? We should seal our agreement."

One corner of her mouth crooked up. "A gentlemen's pact?"

"Something like that."

She hesitated for a moment longer, then tentatively placed her fingers in his. Her hand was hot and dry and so fragile-seeming that James cradled it gingerly. The next moment, she squeezed so hard his eyes widened.

Fragile lady be damned. He squeezed back spitefully. "Vicious minx."

She smiled and withdrew her hand primly. "I did warn you. . . ."

He snorted and poked his head outside to have a word with Barker.

"Doesn't your brother wonder why you keep driving around in his carriage?" she asked once he was reseated.

James was irritated. "Why do you assume it's his?"

"Because he's older. Aren't you his apprentice?"

"I'm an equal partner. And I do a lot more engineering work than he does."

She was visibly surprised. "You must have started straight from school."

He nodded. "George needed my help."

"What about your father? Isn't it a family business?"

"He's dead."

"I'm sorry," she said quietly. "My parents are dead, too."

He pretended not to hear. "We share a house, too. For

now, that is. If this Thorold business turns out all right, I'll have to go. I don't fancy living with newlyweds."

"Miss Thorold seems to prefer you to your brother," said Mary slyly. "If this business turns out all right, perhaps your brother will have to move out."

Amusement gleamed in his eyes. "Do I look the type to ruin my life by falling in love and getting married?"

"Well, if that's your attitude, you'll certainly end up a lonely, embittered old man."

"Oh, I'll marry eventually," he said calmly. "But when I do, it'll be for the right reasons."

"Which are?"

He waved his hand vaguely. "Money. Business contacts. Political connections."

"And in return, your wife would get . . . ?"

His expression suggested that it was an odd question. "A husband, of course."

"That's it?"

"What else do women want? Flowers? Jewels? Sonnet sequences? Children?" He shrugged. "I can manage all that."

Mary eyed him skeptically. "Sonnet sequences?"

"Well, a proper sonnet sequence would be rather time-consuming, but poems are easy. I made up one for Angelica as an acrostic, using each letter of her name. George signed his name to it, of course, but I wrote it for him." He grinned. "You don't believe me, do you?"

"Not a word."

"Well, your name is a bit too short, really, but it takes no time at all. The lady doesn't have to know that, of course."

"Go on, then. Make an acrostic poem with my name."

"All right. Let me see. . . . Maiden with the ebony locks, / Armed with potent charms and looks. / Release me from your potent spell, / Your—er—"

She made a sound that was midway between a shriek and a groan.

He stopped, surprised. "What?"

"Stop the carriage. I'm jumping into the river."

"Is my poem that bad?"

"Your poem is ghastly," she said sincerely.

He looked annoyed, then suddenly relaxed. "You're the most plain-spoken woman I've ever met."

"I'll not apologize for that."

A hint of a smile played across his lips. "I think I mean it as a compliment."

"Oh." She smiled at him—a proper smile this time, that made his cheeks suddenly warm.

He frowned. "At any rate . . . we should discuss our next move."

"Certainly." She was all business once again.

"Tonight was your last chance at the warehouse. They'll be on guard from now on."

A pained look crossed her face. "For some time, at least. Perhaps I—we—could try again in a few days' time."

"Very well, then. We've looked at the private study

and part of the office. Thorold's unlikely to keep his papers anywhere else."

"Not unless there's a third office . . . one devoted to the illicit trade."

His gaze was sharp. "Have you heard of such an office?"

"No," she admitted.

"Right. I'll make some inquiries in that direction, but in the meantime we need a new course of action."

"We'd better hurry. Thorold intends to pack off the family to the seaside as soon as possible. I think it likely that he might be planning something quite soon and is therefore getting them out of harm's way." It was the closest she could come to telling him about the seventeenth of May — the deadline set by the Agency.

"Using the heat as an excuse?"

"Yes. He and Michael Gray intend to remain in town, of course."

James shot her a look. "Gray. Of course. Was it he who told you?"

"Not exactly . . . . I overheard a conversation."

"Between Gray and Thorold?"

"Involving Gray," she said carefully.

"And he was definitely speaking for Thorold?"

"Yes."

"I see." James brooded on that for a moment, then shot Mary a suspicious look. "You seem rather intimate with Gray. What else has he told you?"

She hoped the rush of warmth to her cheeks did not signify a blush. "I am scarcely acquainted with Michael Gray," she said stiffly. "I *accidentally* overheard a conversation of his earlier today, and I'm sharing the information. According to our agreement." And if she'd been inclined to part with the rest of the information, his suspicion had just canceled that.

He raised his eyebrows sarcastically. "Naturally."

"You don't believe me, of course."

He leaned back, legs and arms crossed. "Why should I when the evidence of my senses suggests otherwise?"

"The evidence of your senses? More like your fevered imagination!"

"He came flying to your rescue after you burned your hand, and carried you off into a private area of the house. You blush whenever I mention his name. You're blushing now. *And* you're on a first-name basis with the man," he said flatly.

"And on this circumstantial evidence, you call me a liar!"

"Aren't you?"

"I don't know why I imagined such a collaboration might be possible," she muttered. "Let me down."

"You don't even know where we are."

"I don't care." She reached for the door handle.

He grabbed her wrist, and she chopped at his hand. With a grunt of pain, he wrestled her back into the seat, twisting aside just in time to avoid a knee to the groin. "Stop fighting, you idiot!"

Suddenly, she went limp. Her whole body was trembling, and her cheeks were flushed a deep pink.

"Histrionics are becoming a habit with you." He placed one hand on her forehead. She was burning up.

"What are you doing?"

Instead of answering, he picked up her left wrist. The burned skin was still red and puffy, but there was something new: a row of four crescent-shaped marks that had broken the skin. They were unpleasantly discolored and swollen.

"Let me guess: You feel light-headed? Weak? Overheated?" She nodded each time, and he sighed. "It's because you have a fever." He indicated the infected punctures. "This must be Angelica's work."

She said nothing.

"It's a good thing George keeps a flask of whiskey in the carriage."

She stared at him. "This is hardly the time for a drink."

"You stubborn idiot," he said amiably, fishing around in his pockets. "I told you a physician ought to look at your burn."

"It was healing nicely enough before. . . ."

He raised an eyebrow. "What? Before Angelica clawed you? Rather vindictive of her . . . although I'm sure you deserved it."

Mary eyed the row of things he had laid out on the seat: a flask of whiskey, a pocket knife, and a handkerchief. "Oh no. You're mad if you think I'll allow you to slice my hand open."

"Don't be an idiot. It's got to be drained and cleaned."

"Stop calling me an idiot!"

"Then let me clean your wound before it goes septic and kills you!"

She sighed and held out her hand. "I'm not a liar."

He half smiled. "You funny thing. Brace yourself," he added, opening his penknife. "This will hurt."

Eleven

Thursday, 13 May

She had forgotten to close the blinds. When the first rays of sunlight warmed her eyelids, Mary's eyes popped open. She half sat up in a rush, then slumped back against the headboard. How much of last night had been a dream? Running from the warehouse . . . James Easton looming up out of the shadows . . . that strange argument . . . James cleaning her infected wounds with whisky and a pocketknife! He'd accompanied her back to Cheyne Walk and stood watch as she scrambled back into the house.

Before going to bed, she'd bandaged her hand and taken some willow-bark powder to combat the fever. Now as she sat up, listening to the servants' pattering footsteps, she realized that she felt better than she had in some time. Not rested, of course—she'd been up for two nights running. Yet her body didn't ache as much, and she felt more clearheaded.

Her bedroom door opened on a violent shove, and the

kitchen maid appeared, slapping a cup and saucer on the bedside table. "Tea." It was closer to a snarl than a word.

Mary smiled gratefully nonetheless; she was parched. "Thank you, Cass."

The girl remained stone-faced. "Mary-Jane-says-there's-trouble-with-the-hot-water-pipes-and-will-you-have-your-bath-in-here-miss."

"Of course." They were always having trouble with the pipes, and this announcement was part of the morning routine. As she bathed and dressed, Mary considered the new complication of James Easton. (They'd arrived at first names last night at some point between their wrestling match and his supervision of her predawn scramble through the window: a series of humiliations she shuddered to recall.) He'd demonstrated that he was active, intelligent, and—she hated to admit it—not incapable of kindness. After all these good years at the Academy, she was still so surprised by kindness. But, Mary reminded herself, he was also arrogant, rude, suspicious, and convinced of the natural superiority of men. She *quite* pitied Angelica for preferring him to George.

She needed more willow bark, so took the servants' staircase down to the housekeeper's office. As she rounded a corner, she very nearly walked into a tall, grimy man who was loitering in the corridor. Judging from his clothing, he belonged to the stables and ought not to be in the house at all. She blinked up at him, waiting for him to mumble his excuses.

Instead, he stared down at her with glazed eyes. A slow grin stretched his bristly face. "Well, if it ain't the new missy. . . ." His breath reeked of gin.

Mary drew herself up to her full height and met his gaze directly. "You must be lost. I suggest you return to the stables by the kitchen door."

His jaw sagged in mock offense. "Wouldn't hurt you to be friendly-like, miss," he mumbled, swaying slightly. "Never pays to make enemies with the lower staff, y'know."

Despite herself, Mary was amused. After all, it was rather good advice, no matter who was giving it. "I'm not being unfriendly," she pointed out. "But you certainly ought to leave the house before one of the family finds you here."

He flapped one hand at her carelessly. "Shows h'little you know," he said with a leer, leaning comfortably against the wall. "Nobody says boo to old Brown . . . least of all you, missy."

"And why is that?" As soon as she heard her own sharp tone, Mary regretted the question. What was she doing bandying words with Mrs. Thorold's coachman? Now that he'd identified himself, she knew why she hadn't recognized him: he had never come into the house before today, and she never rode out in the carriage. Straightening, she made to move past him, but he blocked her way with a slight, lurching stagger.

His grin acquired a tinge of menace. "Like I said,

missy, no call to be uppity. You'll be civil to old Brown if y'know what's good for you."

She flicked a quick glance toward the staircase that led down into the scullery. There were voices below—certainly Cook and a maid or two were down there—but no convenient footsteps coming toward them. Even the footmen seemed to have vanished. Should she simply flee to the drawing room and pretend she'd never encountered Brown?

He laughed at her obvious discomfort. "See now? Civility don't cost nothing."

Reining in her temper, Mary continued to stand tall. "I have been nothing but civil to you," she pointed out. "More civil than you to me."

He grinned and shook his head. "You're a fine one, missy. I like your temper."

He must be more drunk than he seemed. "You are impertinent." Once again, she made to walk round him but a long arm, encased in musty-smelling tweed, shot out to block her path. She swallowed. If he so much as brushed her sleeve, she'd hit him. But until that moment, perhaps it was best not to provoke him.

"Let me pass," she said, keeping her voice—and, she hoped, her temper—low.

"He's a lucky swine, that gent," Brown said admiringly, propping up the wall now. From his posture, he could have been chatting her up in a pub. "Talk about eating one's cake and having it, too. . . ."

"I haven't the faintest idea what you mean." The words came out automatically, prim and clipped, but she couldn't help stiffening slightly. He couldn't possibly . . .

" 'Course y'know what I mean," scoffed Brown. He lowered his voice meaningfully. "You and your chappie. I saw you this morning, scrambling in the window at dawn wearing your little breeches. And I saw him, too, keeping lookout. Only he was too busy looking at you to see me watching over the whole scene." Brown emitted a fat, satisfied chuckle.

Mary's stomach churned with fear while, perversely, a subtle current of satisfaction prickled her skin. James had been staring at her?

"Always been partial to the English rose look myself, but you ain't half bad," Brown rumbled, his gaze as invasive as a hand in her corset. "I'm full to busting with admiration for the gentleman: how's he convince a fetching little lady like you to give it away for free?" He gave a low whistle of admiration. "That's a clever bugger, that gent."

Mary swallowed. "You seem to talk a great deal, Mr. Brown."

A spasm of silent laughter made him shake, mouth gaping. When he recovered, Brown wiped his eyes with a dirty cuff and grinned at her. "So it's *Mr.* Brown now eh, missy?" But he seemed pleased, all the same. "I do know a great deal, m'dear. . . . The stories I could tell you about this here family!" He winked at her broadly.

"Really."

"You're not the only skirt sneaking about in this household," he assured her with another confidential wink. "All the fine ladies in London are up to no good, and this household's no exception."

Once again, Mary tried to assess his degree of drunkenness. It was possible that he was always half drunk, she supposed. Or that he used its likeness to his advantage. . . . His eyes were still shiny with gin, but a distinct intelligence flickered within.

"What's going on in that little head of yours?" he demanded suddenly. "You've a particular look in your eyes."

She looked down modestly. "I'm only trying to think, Mr. Brown, whether you intend to report your suspicions to my employer."

"I might . . . but perhaps not, if I get too accustomed to being *Mr.* Brown." He snorted mischievously. "You're a cool customer, girlie—most females would be pleading with me now, not to tell. Ain't you the slightest bit afraid of me, now?"

Mary's eyes were round and innocent as they met his. "Why, I've done nothing wrong."

He snorted but didn't seem annoyed. "You and Mrs. T, both." He nodded at her look of surprise. "Aye, the mistress. Got your attention now, haven't I?"

"You had it before, sir."

Brown chuckled again. "Cheeky sausage."

Mary held her breath. The gleam in his eyes had changed somewhat—still impudent but less lecherous. She hoped. "I believe you're telling tales, Mr. Brown," she said smoothly. "I can't imagine Mrs. Thorold would do anything inappropriate." Surely he meant *Miss* Thorold?

"Then you tell me where she's trotting off to, every blooming afternoon!"

"For her medical treatments surely?"

"Aye, that's what she gives out," he sneered. "But it's a funny lady who goes to a quack instead of havin' house calls!"

"Mrs. Thorold sees a number of specialists."

Brown made a dismissive noise. "I never knew a ladies' physician to set up shop in Pimlico, girlie! She's not being physicked." His eyebrows rose suggestively. "Not in the professional way, that is."

Mary's jaw dropped. "So, you believe Mrs. Thorold is having an affair?" It was a daft question—Brown could hardly have meant anything else—but it was the most improbable thing she'd heard in some time. The sighing, napping, slow-moving lady of the house? The woman who called her husband of two decades Mr. Thorold?

And yet . . . while it seemed more than improbable—impossible, rather—there was a perverse logic behind Brown's suggestion. Why indeed was Mrs. Thorold so eager to drive out to see her physicians when she could barely summon the strength to cut her own meat at dinnertime? She seldom went out for any other reason.

She had no friends. Her dressmaker and milliner came to the house. But her medical advisors forced her to come to them? That, too, was improbable. An illicit affair, as Brown hinted, was the likeliest explanation.

Unless there was a third possibility. . . .

A soft thud to her left made them both jump. Cass stood at the end of the corridor, bucket in one reddened hand, a rag in the other. Her expression was one of extreme interest rather than her usual surliness.

Mary cursed inwardly. Becoming chummy with the coachman wasn't always a sackable offense but add to that gossiping about her employer. . . .

Turning back to Brown, she said firmly, "I refuse to believe that, sir. Excuse me."

"Silly cow," muttered Brown.

She didn't bother turning about to see whether it was aimed at her or at Cass. At this point, she thought she quite deserved it.

Twelve

A re you going for a walk, Miss Thorold?"
Angelica jumped, dropping her kid gloves on the
hall carpet. "Miss Quinn! How you startled me!" She was
wearing an unfashionably deep bonnet that concealed
most of her face, but the bit that Mary could see looked
distinctly flushed.

Mary waited for a reply, but none came. "It's a sweltering day," she observed. "Not very nice for a stroll." She
wasn't exaggerating. The air was dense and stifling, even
in the garden, and the intense humidity and thick skies
promised a ferocious thunderstorm.

"It's not so bad," Angelica said quickly. "I thought I'd
pop out for just a little while." This was nonsense. The girl
never walked if she could drive, and just a quarter of an
hour ago, Mrs. Thorold had gone out in the carriage.

"May I come with you?" asked Mary. "Your energy
puts me to shame. And I do feel as though I neglect you
sometimes."

Angelica's face contorted. "No! Er . . . that is, I know you take quite long walks, and I'll be going quite slowly. . . ."

It was too tempting. "Oh, I'm quite happy to walk slowly," Mary assured her. "And I do hope you'll forgive me for suggesting it, but is it proper for you to walk alone?"

Angelica began to sputter helplessly.

Mary watched her paralysis for a few moments, then took pity on the girl. "I don't suppose it could do *much* harm. . . ." she decided nonchalantly. "I shan't make a pest of myself, Miss Thorold, but perhaps I shall go for a little stroll myself, after all. Have you any errands I might perform for you?"

If Angelica Thorold had been capable of gratitude, it would have shone from her face. As it was, her expression lightened and she said, "Oh! Not today, thank you, Miss Quinn." She bolted for the front door. Then, one hand on the handle, she turned back to Mary. "Er—Miss Quinn?"

"Yes, Miss Thorold?"

"As we're both going for little walks . . . perhaps if Mama asks . . . we could allow her to think we did so together?"

"What harm could it do?"

A tight little smile stretched Angelica's cheeks for a moment, and then was gone. Mary gave the girl a two-minute head start, then slipped outside after her. Angelica had lied, of course: she was walking rather quickly indeed, and it was a good thing she had only two minutes' lead.

Already, she was a little dab of color on the distant side-walk, identifiable only by the distinctive azure shade of her gown.

No matter. Mary closed the gap to about fifty yards. It was early afternoon, and the streets of Chelsea teemed with horses and carriages, delivery men, fruit mongers, flower and match girls, street urchins, dogs, and other forms of life.

The two women walked northeast toward Sloane Square. Angelica attracted surprisingly little attention, considering her expensive dress and secretive manner. Mary was grateful. She could hardly watch Angelica get into trouble without coming to her assistance. At the corner of Sloane Square, Angelica halted abruptly. The man behind her nearly lost the contents of his wheelbarrow in an attempt to avoid running her down and growled at the girl for her sudden stop. Angelica scarcely seemed to hear him, she was scanning the square with such intensity.

Mary drifted to a discreet place behind a pair of flower girls who were gossiping loudly with a charwoman. She hadn't long to wait. A minute later, a slim, fair-haired gentleman touched Angelica's elbow, making her start violently. A small smile blossomed on Mary's lips: Michael Gray. The smile disappeared an instant later when Michael hailed a hansom cab and handed Angelica up.

With the pace of traffic, Mary easily kept them in sight while on foot. She wished she could hear their conversation. Did the hansom offer sufficient privacy for Michael, or did they have a destination? And what on earth were they discussing? If this were a novel, they would be secretly, desperately, in love. It would be against the rules, of course, since Michael was poor and Angelica all but engaged to George Easton. But it would also explain Angelica's jealousy over Michael's flirtation with the paid companion. Perhaps they were now planning how to tell Mr. and Mrs. Thorold about their romance. The scenario seemed possible, although perhaps a bit of a cliché.

But—Mary blinked and nearly stumbled as a second possibility struck her: both could be involved in Thorold's illegal business! Never mind who was leading whom. It too made sense. Michael brought Angelica delicate information from the counting house; they now had to modify their plans because of this projected holiday in Brighton; and they maintained a cool social distance before the family in order to prevent suspicion. And who better than Angelica to carry off an unlikely financial deal? It was the Scrimshaw Principle in action: nobody paid attention to women, especially women in subordinate positions. Michael was automatically suspect as Thorold's right hand. Mrs. Thorold, whether invalid or cunning adulteress, was entirely uninterested in her family. But Angelica was perfect—the rich, idle daughter of a merchant with nothing in particular to accomplish and all the time in the world in which to do it. Her viciousness—the evidence of which scarred Mary's left hand — seemed entirely logical, in this light. Really, Mary chided herself, as a member of the Agency, she was the last person who should under-estimate a woman's capabilities.

It was a long conference. Mary followed the cab on a meandering route through Kensington and around the parks. She contemplated a bold move — *Why, hello, Miss Thorold! Mr. Gray! Fancy running into you two, together, on Rotten Row!* — but decided against it. She needed more information before she could act.

After three-quarters of an hour, the hansom drew up. Michael jumped out, paid the cabman, and issued some firm instructions. Then the cab rattled off, presumably toward Cheyne Walk. Michael walked eastward. His hands were thrust in his trouser pockets, and everything about his posture suggested that he was satisfied with the outcome of the conference. Was it worth following him? What if he went somewhere else before returning to the counting house?

She followed him to the edge of St. James's Park, where he suddenly consulted his watch, put it away hast-ily, and accelerated his pace southward. Mary relaxed. His meeting with Angelica had taken longer than anticipated; he now had to return to Thorold's offices. It was a relief not to have her attention fixed so strenuously on a target. She sighed happily, looked about her, and realized that the soup-like miasma that clung so tenaciously in Chelsea had dissipated here in the park. It was a good omen.

It must have been a successful meeting: for the rest of the day, Angelica floated about the house in a cloud of good humor, playing scraps of Mozart and humming dreamily. It was a marked change from her usual sulks and tantrums.

The family had just finished dinner when Mr. Thorold cleared his throat. "My dears, I have something to say to you."

The ladies put down their dessert spoons, and Michael took a gulp of wine.

"Town is most unpleasant at the moment," said Thorold. "I am very concerned about the effects of the heat and the miasma on your health." He paused to cast a worried glance at Mrs. Thorold. "I have arranged for your removal to Brighton, where the air is pure. You will depart on Saturday and remain there for the summer."

His announcement met with perfect silence. Angelica, whom Mary watched from beneath her lashes, feigned surprise rather well. Her eyes went round, and she pressed one hand to her throat. At the foot of the table, Mrs. Thorold's lips thinned into a flat line. The look she directed at her husband was dark with reproach—even anger.

Angelica cleared her throat. "This is very sudden, Papa. What are we to do in Brighton all summer?"

Thorold blinked. "Why, make a holiday, naturally. The house is situated in a charming location—so convenient for the seaside." The general mood slowly began to seep into his consciousness, and he frowned slightly at Angelica. "Why, I thought you'd be pleased, my dear. I thought you quite enjoyed Brighton last year."

Angelica drew a deep breath, as though summoning a reserve of patience. "I did, Papa. But that was for only a fortnight. And in any case, it's such unexpected news— I must rearrange all my music lessons, and any number of social engagements if we are truly going away the day after tomorrow."

Frustrated now, Thorold looked across the length of the table to his wife. His mouth drooped at her expression. "I—I suppose my good news is unwelcome to you, too, Mrs. Thorold?"

Mrs. Thorold sighed and began a long, meandering bulletin on her health.

Mary leaned back in her chair, her gaze focused on Angelica. The girl wasn't surprised. In fact, she was watching her mother with amused expectation. Had she enlisted her mother's help in trying to remain in town? How had she managed to manipulate the old lady without giving away her own interests?

Mary had a sudden, vivid memory of the coachman's insinuations—suggestions she'd not had a chance to pursue earlier that day. If Brown was correct, Mrs. Thorold's desire to remain in London was deeply personal. Perhaps Angelica hadn't put her mother up to it after all. And it certainly gave a new interpretation to Thorold's anxiety to remove the family from town, as well as his tense expression. Extracting his wife from a shameful entanglement? The Brighton plan suddenly seemed reasonable and urgent.

And if this was truly the case—if Mrs. Thorold was conducting an extramarital affair—her entire role as an invalid had to be a sham! How could she have enough energy for passion and deception while lacking vigor in all other aspects of her domestic life? Mary's fingers tightened round the stem of her wineglass. A grand deception . . . larger than any she'd imagined and, in its own way, possibly even more comprehensive than Mr. Thorold's dirty business. After all, if a woman could dupe her husband, daughter, and household staff about her health, her abilities, her character . . . she was a woman of talent, indeed.

Mary realized that she was in danger of snapping the fragile crystal goblet. With an effort, she refocused on Mrs. Thorold's voice. "I cannot possibly find an internist of Mr. Abernethy's stature in Brighton. It's simply impossible. The same goes for Mr. Bath-Oliver, my cranial specialist, who is the best man in Europe in his field. Then there's the . . ."

As the plaintive list expanded, Mary glanced at Michael. He immediately withdrew his gaze from Angelica.

Finally, Thorold grew impatient. "Very well, Mrs. Thorold, very well. I understand. I am still very anxious to have you all away from this city. This evil stink from the

Thames is becoming absolutely intolerable." He paused. "But if your health would be greatly compromised if forced to leave the care of your physicians. . . . Indeed, if you think the risk of removing greater than that of remaining. . . ."

Mrs. Thorold's eyes glittered, a brief flash of underlying steel. When she spoke, however, her voice was chalky soft. "I do, Husband."

He sighed and closed his eyes. After a minute, he spoke in a strained voice. "That leaves one remaining decision. I shall take the house at Brighton regardless; I should feel more comfortable knowing that you have a place to go in the event that the atmosphere here becomes yet more vile. But you may choose, Angelica, whether you wish to remain in town with your mother or if you prefer to go to Brighton with Miss Quinn for companionship."

He looked at his daughter helplessly. Michael allowed his gaze to return to her. Mary, too, was watching, as was Mrs. Thorold.

Angelica clearly felt the importance of the moment and let it stretch out for a few seconds, luxuriating in her fragment of power. Finally, she smiled at Thorold. "Papa, you are most kind and generous, but I really think I ought to stay with Mama. Surely if the air becomes truly poisonous, you and Mr. Gray will join us in going to Brighton? It cannot be right that we should go to purer air while you remain in danger."

It was a splendid performance: modest, sweet, and

dutiful, just as a daughter should be. If Mary hadn't known better, she would have been tempted to think well of Angelica for nearly the first time since they'd met. As it was, she could only admire the girl's stagecraft. She did not even permit herself a glance in Michael's direction.

Thirteen

Friday, 14 May

After her day of discoveries, Mary found it difficult to fall asleep. Head buzzing with anxiety, she couldn't shut off various streams of speculation about Michael Gray, about Angelica, about the curious lack of evidence pointing to Thorold so far. But when she tried to focus her thoughts, they returned with rebellious persistence to the subject of Mrs. Thorold's "physicians." Mere prurience? Or was the paramour part of the scheme as well? Perhaps—the idea flashed through her weary mind so swiftly she scarcely caught it—they were all in it together: husband, wife, lover? Too scandalous? Too damned impossible given the personalities involved? She didn't . . . perhaps . . .

Sleep ambushed her train of thought. The next thing she knew it was morning, announced by the groan of rusty door hinges.

"Tea." Cass placed the saucer on the bedside table with less than her usual crash.

Mary raised herself on one elbow and squinted at the girl. "Thank you."

Instead of the usual question about her bath, there was a silence. Then, "Is it true then?"

Mary sat up and rubbed her eyes. "Is what true?"

"What Mr. Brown said."

Gad. "About Mrs. Thorold? I don't know." Mary took a sip of tea and looked at Cass. "Do you believe me?"

Cass shrugged. "Dunno."

"Then why did you ask?"

Another shrug. That should have been the end of the conversation, but instead Cass looked at the floor and began to pick at her fingers. They were raw and chapped and scabbed round the cuticles.

"Do your hands hurt?"

A third shrug. "Can't help it. It's all the washing up."

Mary considered her for a moment. "Pass me that jar on the washstand—the one made of blue glass."

Cass obeyed mechanically.

"Sit here." Mary patted the bedside chair. "Roll up your sleeves a little." The cuffs were grimy and tattered, and the child smelled of mutton fat and dirty hair. Was she a child? At this proximity, Mary noticed for the first time that the eyes were old and weary. Twelve, at least. Perhaps even fourteen, in the spindly body of a ten-year-old.

Her hands were stiff at first under Mary's touch, but after a minute she relaxed a little. "That stuff smells nice," she whispered.

Mary nodded and took care not to make eye contact. "It stings a little at first, but it helps." She massaged the little clawlike hands for a few minutes. It was longer than necessary, but they had softened dramatically and Cass seemed in no hurry to go.

"Are you a lady?"

Surprised, Mary looked at her. The girl had intelligent eyes. "What do you mean?"

Cass frowned impatiently. "Just, are you a lady?"

"Er . . . well, I work because I haven't any money," Mary said cautiously. "But I had a lady's education. You know, French and geography and history and all that."

"So your father was a gentleman?"

Mary made a wry face. "No, he wasn't. Why do you ask?"

"'Cause you look like a lady, but you don't behave like one."

"What do you mean?"

"You talk to me. Say 'thank you.' And Miss Thorold would never ask about my hands."

Mary gave the hands a final pat. "I doubt Miss Thorold ever sees you."

Cass shook her head. "No."

Mary waited, but the girl didn't move.

Finally, Cass asked, "Do you think *I* could be a lady? Like you, I mean," she clarified. "Not a real lady."

Mary hid a grin. "Do you want to be ladylike?"

Cass shrugged. "I don't care about French and history. . . ."

155

"But it seems easier than the scullery?"

"Yes."

"It probably is." Mary looked at the alert eyes, half hidden by a tangle of dirty hair. She felt a sudden jolt: she must have looked like this once. "It's getting late," she said, putting the stopper back in the ointment pot. "Come and see me before you sleep tonight; I'll rub your hands again."

Breakfast was a silent meal at Cheyne Walk. Thorold disappeared behind his copy of the *Times* while Michael scanned the other papers for news pertaining to the company. At the Academy, breakfast was simple and communal: porridge eaten at long wooden tables in the company of high-spirited girls. Now, with an amazing array of hot dishes under silver covers and the luxury of silence, Mary wondered how she would ever return to the noisy austerity of the school once her assignment was over. She was spooning quince jelly onto toast when one of the footmen appeared at her elbow with the day's first post.

Mary blinked. "Thank you." It was the first letter she'd received since coming to live at Cheyne Walk, and she recognized Anne's sharp scrawl immediately. A slight prickle crawled up and down her spine, and she broke the seal hastily, her hand shaking slightly as she unfolded the single sheet.

My dear Mary,

I am writing to you using my new portable letter case,
which is most convenient and very practical: it opens
and closes with one simple movement. As I write, sur-
rounded by some three dozen excited senior pupils, I feel
unusually anxious. For two days, due to the heat being
intolerable and unseasonable for this time of year, we
have stopped conducting lessons. I intend to take the
girls to the countryside for a spell, hoping that no nox-
ious airs will affect us there.

Likewise, try to minimize risks to yourself. Perhaps
you'll find a way to raise this subject with your employ-
ers; they must realize that the stench is dangerous to
one's health. Take care of yourself, Mary, dear.

Yours sincerely,
  A.

It was a terrible letter—stilted, imprecise, and
unworthy of Anne's crisp intelligence. Yet it provided
Mary with more information than she'd received since
arriving at Cheyne Walk. The agreed-upon code was
absurdly simple: every eleventh word of the body of
the letter was part of Anne's real message. She and
Felicity had argued strenuously about this, with Anne
favoring something more difficult to decode and Felicity
championing speed of comprehension. Felicity had won,

arguing that Mary would have little privacy and leisure to work out an elaborate code and, further, that the intention of the code was only to protect the information from casual observers. Now, as she sat at the breakfast table munching toast, Mary easily sifted through the faux news to discover Anne's true warning: *case closes three days time take no risks subject dangerous.*

Three days meant that the investigation was running to schedule. It also meant that she was nearly out of time, considering how long it had taken her to achieve so very little. Mary sighed.

"Not bad news, I hope."

She looked up and met Michael's inquiring gaze. "No . . . but timely, considering our conversation last night. My former employer, Miss Treleaven, wrote to inform me that she intends moving her pupils away from London for the summer. She's extremely anxious about the effects of the heat on the girls' health."

He frowned. "Really? Isn't the school quite far north?"

"Yes, in St. John's Wood. But Miss Treleaven's concern for her students is thorough: she is extremely good to them." Too late, Mary realized the unflattering implications of her sentence. "Er . . . much like Mr. Thorold toward his dependents, of course."

Michael scarcely glanced at his employer. "Of course. You must be close to your former headmistress for her to write to you on such a small matter."

"I am," she said guardedly. "I owe her a great deal:

158

She educated me and gave me my first post. Without her, my life would have been very different."

Michael's next remark was cut off by the rattling of Thorold's newspaper, which signaled the end of their meal. As he rose, he said softly, "I am intrigued, Mary. You must tell me more of your history later on."

She only smiled. He was carrying his end of the "flirtation" very dutifully. After breakfast she wrote a short letter, using the agreed-upon key:

Dear Miss Treleaven,

Thank you for your kind and informative letter. The country house sounds a splendid idea: safe and with enough space to let the pupils take exercise and enjoy themselves. Such impromptu holidays, in my recollection, are, indeed, always the most enjoyable. The midsummer Brighton beach holiday we teachers all enjoyed last year lingers as but one of my happiest memories.

Here in Chelsea, the Thorold family is most kind to me. There cannot be many households remaining in which dependents are treated with such generosity. I find Chelsea most interesting and, although near the river, the air is, for me, quite tolerable. Regrettably, I must end this little note now, but hope to hear from you at your earliest leisure.

Yours sincerely,
Mary Quinn

After seeing Thorold and Michael safely away, she left the house at half past nine at a brisk walk, dropping the letter safely in a pillar box round the corner. At this hour, the day was still cool and the river at its least offensive. Even so, she was glad for a light breeze from the north, which carried the smells of decay and sewage away from her. At the corner of Oakley Street, a small lad overtook her, clipping her on the elbow.

"Ouch!" Automatically, she turned to collar the boy: the "accidental" jostle was a well-worn pickpocket's maneuver. She'd used it herself in her youth, before graduating to larger exploits.

"Ever so sorry, miss." The boy tugged his cap apologetically. It was only then that Mary noticed he was neatly attired and surprisingly clean. An office boy of some sort?

"No harm done."

"B'lieve you dropped this, miss." He bobbed to the ground, then offered her a sealed letter.

She opened her mouth to deny it, then noticed the direction on the paper: *Miss M——Q——*. "Oh. Thank you."

"Not t'all, miss. G'morning." And with another tug on his cap, he was off.

Mary glanced about—ridiculously, since she was in a busy street—and tore open the envelope. *Come to my offices. JE.* An address was printed below. She debated his terse command for only a moment. It wasn't as though she had an elaborate scheme of her own. *Three days. Three days. Three days.* The words made a drumbeat in her head.

As she emerged from the omnibus in Great George Street, the first brass nameplate she saw was that of Isambard Kingdom Brunel, the most eminent engineer in the country. But unlike Brunel's offices, those of Easton Engineering were unassuming. In the main room, a row of clerks' heads bent low over desks and drafting tables. No marble, no mahogany: just a high reception desk, behind which a thin, bespectacled man regarded her with suspicion. After a moment, he unprimmed his mouth enough to emit a dusty "Yes?"

"I'm here to see Mr. James Easton."

"What name, miss?"

"Give this to him." She slid the crumpled envelope across the desk.

His nose wrinkled slightly, and he hesitated before grasping the envelope between the extreme tips of two fingers. "Wait here." Half a minute later, he returned down the length of the large room, stiff with reluctance. "If you'll come this way, miss."

Trailed by the curious gazes of the clerks, Mary followed him to the end of the room and through another heavy wooden door. James's office was as spare as the first. He was seated behind a fantastically untidy desk: stacks of papers, rolls of technical drawings, and dozens of little scribbled scraps of paper cluttered its surface. An empty coffee cup teetered at one corner with a half-eaten muffin balanced against the saucer. He was in shirtsleeves.

He glanced up as she entered the room but did not bother to rise. "No interruptions, Crombie," he said to the old man. "Especially not from George." The old clerk grunted and closed the door firmly behind him. After a moment, James set down his pen. "You might raise your veil; I prefer to see a person's face."

Instead, she unpinned her hat and placed it on a corner of his desk. "You're in a charming mood today."

He frowned at the hat. "It's nearly ten o'clock. What took you so long?"

"I can't leave the house before Thorold and Gray do." She began to remove her gloves.

He grunted, then looked her over with a critical frown. "You look ghastly. Didn't you sleep at all last night?"

"I slept adequately, thank you."

"Hm. Must be that dress, then. What color d'you call that?"

"Mustard color. It was very fashionable three or four years ago."

"It makes you look bilious."

"Thank you."

The dangerously soft tone finally penetrated his ill humor. "What's wrong, then? Why are you so polite?"

She blinked dramatically. "I am always polite, Mr. Easton. It is you who express your great importance through bad manners."

"Poppycock. Why don't you sit down?"

"Because you have not asked me to."

With a look of deep irritation, he came round the desk and held the facing chair for her. "My dear Miss Quinn, won't you take a seat?" His voice was heavily sarcastic.

She accepted graciously.

He slumped back into his chair and crossed one leg over his knee. "Now. Have you learned anything since we last spoke?"

She briefly described what had happened at dinner last night. "As the Brighton scheme's been overruled, perhaps we can let that go?"

He nodded. "My solicitor is searching for any legal proceedings in which Thorold's been involved in the past twenty years. He's come up empty-handed so far."

Mary bit her lip. She ought to tell him about Thorold's past entanglements: the suspicion of insurance and taxation frauds, both of which had come to naught. But could she explain her knowledge of such without compromising the Agency?

"I also inspected his will at Doctors' Commons."

"Because you can't have love without money," she scoffed.

He wasn't the least bit offended. "It's all very average and sensible: everything to his wife, if she's alive. Otherwise, a generous life interest to Miss Thorold and everything to her heirs."

"The classic way to fend off fortune hunters."

"Exactly."

"No old friends, business partners, charitable gifts?"

"Nothing extraordinary—a couple of thousand here and there. He named a missionary society and a home for aged sailors—Lascars, specifically."

Mary's eyebrows shot up. "He cares for Asian sailors but not English ones?"

"I suppose the English ones are better provided for. At least they have families and communities here. The Asians who become stranded here really do need the help."

Mary nodded. As a child in Poplar, she'd known a number of Lascar families. Even the sailors who settled in London and married English women were generally poor.

"Lascars could link me to my illegal shipments," mused James.

This was not a subject she wanted to explore. "Ancient, underpaid sailors responsible for smuggling?" she scoffed. "It seems unlikely."

"Not old sailors, no. But there must be younger men who pass through the home—seamen who have recently arrived from the subcontinent."

She looked skeptical. "Why would Thorold trust foreign sailors with his smuggled cargoes?"

"If they're caught, he can deny all knowledge. Everyone's eager to believe that foreigners are responsible for the worst crimes. And the stereotypical connection between Orientals and opium is useful."

They argued the point for a while longer before Mary was forced to concede. She nodded slowly. "I suppose it wouldn't hurt for you to take a look. I'll think of something else to do in the meantime."

He looked surprised. "Aren't you coming with me?"

She stared, stomach churning. "Why? It seems— unnecessary."

"I have a plan. I'll tell you on the way."

Fourteen

They detoured north instead of crossing the river directly onto the Isle of Dogs. He stopped in a seedy alley in Holborn where he jumped down from the carriage, held a muttered conference with a dirty, one-eyed old woman, and climbed back in, his arms full of grubby cloth.

She wrinkled her nose. "Phew. What the devil is all that?"

"It's a dress."

"Oh, no. I'm not putting that on. It stinks of last week's washing up."

"It smells of the people."

"And how will that disgusting object aid our inquiry?"

"One of us is going to distract the warden and the other is going to slip in the back way."

She sighed. "I suppose you'll be going to the front door and I'll be sneaking in the kitchen door? Why can't I be the lady and you the smelly servant?"

"You can't pass as a lady without a maid in tow."

She glared at him for a moment, but his logic was inarguable. "Fine. Close your eyes," she ordered, drawing the carriage blinds.

"It's nothing I haven't seen before, you know."

"You haven't seen mine before."

He grinned but closed his eyes obediently. "You're awfully prim for a woman who runs about in the middle of the night wearing breeches."

It was more difficult than one might expect to change dresses in the confines of a carriage. It didn't help that she had to go largely by feel and that her own dress had so many respectable yards of fabric to its skirts. After a few minutes of struggle, she managed to get free of the mustard-colored creation and thrust it toward James. "Here. Hold this."

"That took long enough," he snorted.

"I didn't say you could look yet!"

"Still not dressed?" It was a stupid question: she wore a light corset over a thin chemise and plain muslin pantalettes. If she stepped out of the carriage, she would probably start a riot.

"No!" She folded her arms protectively over her chest. "Shut your eyes again."

There followed several more minutes of rustling before she said, "All right."

When he opened his eyes, she was tying on a much-battered bonnet. "The color suits you."

"I don't look bilious?" She grinned back, despite her trepidation.

They drew up round the corner. "I'll meet you back here in half an hour."

The Imperial Baptist East London Refuge for Destitute Asiatic Sailors was located in Limehouse, near the East India Hospital. Composed of two grimy redbrick terraced houses knocked together, it was identified by a large, tarnished brass nameplate on the front door, next to a similarly neglected bell. Eyeing its sad façade, Mary was suddenly relieved that she wasn't the one providing the distraction. The last thing she wanted was to be seen here.

She picked her way through the alley that ran behind the row of houses. It was full of the usual rubbish—scraps, slops, ashes—and heavy with the odor of rot. The back door of the refuge was no better and no worse than any other in the row. Its paint was blistered and peeling off in sheets, and the window beside it was boarded up. But the doorsill had been recently swept and the ash can stood neatly to one side. It was an odd blend of tidiness and disrepair.

She listened for a moment outside the door. Nothing. Somewhere deep in the house, she could hear activity— a bell ringing, footsteps, a door creaking open. But nothing immediate. She was unsurprised when the doorknob turned easily beneath her hand.

As she'd expected, she stepped into the gloom of the

scullery. The walls were naked brick, the floor bare stone. She listened intently once again and caught a murmur of male voices. Footsteps—two sets? And then a door closing on the voices. There was still no movement at the rear of the house.

If she were hiding illicit cargo or papers, where would they be? In the uppermost corners of the house, probably. The cellar was surely too damp and full of vermin. And if the papers were in the warden's study . . . She'd worry about that later. Gliding through the kitchen proper, she passed into the main corridor, glancing about cautiously. The house was dim and still and surprisingly cool, given the weather. Small patches of mold blossomed in corners, and rust-colored water stains took the place of wallpaper. Beneath the sweet smell of damp, there was a sharp, warm odor: Asian cooking, medicines, textiles . . . the Far East condensed into a domestic scent. She was suddenly, forcibly, reminded of Poplar. Of home.

The staircase was uncarpeted, and she trod carefully, trying both to be quiet and to control her shaking limbs. On the second-floor landing, there were three doors. A neat opening had been cut into the wall at the top of the stairs, linking the landing with that of the adjoining house. It was presumably a mirror image of this one.

Where were all the old sailors? Were they turned out until nightfall? She chewed her lip. If she attempted to walk into a bedroom, she might disrupt a roomful of innocent old men. She might discover crates of smuggled goods. She might find Thorold himself, counting out his piles of gold. . . .

She had to act before she became too skittish. She chose the back bedroom, on the grounds that it was the nearest. Nothing was audible through the thin wooden door, and when she turned the doorknob, the hinges creaked only slightly. A small window admitted a modest amount of grayish daylight—enough to reveal a double row of little cots, very close together. They were narrow and low, each with a threadbare blanket folded neatly atop the lumpy straw mattress. No pillows. A small, open crate holding personal effects sat at the foot of each bed. The floor was bare wood, worn smooth through use, and swept clean. The room smelled of tallow candles, lye soap, and decay.

With a shudder, she closed the door and passed on to the next room. This one, at the side of the house, had no window. With the aid of a candle, she discovered that its contents were basically the same, except that there were even more beds, pushed so close together they all but touched. The room was perhaps less clean than the first; the old-man smell was stronger and undercut with opium.

When the third and largest bedroom yielded only the same pathetic contents, Mary began to doubt herself. What was she doing, intruding on the privacy of these respectable, poverty-stricken old men? There was no space in this threadbare little charity for the things she and James had imagined . . . and if there were, wouldn't the residents ask questions? She'd counted twenty or so beds in this side of the house. If she assumed the same for the other half, there were perhaps thirty-five to forty-five residents in total. They couldn't all be helpless, doddering old fools. Either the stolen goods and papers weren't kept here or they were stored in a separate part of the house. Perhaps the cellar, after all. Or the warden's office itself.

She had just made up her mind to descend when she heard footsteps on the staircase. Ascending, of course. Damn.

"Who are you? What are you doing up here?" The voice was male, elderly, scolding.

She let out a silly little bleat. "Oh! Beggin' your pardon, sir . . . I was lookin' for the gentleman what manages this place." A swift glance showed her a thin Chinese man in his sixties, at least, but spry-looking. "That you, sir?" She bobbed deferentially for good measure.

His frown was apparent in his tone. "How did you come in?"

"Th-through the kitchen door, sir. I was looking for a place, you see."

"The warden's office is on the ground floor." His tone was stiff, suspicious.

Mary poured on the Cockney charm. "I didn't mean no harm, sir: I'm just lookin' for a place, see? Ain't many jobs for a good girl round here." She looked up, trying for an expression of dim-witted hope. "You the warden, Mr. . . . ?"

The man pressed his lips together. "Chen. I am."

"Oh!" She made as though to dash at him, and as she'd expected, his sharp hand gesture held her back. "Oh, do give us a job, sir. I'm ever so hardworkin', except I ain't been able to, what with my sister so poorly, and—"

"Come downstairs, young woman."

She faltered to a stop and, obeying another curt gesture, preceded the warden downstairs. They went into a room at the front of the house, just off the main corridor. It was as sparse and faded as the rest of the refuge, although here someone had attempted to decorate. The walls were covered with a dark, fern-patterned paper that was now beginning to peel loose from the damp. Velvet curtains, drawn open to admit thick daylight, clashed with the greens of the paper and the tattered carpet. But the focal point of the room was a garish oil portrait of an obese merchant with jaundiced eyes and improbably pink cheeks. The heavy gilt frame bore a nameplate: *Wm. Bufferton (1801–1852), A Good and Faithful Servant and a Man After God's Own Heart.* Lip curled with distaste, Mary turned from her inspection of the painting to meet the sharp gaze of the warden.

He pointed to a rickety wooden chair. She sat.

He remained standing. "You say you are looking for a place?"

"Y-yes, sir."

"Doing what?"

"A-anything, sir." She curled her hands into the folds of her skirts. "Maid-of-all-work, sewin', anythin' what needs doin' round the house."

His gaze dropped to her lap. "Indeed."

In the long silence that followed, Mary dared not look up. She strained her peripheral vision for clues, but no telltale sound or movement came from Mr. Chen. The room seemed perfectly still. She counted to twenty, then to forty, then to sixty. A clock in the next room chimed half past the hour.

When at last he spoke again, his voice was crisp and startling. "I don't believe you." Instinctively, Mary drew breath to protest, but he shook his head gently and she closed her mouth again. "You are not looking for work," he continued, more mildly. "Your hands are too soft; they are not a servant's hands. You are looking for something else."

Her stomach turned over. What was wrong with her? Why couldn't she find the words to bluff her way out of here? And was he at least confirming that the smuggled goods were hidden here? How could she get out to inform the Agency? Surely James would sound some sort of alarm if she didn't return. Amid the whirl of her thoughts, the warden's next remark astonished her completely.

His question was simple enough: "Who are your people?"

But he said it in Mandarin.

Mary stared at him for a moment, the color rising in her cheeks.

The warden smiled slightly at her bewilderment and tried in Cantonese. "You cannot speak your language?" He shrugged and switched back to English. "What is your father's name?"

She swallowed hard. It was everything she'd feared in coming here today. Everything she tried not to think about.

Just like that, he'd laid bare her secret.

Fifteen

"There is no need to be afraid, *Ah Mei*." His use of the courtesy title was surprising and compassionate. She hadn't been called "little sister" since she was a child. "Many young people come here looking for their families."

She drew a deep breath, suddenly shaky. Her palms and armpits were damp with a perspiration that owed nothing to the weather. "I'm sorry I lied to you, *Ah Gor*." "Elder brother"—a term of respect—came back to her without thought, without effort. She didn't know that bit of her had survived.

"Why did you lie?"

"I was—afraid." That much was true. "I knew I shouldn't have gone upstairs." Also true. Despite her shame at being caught—at being recognized—the truth felt better.

"You are looking for something. Information."

She nodded cautiously.

He paused and studied her face. "You are half-caste."

She couldn't control the heat rising in her throat, the rush of blood scalding her cheeks. "My mother was Irish."

"And your father was a Chinese sailor."

It wasn't a suggestion. Belated panic bloomed in her chest, spreading swiftly to her stomach, her suddenly shaky limbs. Her pulse was too rapid, too loud—it drummed in her ears, deafening her to all other sounds. She hadn't thought about her parents in years. Certainly not that aspect of them . . . and of her own identity.

Mr. Chen was still watching her, his face guarded. He awaited her response. Was it too late to flee? He was old. She was quick—and a coward if she ran away now. Again.

Mary lifted her chin. "Yes." Shame, relief, a curious sense of both defiance and disgrace, flooded her body. It was, in some ways, liberating to share her secret—to acknowledge her real identity—for the first time since her parents had died. Not even Anne and Felicity knew this. Yet the act of confession was also frightening. Humiliating even.

"Your father is dead?"

It still hurt to think about it. "He died at sea."

He made a small, elegant gesture. "Tell me."

It was a simple request, but Mary's mind went blank. She hadn't allowed herself to think about her father for years. Now, staring into Mr. Chen's shrewd eyes, she had no idea how to begin.

"He was a good father?" he asked gently.

She nodded.

"You were quite young when he died?"

"Eight years old. Perhaps seven."

"So you remember him."

Mary closed her eyes and her father's face floated in her memory. A handsome man with a shy smile. "He was kind," she said. "We used to go for walks by the river and he told me about his boyhood in Canton." She smiled. "People in Poplar called him Prince, because he looked a bit like Prince Albert."

Mr. Chen blinked and leaned forward slightly. "Do you know his Chinese name?"

Mary frowned. "No one ever called him by it. Our family name was—is—Lang, but I can't think of his given names."

Mr. Chen's breathing quickened. "Take some time," he said with determination.

Mary blinked. "But you wouldn't know anything about him . . . would you?"

"That depends on who he is."

"But he died at sea! His ship was wrecked, and someone from the company came round. . . . They gave us some money—his wages." Her hands were trembling and her face hot. She remembered that day. But there was something about Mr. Chen's expression. . . . "You can't know! How would you know anything?"

"Calm yourself," he said sternly. "I cannot tell you anything about a man whose name you cannot remember."

Various syllables swam in her mind. She'd never

learned Mandarin or Cantonese, apart from stray words and phrases, never had the patience to learn to write in Chinese characters. She felt a sudden stab of anger with herself for having let it go. She was the last living scrap of her father, the only person left to remember him, and she couldn't even recall his name. She closed her eyes and focused. Out of the crowd of difficult sounds that teemed in her mind, she suddenly said, "Lang Jin Hai."

He looked at her steadily. "You're certain? Lang Jin Hai?"

"Yes." That was right. It meant "golden sea."

Mr. Chen's eyes kindled with a strange excitement. "Then you are Mary, his only daughter."

She could only stare at him. It was shocking enough to be identified as half Chinese, but for this man to claim to know who she was . . . ? It had to be a trick. Finally, she managed to whisper, "Impossible."

He did not appear offended. "How so?"

"How could you—my father—years ago . . ." She couldn't find a single coherent sentence. Suspicion, hope, fear, and confusion all jumbled her thoughts. "It's impossible," she said again.

Mr. Chen smiled slightly. "You left Limehouse when you were quite young, and you have been passing in society as a white Englishwoman ever since."

How could he know so much about her? She scrambled to her feet, but her knees were shaky and she ended up clutching the chair for support.

The old man stepped back and held up his hands. "I will not attempt to keep you here, Miss Lang. But is it wise to run away from an explanation?"

If she closed her eyes, the room would begin to spin. Mary kept her gaze focused on Mr. Chen, and something in his expression reminded her, oddly, of Anne Treleaven. Perhaps it was also the situation: she felt twelve years old again, angry and lost and on the verge of something new and frightening. She gripped the chair harder and said hoarsely, "I'm listening."

"It is obvious to me that you left Poplar at a young age because you do not appear to understand how very small our Chinese community is. There are perhaps two dozen Chinese sailors who have settled here and married white women."

That much made sense.

"You are not part of our community; you speak only English; you were surprised—even upset—to be recognized as mixed race."

She longed to defend herself, although what he said was true. Nevertheless . . . "I'm not ashamed of having a Chinese father," she said carefully. "But most English are bigoted: they think that foreigners, especially those with darker skin, are inferior. They think we have weak minds and poor morals."

"Of course; that is something against which we all struggle here."

"But my life is among the English now. If I told them

of my mixed blood, it would change the way they think about me: it would prevent my finding work, other than the most menial and poorly paid service; it would alienate my friends; others would despise me and treat me as less than a person. I can't afford that!"

"Yet that is the fate of most Asiatics—indeed, most dark-skinned people—in this country. You are unusual only because your race is not so strongly written in your features. Compared to most young Chinese women, you are doubly blessed and cursed: you have the luxury of being able to deny your heritage if you choose."

She flung out her hands, trying to make him understand. "But I'm not fully one of them either! To the Chinese, I'm only half Chinese, and to Caucasians, my blood is tainted. I have no family—no one like me—I don't belong anywhere!"

He looked at her for a long moment. "I see your point. Although I hope that one day you will come to believe differently."

Mary looked at him, bewildered. "But how . . . ?"

He ignored this. "So in order to gain employment, you severed your connections with Poplar and Limehouse and began to pass as Caucasian."

She nodded slowly.

"And people believe that you are an English girl?" His voice was gently skeptical.

"Not English, though often they are satisfied when I tell them my mother was Irish. Others assume I have some French or Spanish blood, or some other continental mixture." Her mouth twisted. "And while Europeans, too, are suspect in many circles, they still rank higher than—the truth."

The word *truth* hung in the air, heavy and burdensome. As a young girl, someone—her mother?—had tried to teach Mary that "the truth shall set you free." She didn't see how that could possibly be the case. It was just another cliché for the naive—or the privileged.

Mr. Chen cleared his throat gently. "We have digressed. I remember your father because he was an unusually tall and handsome fellow; everybody knew who he was, even if they did not know him personally."

She forced her mind back to the present question: how Mr. Chen knew who she was. Yes, his explanation seemed logical.

"I only met your father a few times, and once I met you, too. I doubt you will remember; you were a small child of three or four." He smiled slightly. "But you are recognizably the same child, Mary Lang."

She took it in slowly. Her mind felt sluggish, as though working at a fraction of its usual speed. Everything seemed to make sense. Too much sense?

A sudden thought darted into her mind. "If that's the case," she said, her voice high and harsh, "if you care so much for the Lascar community, why didn't you help us after he died? Why did you leave my mother to suffer and to starve, and to—to—" She was shaking now, with anger.

Mr. Chen's expression was somber. "That was a tragedy."

"Of course it was! But it needn't have happened!"

He sighed and pinched the bridge of his nose. "You are correct." He paused for a while, then said, "After your father was reported dead, a lady from a nearby church went to see your mother. She wanted a maid-of-all-work, and she offered to buy you.

"Your mother was extremely angry. She refused the offer and ordered the lady to leave at once. The lady was very offended and decided that if your mother would not accept her offer, which she thought generous, your mother should receive no assistance at all."

He seemed to have an answer for everything. And yet . . . "What about you?" she asked stubbornly. "You knew so much, but you refused to help us, too?"

Mr. Chen looked ashamed. "I was afraid. The lady's church helps to support this refuge. I feared that they would refuse to donate to the refuge if we helped you."

His shame seemed genuine. As his words filtered through her, Mary realized that she believed him. Slowly, she sat down again. Her hands ached from clutching the wooden chair so fiercely. "So you knew my father."

He rose and went to a tall filing cabinet. "For several years now, I have kept a file of 'lost Lascars'—men who vanished on sea voyages. Although sailing is a dangerous profession, there have been a number of mysterious disappearances of foreign sailors in particular, all surrounded by rumor. The men at the docks gossip, you understand. These lost Lascars have certain things in common. I believe your father was one of that group.

"But he was also different," continued Mr. Chen. "Before setting sail in 1848, your father paid me a visit. He felt quite strongly that he might not return from that voyage, but he didn't want to alarm your mother. He left this cigar box in my keeping. He told me that if he returned, he would reclaim it; if he did not, I was to give it to you when I thought the time was right." Mr. Chen looked somber. "I was too afraid to help your family, and I failed to give this to you before you disappeared. I cannot forgive myself for those failures. But you are here now.

"Your father loved you dearly, Miss Lang. This is his legacy to you."

So many questions crowded her mouth, but Mary couldn't take her eyes from the cigar box. She simply stared, terrified that this was a hoax—or that the moment she stretched out her greedy hand to touch the box, it would vanish or crumble.

The muffled sound of the doorbell interrupted them. "I shall leave you here to examine your inheritance," said Mr. Chen gently. She couldn't manage a reply, but when she next looked up, he had vanished.

The cigar box was tied roundabout with twine. As Mary unfastened it, she suddenly remembered her father teaching her to tie different knots: bowlines, figure eights, reef knots. Her hands shook as she raised the lid, nearly tearing it from its cardboard hinges. The topmost item was an envelope addressed simply to "Mary" in careful, childish handwriting. From it, she removed a half sheet of paper and a separate twist of newsprint containing something seedlike.

My dear Mary,

First, and most important, I love you. I am proud of you, and always will be.

I'm departing on a dangerous but necessary journey. In this box, I leave some information that may one day be important to you. You can trust Mr. Chen to help you with it.

I must go. Take care of your mother and your new brother or sister, and help them to remember me.

Your loving Papa

It was so brief. Mary reread it half a dozen times, willing it each time to say something more. More about himself, more about her, more about anything at all. She didn't realize she was crying until a tear splashed onto the page, blurring his signature.

That made her cry all the more, and her fingers shook as she opened the crumpled knot of newspaper. Inside was something she'd entirely forgotten: a small pendant of carved jade, no longer than her thumbnail. It looked like a piece of fruit—a pear, perhaps. Its chain was tarnished from long disuse, but she remembered it with a fierce stab of possessiveness. It had been hers—hers from long ago. A piece of her Chinese heritage, which she had worn on holidays. But what was it doing here? Why had her father set it aside so carefully, in a place where she might never have found it?

A quiet knock on the door made her jump and wipe her face hastily. "Yes?"

Mr. Chen came in. "I'm sorry to interrupt you, Miss Lang, but I need this office to receive a business caller. Could you step into the parlor? You may take as much time as you like there."

The word *time* suddenly recalled the whole situation. "I must go!" she gasped. How long had she been inside now?

"Really, Miss Lang, you needn't leave."

She tried for a smile. "On my own account, I must." She looked down at the cigar box. It held another envelope, inscribed to her mother, and a roll of documents held with another piece of twine. "Mr. Chen," she said, "may I leave this box with you? I can't take it with me now."

"Of course. It has awaited you for a decade; it will wait a little longer."

Mary repacked the box, hesitated, then took out the pendant and put it on, sliding it beneath her collar. "Thank you," she said huskily. "I'll be back soon."

Mr. Chen bowed slightly. "Until next time, Miss Lang."

Sixteen

From the privacy of the carriage, James surveyed the scene before the Lascars' refuge with narrowed eyes. He'd prolonged his interview with the warden to the point of inanity before retreating to the carriage. And now he'd been waiting for an additional half hour. It felt like much longer.

His gaze wandered to Mary's pocketbook, neatly propped on the facing seat. Did he dare? It was certainly unfair, ungentlemanly, taking advantage, whatever one liked to call it. . . . What the hell. It was what Mary did. Aside from the usual bits and pieces — a couple of penny stamps, small coins for the omnibus, a clean handkerchief — there was a letter, postmarked yesterday.

James scanned it rapidly. *My dear Mary, I am writing to you using my new portable letter case, which is most convenient and very practical.* . . . What a nonsensical note. And what would Mary care what the old biddy did with her charges?

He had already replaced it when something made him pause. Something nagged . . . he couldn't quite place it. He reread the letter. What kind of headmistress gloated about a writing case when she believed her pupils' health was at risk? And who was the woman anyway? He'd have to verify an Anne Somebody as a teacher. He held the sheet up to the light of the window, all the while mocking himself. Invisible ink and encoded letters were the stuff of children's adventure stories, not real-life investigations. Yet everything about Mary seemed a bit like an adventure.

A faint trace of lemon soap lingered in the carriage — a scent that immediately called to mind the image of Mary, wearing only her underclothes, her bare shoulders and arms luminous in the dim carriage. He hadn't meant to gape like a schoolboy. Yet he wasn't sorry that he had.

The sight of a large bay mare interrupted his musings. It stopped before the Lascars' refuge and its rider, a handsome blond gentleman, was instantly familiar to James. He scowled and drew back from the window, scanning the streetscape as he did. Sure enough, a sandy-haired butcher's boy soon appeared, dangling a basket from one arm. The boy stopped in the street, squinting at an order sheet and mouthing the items to himself. James smiled at the sight of his young accomplice: Alfred Quigley certainly had a flair for the dramatic.

When the horseman vanished inside the refuge, James checked his watch. Mary had been inside for nearly an hour. Now, with the unexpected arrival of Michael Gray, she would certainly need at least another quarter of an hour. Very well: he would reserve judgment and be productive. Think of the myriad other things he had to do today. Think of ways to find answers to his own queries. He stretched his long legs, then refolded them and realized he was grinding his teeth.

When Mary reappeared, through the front door this time, she moved as though in a trance. Her expression, normally alert, was utterly distracted. Before Barker could fold out the steps for her, James seized her by the forearms and lifted her bodily into the carriage.

She landed on the seat with a thump that raised dust from her skirts, but she didn't protest. "You must be tired of waiting," she said.

"A little." His tone was surprisingly even, all things considered.

"I'm sorry." She sounded uncharacteristically meek, but wouldn't look him in the eye.

He waited, a muscle twitching in his jaw. "Well?" he finally demanded.

"Oh—you want to hear what I learned." Her eyes were red. Dust, perhaps.

"Yes."

She stared out the window for a moment and seemed to focus. "Close your eyes," she said. "I'll tell you as I change."

James covered his eyes for good measure and listened

impatiently to her brief description of the building and the sailors' rooms. "That's all you saw? What took you so long?"

"Well, the warden caught me. I had to pretend I was looking for work. It's a good thing we got the costume." She finished buttoning her dress and ensured that the pendant was tucked out of sight.

"I suppose—" she broke off when she noticed Anne's letter lying on the seat beside her. With a slow movement, she retrieved it and stared at it, puzzled. "This is . . . how did . . . ? You—you swine! You rummaged through my personal possessions and read my private correspondence! How *dare* you!" Her eyes narrowed, glittering with anger; her body was tense and poised to spring.

James felt a prick of shame, which he quickly smothered under righteous anger. "You are scarcely in a position to accuse me of underhanded behavior," he retorted. "What about your secret meeting and the reason you were so long in the refuge?"

"Are you mad? What secret meeting?" Her face was flushed and she looked defensive. Guilty, even.

"I'm not a fool!" he roared. "It's perfectly clear that you were up to something in there. How else could you have stayed so long, asking for work?"

"I did what we agreed! If you'll recall, it was your plan!"

"I must have played right into your hands. It was purely by good fortune that I saw him arrive at the

Lascars' refuge. It was a clever move, getting me to suggest the place! It's a pity you weren't as careful about packing me off after I'd created that useful diversion. *I saw him*, Mary!"

"You saw him arrive?" Now she seemed genuinely perplexed. "What on earth are you raving about?"

He curled his lip. "More denial? I thought you cleverer than that, Miss Quinn."

"Oh, I could just scream. For the last time, *Mr. Easton*, I have no idea who you're talking about. You suggested we explore the Lascars' refuge. You made the plan and bought those stinking rags. I followed the plan. And now you're accusing me of meeting somebody who is clearly a figment of your imagination!"

"Michael Gray is a figment of my imagination? Tell that to your precious employer."

"Michael Gray?" She really was outraged now. "At the refuge? What utter bosh!"

"I suppose it'll turn out you're all in it together, the whole damned family, for some arcane reason I haven't yet worked out."

"You're completely obsessed with the man. Actually, no: you're obsessed with the idea of my being in league with Gray."

Oh, what he wouldn't give to shake the woman. Being a gentleman was a distinct disadvantage at moments like this. "So you deny that you met Gray at the Lascars' refuge?"

"Of course I deny it, you blockhead!" she howled. "How could I have met him? He wasn't there!"

"'Blockhead'?" James felt his control disintegrate. "You devious little —"

"Stop the carriage! I'm getting down!"

"Gladly!" he snapped, thumping the roof energetically. He didn't care where they were; he'd gladly drop her into the Thames itself.

Mary flung open the door as the carriage slowed, and he saw that they were indeed beside the river, which shimmered like oily tar in the midday light. Its odor of rotting waste invaded the carriage, making them gag violently.

"Shut the door," choked out James as soon as he could speak.

Mary looked green but prepared to climb down from the carriage. He caught her by the elbow and pulled her back inside. "Stay."

She seemed too queasy to argue and slammed the door smartly as the carriage accelerated westward. James could only imagine how Barker was getting on, out in the open air. There was a long silence as they both battled nausea, handkerchiefs clasped over their noses.

After several minutes, Mary took an experimental breath. "It's not so bad now."

"Good." Yet when he put away his handkerchief, he was assaulted anew by the thick stench. He re-covered his nose again and attempted to breathe normally.

Mary frowned. "Are you going to be sick?"

"No." His saliva tasted intensely salty.

"You look chalky."

"I'm *fine*," he said with a scowl. Why had she recovered, while he was still carrying on like a delicate maiden aunt? The last thing he wanted was to vomit in front of her.

After a pause, she cautiously offered him her hand-kerchief. He took it reluctantly. Her lovely lemon scent helped more than he'd care to admit.

"How do you do it?" he mumbled through layers of linen.

"Do what?"

"Live at Cheyne Walk. All the Thorolds."

Mary considered. "Well, Miss Thorold doesn't care for it. Mr. Thorold says the river made his fortune, so he's loyal to it. And Mrs. Thorold seems unaffected by the stench."

"The newspapers are calling this the Great Stink, you know."

"The Thames never smells good."

"But it's never smelled this bad," he countered. "Even the ferrymen have stopped working."

It was true: the usual fleet of small river taxis was nowhere to be seen. "Is it true what they say about the cause of the stink?"

"Human refuse, dead animals, rotting vegetation, waste from tanneries and chemical works, and God knows what." James had seen all these things—and more—while working on the tunnel excavations.

"But the Thames has been full of that for ages. Decades."

"It's been getting worse," he said. "More people create more refuse. And it's not just dead cats and other rubbish in there now: all the toilets in London flush directly into the river."

Mary shuddered. "So the heat isn't causing the stink; it's merely making the normal stench worse."

James nodded. "We'll have to find a solution soon. London's growing so quickly."

"But how can we clean the river? And where will all the refuse go?"

"The simplest solution is to send it elsewhere—build underground pipes to take it away—and stop allowing the factories to dump their waste into the river."

"Underground pipes? I suppose that's where you and your brother come in."

He lowered the handkerchiefs cautiously. "Or Brunel. Or the dozens of other engineers who will want to do the work."

She looked at him for a moment. "Aren't you very young for an engineer?"

Why did people always remark on that? They either thought him too young to do his job or too mature for his age. "I began my apprenticeship when I was fifteen. I'm nineteen now." And speaking of age . . . he frowned at her critically in the gloom. "Aren't you very young for a lady's companion?"

"I'm twenty." She changed the subject abruptly. "Where are we? I suppose it's safe to get down now."

He held out a hand to stop her. Their argument seemed childish after the interruption, but he had to know. "Mary, he *was* there."

"Gray? When?"

"While you were inside, Gray rode up. He entered by the front door. You remained inside for another quarter of an hour."

She frowned. "He *rode*? That bay mare that was tethered outside?"

"Yes!"

"But why didn't you say so?"

"We're not going to fight again, are we?" He grinned.

One of her rare, full smiles transformed her face. "It didn't actually come to fisticuffs."

"For which my nose is grateful."

"Your bruise is healing quickly, I see."

"Yes. And your hand?"

"Much better, thank you."

The carriage drew to a halt. Barker swung the door open noiselessly and unfolded the steps. "Lawrence Street, Miss Quinn."

She hesitated a moment, then said, "I'll keep you informed."

"Likewise."

* * *

After dinner each evening, the ladies retreated to the drawing room while Thorold and Gray drank port and ate Stilton in the dining room. Mrs. Thorold tended to nap in her armchair while Angelica played the pianoforte. This evening, however, Angelica couldn't settle. She rustled through sheet music, tossed it aside, and settled down to mope by the windows. She'd been like this all day.

"I think I'll get my sewing basket," Mary finally said. "May I fetch you anything?"

Angelica didn't even turn her head.

Mary gently closed the drawing room door behind her. It was quiet on the landing. By now, the servants were in their own hall having their evening meal. Downstairs, the dining room doors stood open. Not normal practice, but given the stuffy weather, not a bad idea. Yellowish gaslight spilled into the hall, along with low, intense voices.

"With all respect, sir, you ought to reconsider the Brighton scheme."

"I've already told you. It's not possible."

Mary paused, one hand on the balustrade. This was even better luck than she'd hoped.

"I realize the ladies prefer to stay in London, but under the circumstances—"

"You heard that family conversation, Gray. Mrs. Thorold made herself very clear. It is not a question of preference but medical necessity."

"There is a medical case for getting her out of the

city, sir. Could she not consult other physicians in Brighton?"

A pause. Then, "Don't interfere in matters you don't understand."

"Sir, I—"

"Enough!" The sudden anger in Thorold's voice was startling. "I have informed you of my decision; it is not reversible."

Gray's voice was hard now. "I went to George Villas today, sir."

Another pause. "You what?"

"George Villas, Limehouse. Site of the Imperial Baptist East London Refuge for Destitute Asiatic Sailors. Sir."

"Why the devil should you go there? It's not one of your responsibilities."

Michael was speaking now with heavy emphasis. "I was following up some irregularities in last quarter's accounting." He paused for effect, but Thorold made no attempt to speak. "I wondered, sir, why the company was paying for the . . ."

A servant's footsteps in the corridor made both men pause. Then Thorold said coldly, "As I said, that is outside your purview, Gray. If you want to keep your job, you'll mind your own damn business."

Silence.

"Do I make myself clear?"

"Yes, sir."

Mary paused a moment longer, but the conversation

was clearly over. Even so, it was a piece of luck. She hurried upstairs to her bedroom and turned the key in the lock. She scrabbled around for a minute, trying to find her candle, when suddenly a gravelly voice said, "I've a rushlight in my pocket, miss."

Mary stifled a scream. When she could speak again, shock made her severe. "Cassandra Day! What on earth are you doing in my bedroom?" Her fingers closed round the box of lucifers. In the sudden flare of the match, she saw Cass crouched on the floor by the washstand, her knees drawn up under her chin. Judging from the way the girl blinked and squinted, she had been sitting in the dark for some time. Mary took her time lighting a second candle.

"Now. What's all this about?" she asked crisply.

"Don't be cross, Miss Quinn: it's important."

"What's important?"

Cass stood awkwardly, twisting her hands in her apron. "Something I heard today. I didn't know how else to tell you."

"Won't you be missed from the kitchen?"

"I've washed up the pots, miss. Cook gave me leave to mend my aprons."

From the look of the specimen she was wearing, she needed the time. Mary nodded. "All right, then. Sit down. I'll work on your hands while you tell me what you heard."

Even in the dim light, she could see Cass flush with

satisfaction. She sat gingerly in the cane chair, careful not to let her skirts touch the clean bedding.

"Now." Mary opened the small jar of salve. "What's this news?" Cass squared her narrow shoulders and took a deep breath. "Early this morning, I was polishing the silver in the butler's pantry."

Mary frowned. "That's a footman's job." Being outside the scullery—never mind handling the heavy, ugly, and very expensive family silverware—was a significant breach of domestic discipline. If caught, Cass would have been dismissed on the spot.

"Yes, miss. It's 'cause Cook's sweet on William. She told me to do it while she made him a hot breakfast."

"Hm. All right, then. You were polishing the silver. What time was that?"

"The clock struck seven a little after I began, and just as I was finishing, Mr. Gray came down to the breakfast room. The connecting door was ajar, but I didn't want him to see me and ask what I was doing there, so I hid behind the door." She blinked rapidly as Mary smoothed salve into a raw cuticle, but she didn't flinch. "The newspapers were already on the table, but instead of reading them, he began pacing up and down the room. I didn't think much of it; I only wanted to finish the polishing and get back to the scullery. It wasn't until I heard Mr. Gray say, quite loudly, 'What on earth are you playing at?' that I began to pay attention. He said it to Miss Thorold, who told him to be quiet."

Mary's eyebrows shot up. "Was Mr. Thorold in the room?"

"No, miss. It was still before eight, you see, and he normally comes down at a quarter past eight."

"Go on, please."

"I've never seen Miss Thorold before luncheon, so I was very surprised; I thought perhaps I was mistaken, but I could see a little slice of the room through the side of the door—you know, where the hinges are—and I could see her. She was still in her dressing gown, and her hair was all down. She's very pretty, isn't she, miss?"

Mary nodded. "Yes."

"Anyway, Miss Thorold and Mr. Gray began talking about something. He called her Anj and she called him Michael. It wasn't the usual sort of family conversation: more businesslike than friendly." Her brow creased. "I couldn't hear what they were saying. They were in the farthest corner of the room, near the windows, and muttering with their heads together. But he finally said, 'I'll arrange it as quickly as possible.' And she said, 'The sooner the better.' Then they muttered some more."

Mary gave Cass's hands a final light rub and corked the salve. Although she was glad for confirmation of the connection between Michael and Angelica, she couldn't see why Cass had chosen to speak to her about this. But the girl's next words got her full attention.

"Then Miss Thorold said, 'What of Miss Quinn?' Mr. Gray didn't seem to know what to say, but he finally said,

'She's no threat; you know that.' They were both quiet for a minute or two, and then he said, 'If it comes to that, what about George and James Easton?' And Miss Thorold sniffed and said, 'Let them be for a while.'"

Mary glanced instinctively at the door. Naturally, there was no sound or movement in the corridor outside. "Then what happened?"

Cass shook her head unhappily. "Nothing, miss. Just after that, there was a noise in the hall and Miss Thorold left the room. I heard her slippers, but I don't know where she went. And a few minutes later, Mr. Thorold came into the room, and you did, too."

Mary digested the new information for a minute before something else occurred to her. "Were you trapped behind the door in the butler's pantry for the whole breakfast time? After I came down, too?"

Cass looked impish. "I didn't mind; it was a nice rest, miss."

Downstairs, the grandfather clock struck ten, its tones penetrating the closed door in a muffled way. "Speaking of rest, you ought to go to bed."

Cass rose obediently. "Yes, Miss Quinn."

"Thank you for telling me what you did."

Cass shook her head vehemently. "I had to tell you, miss."

They left it at that.

*　*　*

Lying in bed that night, mulling over the day's events, Mary found it impossible not to speculate on the contents of the cigar box from the soldiers' home. It would contain an account, certainly, of where her father had gone—perhaps with a map. It would explain why he had feared for his safety and who was responsible for his endangerment. It might tell her more about who he was—and, by extension, about herself, too. What would she do with that knowledge? How would she negotiate the truth about her father and fit it into her life now? She hadn't a clue. But soon, she'd know. She'd have some of the answers she so needed.

Mary fell asleep wearing the pendant, her fingers curled round the jade carving. She longed to examine her father's papers and rather resented the current case that stood in her way. Yet she had a duty to perform. And, as Mr. Chen had pointed out, she had already waited a decade. *Two days,* she told herself. *Two days left.*

Seventeen

Saturday, 15 May

Despite the turmoil of the previous day, Mary had slept well. She had ample time before breakfast to post a brief note to James describing the conversation between Michael and Mr. Thorold and suggesting a meeting after luncheon that day. On her return from the pillar box, she found Michael alone in the front hall, dressed to go out and looking worried. On seeing her, he turned pale and promptly dropped his walking stick with a loud clatter.

"Good morning, Mr. Gray. Beautiful day, is it not?" Of course it wasn't: it was humid and gray, and the air was already thick with the noxious smell of the river.

"Yes, glorious!" Michael returned automatically, bending to pick up his cane.

Hah. With elaborate gestures, Mary stripped off her gloves and unpinned her hat, watching him in the mirror. "What have you planned for today, Mr. Gray?" She spoke quite loudly. "Anything of special interest?"

He frowned and moved as if to shush her. "No—only the usual, I assure you."

"*Only* the usual?"

"Yes." His voice was hoarse.

She smiled coyly. "How very modest of you, Mr. Gray."

He glanced upstairs with something close to desperation. "I'm afraid I don't understand you, Miss Quinn."

On impulse, she whirled about, all mock flirtation arrested. She took five rapid steps across the hall, bringing her face to face with the unfortunate secretary. "I mean, sir, your clandestine meetings with Miss Thorold."

He was visibly staggered. "I—that's the most absurd accusation—"

Her quiet voice sliced through his bluster. "Two days ago, at the park? And yesterday morning, in the breakfast room?"

Silence. His Adam's apple bobbed rapidly. She kept a careful eye on the hand that clutched the cane, white-knuckled. "Did you really think to use me as your dupe, Mr. Gray?"

His eyes were wide, frantic.

"It's such an old ploy, flirting with the poor, desperate paid companion. She'll be putty in your hands and not notice a thing." She narrowed her eyes. "Isn't that right, Mr. Gray?"

His face was a dull red. "Miss Quinn . . ."

"Save your breath!"

Obediently, he fell silent.

"And, of course," she murmured, "these meetings are partly related to your visit to the Lascars' refuge yesterday."

Once again, he was shaken. He made no attempt to confirm or deny her statement—merely stared at her, pupils dilated.

Mary waited. She needed answers, information, *something*. What was the plan? The silence stretched out, filled only by the steady tick of the grandfather clock.

Finally, he muttered, "I suppose you're going directly to Thorold with all of this."

She held his gaze for another moment. She was good at bluffing; always had been. Yet she still lacked enough information to act decisively. Perhaps showing her hand had been a mistake.

"Let's be off." The voice came from the staircase, low and tense. It was so unlike Thorold's usual friendly bluster that Mary only recognized the speaker when he came into view.

She bowed to him graciously. "Good morning, sir."

His gaze skimmed over her blindly. "Morning, Miss—er—hm." He wrenched open the front door. "Now, Gray."

Michael fell into step behind him, his frantic gaze still fixed on Mary. Good. Let him fret. With her sweetest smile, she bid them both good day and passed on into the breakfast room.

James was even more efficient than she'd hoped. Mary had just consumed boiled eggs and hot rolls and was sipping a cup of chocolate when a footman approached her, bearing a small square of white on a tray. "By messenger, Miss Quinn."

The note—if it could be dignified with such a term—was addressed in James's strong hand and entirely in character: *Agreed.* Incredulously, Mary turned the sheet over, looking for even one stray dot of ink. "I don't suppose the messenger is waiting for a reply," she said drily.

The footman's face—was it William or John? It was difficult to tell when their hair was powdered—was perfectly impassive. "No, miss."

She crumpled the note into her pocket just in time for Angelica's entrance. At the sight of her companion, Angelica stopped short. "Oh." Although it was only just nine o'clock, she was fully dressed in a pretty but plain gown with her hair pulled neatly back and up. It was such a contrast to her usual elaborate and late toilette that she blushed and seemed to feel the need to explain herself. "I was just . . . going to have a cup of coffee before going for a walk," she said lamely.

Mary nodded. "It's not a bad morning for a walk."

Angelica seized the neutral statement with relief. "Is it? Nicer than yesterday, I hope." She filled a plate from the buffet: eggs, bacon, kidneys, tomatoes, a hot roll, and a muffin. When she sat down, as far from Mary as possible, she blinked at the contents of the plate in surprise.

Mary hid a smile. "Shall I pour a cup of coffee for you?"

Angelica looked chagrined. "Oh, there's no need."

But Mary was already up, and when she set down the cup, she noticed that Angelica was biting her lips. "Have you anything planned for today?"

Angelica blushed deep pink and dropped her fork on the carpet. She looked as though she might burst into tears. "What do you mean?" The question began as a hiccup and ended in a gulp.

It was fascinating, really, to see her so thoroughly rattled. What on earth had happened? Or was about to happen? Mary was beginning to feel like a bit of a bully. She had planned to grill Angelica on her movements but instead changed her question to, "Any invitations, or anything I can help you with?"

Angelica shot her a look that bordered on grateful. "No, I thank you."

"If you would be so kind to excuse me, then. . . ."

"Of course. I shall not require your company today."

Mary rose. She had to pass Angelica before exiting the breakfast room, and as she drew near, the girl held out an uncertain hand. "But I—that is, I do hope—Miss Quinn . . ."

"Yes?"

"I do hope that we may become better friends?"

Mary stared at Angelica's outstretched fingers—the

same fingers that had attacked her burn. This must be a ploy to distract her, akin to Michael's flirtation. Yet just as Angelica began timidly to withdraw her hand, Mary took it, and they shook hands. "I hope so, too."

Half an hour later, the front door clicked open and then shut with a sharp bang—an indication of Angelica's nervousness. Mary needed only a moment to don her hat and gloves. In fact, she was almost too soon: when she opened the door, Angelica was still only sixty yards down the street and glancing behind her in the guiltiest manner imaginable.

Angelica took the same route she had two days ago, arriving at the corner of Sloane Square. Michael was already there, waiting for her. They exchanged a few words before he helped her into a waiting hansom and they joined the slow plod of vehicular traffic. Mary did likewise.

To her surprise, Angelica and Michael drove northeast. The broad thoroughfares and garden squares of Belgravia took them through Green Park and up into the pungent, chaotic density of Soho. They worked their way up the Tottenham Court Road, gliding through Bloomsbury into marshy Pentonville. When they reached the red-bricked density of Holloway, Mary was beginning to wonder whether she had enough in her purse to pay for this extended tour of the unbeautiful northern suburbs of London. Worse yet, had Michael and Angelica spotted her, and were they leading her on a wild-goose chase? She was genuinely surprised when their cab drew up outside a squat Anglican church just off the Seven Sisters Road.

Michael alighted, looking serious. As she descended from the cab, Angelica looked even less at ease: although veiled, her stiff shoulders and folded arms showed what she thought of the streetscape. Michael paid the driver. He and Angelica conferred for a moment, he appearing to lose patience and she finally settling matters with a sharp nod. With a glance about—Mary remained in her cab—Michael gave Angelica his arm and led her inside.

After a few minutes, Mary deemed it safe to follow. The street was busy with itinerant vendors—watercress girls, rag-and-bone men, and such—and a hundred yards down the street an organ grinder had set up, to the delight of a houseful of children, all leaning precariously from a first-floor window.

Inside the building it was dark, and after raising her veil, it took a moment for Mary's eyes to adjust to the gloom. The church was deeper than it looked. Michael and Angelica were nowhere in sight, but as she passed through a second set of doors into the sanctuary, she saw at the farthest end a middle-aged man in a cassock, leafing through a prayer book.

A slight rustling by her elbow made her turn and look . . . down. Although slightly below average height, Mary found herself towering over the old widow on her right. The woman was dressed in heavy black mourning, and in the gloom of the church, her face had a waxy, greenish tint.

"You'd like a pew, dear?" The woman's voice was thin and cracked.

Of course: the pew attendant. "Thank you, but I only came in to light a candle and have a quiet moment."

The old lady's face seemed to deflate, and she quickly turned away.

"Oh—wait!" Mary fished a few coins from her pocket-book. "Please—take this." How careless of her to forget. Being a pew opener was one of the few privileges of widows, a sort of publicly acceptable form of begging.

The woman's hand snapped closed round hers with fierce eagerness and she gasped, rather than said, "God bless you, m'dear."

Mary was trapped by the woman's grip for several moments. "Not at all," she said gently, easing her hand free.

"You've not come for the service, then?"

What sort of church service? "Not really . . ."

"Ah. I thought as much. When you see two like that, slippin' in so sly, you can be sure they'll not be followed by family." Her eyes, now rather animated, raked Mary up and down. "Not that you look like family, dark like that; Scotch, are you?"

She had to be certain of the woman's meaning. "You're referring to the couple who just came in?"

"Of course! Fine-lookin' pair, them two." The woman

squinted into Mary's eyes. "Not Scotch, eh? There's a deal of Italians now livin' down Soho way, so m'niece tells me. But you sound English."

"My mother was Irish," Mary said automatically. So much for Michael and Angelica being involved in her father's schemes.

The woman crowed. "Irish! I should've knew it. Black Irish they call it, don't they? You've got that look to you—feisty, like. Eh? The young couple? Ah, they'll be back. Parson's nearly ready, now." Then she suddenly looked panicked. "But you'll let me do the witnessin', won't you? You wouldn't take that from me, would you?"

"Of course you must be the witness," she said. "I'd rather stay back here, where it's quiet."

The woman's eyes softened. "You're a good girl," she whispered urgently.

At the other end of the sanctuary, the priest cleared his throat. His voice carried clearly through the still room. "Are you ready, young people?"

"Yes, sir."

Mary's head swiveled at the sound of Michael's voice. He and Angelica stood facing the minister, stiff and formal. Angelica's veil was still closely draped about her face, but the figure was certainly the same.

Mary stepped into the shadow of a pillar. If she stood quite still, it was unlikely the priest would notice her. He had the squint of a nearsighted man.

"Have you witnesses?"

Michael glanced about impatiently, and Mary held her breath. But his gaze skimmed past her to the shrunken figure of the pew attendant, slowly making her way up the aisle. "There's one: Mrs.—er . . ."

"Bridges," said the pew-opener hopefully. "Old Martha Bridges at your service."

"Right. But where is the beadle?"

"Mr. Potts has his day off today," said the vicar. "I'm sure I mentioned to you in the course of our last conversation that he has the day off every other Saturday."

Michael's face clouded. "It slipped my mind. But what about the sexton?"

"Oh, but poor old Marshall is laid up today," said Mrs. Bridges. "Diggin' a grave last night, and he threw his back out ever so painfully. He's at home now."

"Have you no other witnesses?" Michael's voice rose. "No second pew opener or cleaner?"

Mrs. Bridges bristled. "We're a small parish, sir."

The vicar blinked slowly. "Am I to understand that you brought no witness?"

"No. I mean, yes." Michael raked a hand through his hair. "I suppose we'll have to try to pull someone out of the street. . . . Any passerby will do, I hope, Vicar?"

Angelica's grip tightened on his arm. "Michael, for God's sake." The priest flicked her a brief look of reproof. "We're in the middle of—of I don't know where. We can't just run about the streets asking people . . ."

"We haven't a choice, darling." Michael's voice had an

211

edge of temper. "I'm sorry—I've made a blunder. But we can't change our minds now . . . can we?" The last two words were heavy with meaning.

Angelica sighed. "This is a farce."

There was a charged pause. Michael and Angelica stared at each other as though frozen. Mrs. Bridges seemed crushed at the loss of her tip. The priest simply looked cross. Behind her pillar, Mary held a quick debate. This might be what James wanted for his brother, but it all depended on information they didn't yet have. Should she intervene? If Michael and Angelica wanted to marry, they would manage it one way or another. If there was ever a time for decisive action. . . .

She stepped out from behind the pillar. "Good afternoon, Miss Thorold; Mr. Gray."

Eighteen

The effect was, as Angelica said, farcical. Four faces turned to watch her swift strides down the aisle, mouths agape. Four voices spoke as though in an amateur theatrical, overlapping and interrupting each other.

Angelica (defiant): "You wouldn't dare!"

The minister (confused): "I take it you are acquainted with this young couple?"

Michael (ashen-faced): "For God's sake, Mary. . . ."

Mrs. Bridges (bewildered): "But I thought you said . . ."

"I'm sorry to interrupt the service, Vicar, but might I have a word with Miss Thorold and Mr. Gray?" When the priest only nodded, Mary added, "In private?"

He blinked, as though prodded. "C-certainly. Would you care to use the vestry?"

"Thank you, no," she said brightly. "This spot right here will do."

He and Mrs. Bridges had moved only a few yards away when Angelica exploded. "Of all the sneaking, petty, hateful things!"

Michael jumped and gaped at his bride, pure shock paralyzing his face.

She jerked her veil back, the better to attack. Her eyes were narrow slits, her face contorted with rage. "You will not stop us! I *will not* permit you to spoil everything!"

Shaken, Michael took a firm hold on Angelica's arm. "Mary, I know this looks bad. It's highly irregular, but please . . . is there anything I can do to persuade you that I have Angelica's best interests at heart?"

"You're a lying nobody," snarled Angelica. Her body was tensed to spring, restrained only by Michael's grip. "The vicar would never believe your word over mine even if we hadn't a special licence!"

"An inaccurate special licence?" asked Mary. "You're only eighteen; you can't marry without your parents' permission until you turn twenty-one."

Angelica's eyes bulged, revealing a striking resemblance to her father. "You can't wait to ruin my life, can you? You're jealous of me! You want Michael, but you can't have him!"

Mary glanced at Michael, who was trying not to look embarrassed. He failed at every moment. "Actually, I don't. You're very welcome to him."

Angelica's face suddenly crumpled, and she began to sob. Her words were mangled, but it was clear that she was desperately angry and frightened. Michael tried to soothe her, but that only made her cry all the harder.

Mary sighed and consulted the church clock. After three minutes, she spoke in her crispest voice. "That's enough now. Stop bawling, Miss Thorold."

Startled, Angelica glared at Mary—but her tears slowed to a trickle.

Michael drew a long-suffering breath. "Miss Quinn—Mary—you must believe me: I love Angelica and I want only what is best for her. I am no mean fortune hunter. I—I came to care for her long before I knew anything of her family or her social position . . ."

It was the old story: an absolute cliché. They had met in Surrey while Angelica was at finishing school and carried on a long, secret correspondence after she returned to London. Michael had deliberately sought employment with Thorold in order to be closer to her. Now, with increasing pressure on Angelica to marry George Easton, they had finally decided to elope.

Michael's narrative was long and emotional, and when the church clock tolled noon, Mary hastily interrupted him. "I believe in your sincerity, Michael." He looked pathetically grateful. She turned to Angelica. "And I am a realist: if I were to report this to your parents, it would only harden your resolve." She hoped she was doing the right thing. "If you wish to be married today, I will serve as your second witness."

Two pairs of eyes went round with shock. Two lower

jaws dropped open. Michael regained speech first, and he impulsively clutched at Mary's hands. "My dear girl—bless you."

The formal ceremony was as short as legally possible. No sooner had the vicar supervised the signing of the register than he gathered up his prayer book, nodded curtly, and swept off to the vestry. Mrs. Bridges received her tip with a curtsey and loitered about, flicking at bits of imaginary dust with her handkerchief until Angelica's glare sent her scurrying for cover beyond the sanctuary.

The newly married couple turned to face Mary, flushed and giddy with pride. "Mary, I thank you with all my heart for this great kindness." Michael's voice trembled with emotion. "I'm terribly grateful that you're willing to jeopardize your place in order to help us."

Mary smiled. "It won't be a place for long with Miss Thorold married."

Angelica forced a stiff smile. "We could try to help you find another." Michael nudged her, and she added, shame-faced, "Miss Quinn, I must apologize for my remarks earlier . . . and for other things." She gestured discreetly, sheepishly, to Mary's lightly bandaged hand. "I hope you can forgive me."

It was much more than Mary had expected. "It must have been a shock to see me pop up."

They shared a relieved laugh, and the conversation turned, for a few minutes, to lighter subjects. The chiming of the clock, signaling half past twelve, prompted Mary to return to business. "What are your plans?"

"We intend to keep the marriage a secret for a while," Angelica said slowly. "Although if Mama really presses the matter of George Easton, we'll have to tell her then. But now you've helped us, you won't tell anyone, will you?"

Mary gave her word.

"And there is the question of my post," added Michael. "I am actively seeking another. Not just because of our marriage," he added hastily, with a glance at Angelica. "I have become increasingly anxious about Thorold and Company in recent weeks, and I would have been on the lookout for something else in any case. But this"—he squeezed Angelica's hand proudly—" this has decided me."

Mary's ears pricked up. "Anxious about Mr. Thorold's success? Surely not."

Michael looked pained. "Oh, well . . . trade is never very certain . . ."

Oh, no. He wasn't escaping that easily. "Yet Mr. Thorold is a well-established merchant. Even if trade slackened, other companies would suffer before his." She turned to Angelica. "Isn't that just what your father was saying at dinner a few nights ago?"

Angelica nodded vigorously. "Oh, yes. He's always said so."

Michael looked pained. "Well, darling, we did talk about those other matters. . . ."

"Other matters?" Mary made her eyes wide and ingenuous.

The newlyweds blushed, but Mary kept her gaze fixed firmly on Michael.

He spoke reluctantly. "Some weeks ago, I noticed a number of discrepancies in the firm's accounting. I was quite sure that they were only clerical errors at first, but when I brought them to Thorold's attention, he told me not to worry about them; that he would sort them out.

"It wasn't typical behavior, of course. As his secretary, I would normally oversee such corrections. But I let matters alone. It was only the other week—perhaps a fortnight ago—that I happened to glance at our quarterly accounts and noticed that the errors were still there." He paused, and Mary made a deliberate effort to relax her posture. "Naturally, I mentioned them to Thorold again. He's a busy man, and sometimes the odd thing slips his mind. But he told me—quite brusquely—that things were in order and I was to mind my own d——" He glanced at Angelica. "To mind my own affairs." He paused again and seemed suddenly to recall himself. "I'm sorry to burden you with all this," he said hastily. "You can't be interested in the details of the trading house."

"But of course, I am concerned about you and Angelica," Mary said gently. What she really wanted was to shake the information out of Michael Gray.

"Well . . . the long and short of it is that something's not right. There have been odd sums paid to diverse people. Highly irregular sums."

"He's a very generous man," Angelica put in defensively. "He gives money to all sorts of people."

"That's true, darling. . . ." Michael winced.

"One of the largest sums went to a refuge for aged seamen!" she persisted. "That's obviously just charitable giving!"

"Ye-e-es," said Michael. "But it's the confusion in the accounting that makes me nervous, darling."

"Yet Mr. Thorold seems to think that matters are as they should be?" Mary tried to sound casual.

Michael fidgeted nervously. "Not as they should be; as he wants them."

"That is a very serious accusation," said Mary.

He sighed. "I know it. I'm not in a position to criticize the man, naturally. I think the best I can do is clear out."

She wanted to scream. "Surely," she said, striving for a reasonable tone, "the thing to do would be to go to the authorities? You have, after all, seen the proof of this . . . inaccuracy."

Michael smiled grimly. "In a perfect world, naturally. But I have my wife to think about . . ." He smiled at Angelica as he uttered the possessive phrase. "And our future family. Who would engage a secretary who goes snooping for trouble and then denounces his employer? In my line of work, loyalty is prized above most other traits."

Mary shifted impatiently. "Perhaps you could convey the information to a third party? Anonymously?"

Michael looked thoughtful. "That's an idea . . . although poor Anj's family would still be in the soup, then."

Angelica looked anxious. "I see your point, Miss Quinn. But it's a dreadful position. I feel such a traitor even listening to Michael's concerns about my father. And there's my mother to think about. Her health is so precarious."

Was it? Mary was tempted to question her about that. Had Angelica never wondered about the inconsistencies in her mother's behavior? Or was Angelica merely returning Mrs. Thorold's favor: being entirely self-absorbed and letting everyone else go his or her own way? But this was neither the time nor the place for that conversation. "Yet it seems wrong to say nothing!" she persisted.

Michael nodded uncomfortably. "You're right. I have . . ." He trailed off, considering something. "This is confidential, you understand."

Mary nodded, trying not to appear too eager.

"I have taken copies of the account and a few relevant documents. They're not notarized or official in any way. . . ."

"Yes?" she prompted. "They're unofficial, of course, but quite complete?"

He nodded. "I'm keeping them in a safe place."

"Not at the house, I hope?" Mary asked in what she hoped was a naive voice.

Michael looked startled. "The warehouse? Good Lord, no!"

"I meant the family home."

"Oh." Michael looked crafty. "Well, let's just say that they're well hidden." He cast a tender look at Angelica. "Aren't they, darling?"

"Yes. I was against it, at first," Angelica added. "But the longer I've considered the matter, the more important I believe it to be. One day, Michael might be able to persuade Papa to do something; to make things right."

Well hidden? Between the two of them? Mary had a sudden idea where. "Do you have all the files you need in order to persuade Mr. Thorold of your serious intentions?"

Michael nodded. "I have enough to cause the authorities to look into matters."

"One day," added Angelica firmly.

Nineteen

With Mrs. Thorold still in her room and Mr. Thorold long departed for the office, only the servants were present to note Mary's return to the house at Cheyne Walk. To them it would seem as though she'd gone out with Angelica but popped back to retrieve something. And, in a way, she had.

She went directly to the drawing room, to the music chest beside the pianoforte. Some of the sheet music was printed and bound, but much was painstakingly hand-copied by Angelica and the pages pinned or clipped together. Her enthusiasm for music was striking. Most young ladies' music collections consisted of simple verses set to pretty tunes. In contrast, Angelica favored a challenging repertoire from modern composers—Mendelssohn, Chopin, and especially Schumann. As she searched, Mary wondered what it must be like to be Angelica: pretty, spoiled, and destined for marriage. Had she ever wanted anything more? Perhaps to be a musician, like Clara Schumann?

Mary couldn't shake the idea that Angelica's tantrums and sulks might themselves be a form of unhappiness.

Near the bottom of the music chest, Mary found a pianoforte concerto by Schumann. It had been specially bound in handsome maroon leather and dedicated *To A.T. on her eighteenth birthday, from M.G.* The gift of Angelica's favorite music given by Angelica's favorite admirer. The kick of her pulse told Mary that this was it. Sure enough, folded into the back were a dozen or so loose sheets of paper, closely covered in neat handwriting. She scanned the pages carefully. Balance sheets—records of payment—notes on shipping insurance—and, crucially, letters between Thorold and an employee of Lloyd's. Yes. There was enough information here.

The drawing-room clock struck one thirty, and Mary remembered that she was due at James's office. There was no time to make a copy, and removing the whole sheaf would distress Michael and Angelica if they checked on it. As a compromise, Mary took a small selection of documents. Three or four sheets of paper, she reasoned, would not be quickly missed. She stuffed it into her pocketbook, thinking longingly of her father's roll of documents. In two days, this would be over and she could return to the refuge to learn more. In the meantime, it was simpler not to think about him at all.

When Mary turned up at Great George Street, James was waiting in the entrance area. He didn't greet her but instead took her arm, marched her briskly into his private office, and shut the door firmly.

"What's the matter?" Mary was amused.

"I don't want my brother to recognize you."

"I'm only a servant," she said. "I doubt he'd recognize me if I looked him straight in the eyes and told him my name."

James grinned. "Oh, he remembers you. After what you said about the Crimean War last Sunday, he thinks you're an evil influence who oughtn't be allowed within a hundred yards of Miss Thorold."

"Oh." This morning's events would only confirm George's opinion of her.

"That's it? 'Oh'?"

"What do you think?"

That wiped the smile from his face. He looked at her for a long time, his eyes unreadable. "I think you're trouble," he said slowly. "But you're very interesting."

Mary felt herself blushing under his scrutiny. She didn't know how to respond, so she sat down and removed her gloves.

James cleared his throat. "How are your inquiries coming on?"

"I've located copies of some documents pertaining to some fiscal irregularities in Thorold's company." She produced her "borrowed" pages. "This is only a sample. They should be sufficient to show evidence of financial dishonesty . . . enough, at least, to warrant searching further."

He leaned forward to study the sheet. "Tell me more."

"This is an internal memorandum from Lloyd's of London, the insurance firm, tallying Thorold's claims over the past five years. Taken separately, each claim seems ordinary; modest, even. Yet they occur a bit more frequently than the average, and they happen over a sustained period of time."

"So either Thorold has rather poor luck or he's making fraudulent claims."

"Precisely." She waved a second page at him. "Lloyd's seems to have begun an internal investigation. They daren't accuse Thorold of anything without proof, of course, but they're suspicious and they're doing their research. And this is where things become interesting: The investigation is assigned to a Joseph Mays. A fortnight later, Thorold begins to write checks to one J. R. Mays. Here, and here, and here."

James whistled low. "Rather large sums, considering the frequency."

"How much would Joseph Mays earn at Lloyd's? Two hundred a year?"

"Much less, I think. So Thorold is more than doubling the man's salary."

She nodded. "But he's still ahead: the payouts to Mays are cheaper than having his insurance claims denied."

"D'you think Thorold's ships really sink that often? What could possibly be happening to them?"

"He might be lying about their sinking. Double collecting."

He frowned. "That's the simplest solution. . . ."

"But?"

He took his time framing the question. "But what if he really was sinking them? Not deliberately, of course, but by overloading them—out of greed or carelessness or false economy."

As he spoke, a long-forgotten memory flashed into Mary's mind. A man in a suit standing at her mother's door in Poplar. A man explaining that her father was dead because the ship had capsized in a storm. Her mother refusing to accept what the man said. Neither adult had realized she understood every word.

Mary's face flooded with heat and the backs of her eyes prickled with tears. She would not cry. Not here in front of James.

"Mary? What's wrong?" His voice was unusually kind, which only made things worse.

"N-nothing. It's just a bit warm in here."

"It is." He covered her hand with his. "Are you certain it's the heat?"

She cleared her throat and pulled her hand from his clasp. "Of course. Where were we?"

He gave her a long, steady look but when she glared at him, he shrugged. "All right. I suggested that Thorold might overload his ships, causing them to sink." He paused, studying her face. "Mary? Are you sure you're feeling well?"

"Er—yes." *Concentrate!* "If the ships are grossly over-loaded, they'd ride so low in the water that it wouldn't take much of a storm to sink them. They're called coffin ships among sailors." It was difficult not to sound bitter.

"Thorold once told me he preferred to engage foreign crews because they're cheaper. The other benefit is that if the ships go down, there are fewer people to ask questions of him in England."

Mary's eyes hardened. "Hence the donations to the Lascars' home."

"Buying his way out of guilt?"

"It rather looks that way."

In the grim silence that followed, Mary's stomach rumbled loudly. She tried—and failed—to cover it with a cough.

James glanced at his desk clock. "It's quite late; will you let me give you some luncheon? Afterward, we might have a look at the register."

"Oh, no. I couldn't. Indeed, I'm not really—" She was betrayed by another vigorous stomach growl and subsided into silence.

He grinned provokingly. "You couldn't, because ladies never eat except as a social diversion. Nor do they drink, sleep, or have other gross, vulgar, human functions. I know."

She had to smile at that.

"Come on, then. I haven't lunched either. Won't you join me?"

"I can hardly nip down to the pub for a sandwich and a pint," she reminded him.

"Damned inconvenient, isn't it? How *do* ladies manage?"

"We go home," she said tartly.

"And if you're far from home?"

"We faint from inanition, of course. I'm surprised you didn't know that, too."

Twenty

They lunched quickly on sandwiches and pints of ale brought in from a nearby pub. They didn't talk much, but it was a friendly silence. Afterward, James smuggled her out of the office (they could hear George somewhere, practicing a syrupy ballad on his accordion) and down to the curb, where they hailed a cab.

When he handed her up into the hansom, she couldn't repress a small smile. "That's the first time you've offered your assistance."

"It's the first time you've let me," he murmured, settling in beside her.

The light was yellow-gray, bright enough to make one squint but without the appearance of actual sunshine. In its unflattering glare, all of London appeared dingy. Even new buildings, like the Palace of Westminster with its unfinished clock tower, looked sad and weathered. As the cab prepared to negotiate a slow left turn up Parliament Street, Mary suddenly jumped.

"What is it?"

She leaned back as though avoiding scrutiny. "Look."

James couldn't see anything special in the usual scrum of unwashed humanity, hard-worked animals, yapping dogs, and clouds of dust jammed into a few hundred square feet. He leaned closer to Mary. "What am I to look at?"

"The carriage about to pass us on the far side of the road. It's the Thorolds'."

"That's straightforward enough."

She shook her head impatiently. "No, it's not. Thorold never takes the carriage. He and Gray used to take the ferry. Now they ride."

"Thorold loves that stinking river, doesn't he?"

She ignored that. "It must be Mrs. Thorold in the carriage."

"I thought she was an invalid."

"She is." The Thorold carriage trundled past, southbound. "Damn, damn, damn!" She turned to him. "Quickly, we must follow them!"

"I thought we were after Thorold."

"*Please*, James. The driver won't listen to me with you here."

With a resigned look, he gave the cabbie his mysterious instructions, and the cab immediately began a slow U-turn, much to the irritation of a flower girl they nearly bowled over. She was still shouting curses after them as they joined the thick stream of traffic oozing slowly down toward Millbank. They were only five or six vehicles behind the Thorold carriage.

"Tell me again why we're following a hypochondriac housewife about town?"

"Doesn't it strike you as odd that Mrs. Thorold should be driving across Westminster Bridge? She hasn't a single reason to be in the area."

"It could be a similar horse and carriage," he said reasonably.

"I recognized the coachman, Brown."

"I still don't see your point."

"She drives out most afternoons, either for an airing or to consult one of her physicians. If you wanted air, would you drive to Lambeth?"

"No, but perhaps she's going to the physician's."

"She's a long way from Harley Street."

"He might be one of those homeopathic snake-oil types. They're fashionable, and they set up shop in all sorts of peculiar districts."

"Well, Brown thinks something's amiss. He says she goes to a private house in Pimlico on most days."

"And you believe him?"

"Why would he lie?"

"Perhaps for the pleasure of gossip, or because he thought it was what you'd like to hear. When did you question him, anyway?"

"He made a point of telling me one day, by the kitchen stairs."

He felt a stab of irritation. "Sounds as though he'd have said anything to attract your attention."

"Oh, please. He was dying to tell somebody, and I was the first candidate to come along."

"Hmmph. What else did he tell you?"

"He intimated that Mrs. Thorold was having an affair." Mary blushed at the memory of Brown's other suggestion: that she and James were lovers. Then she was promptly annoyed with herself for blushing.

"What nonsense."

"Hm? Oh!" She forced her attention back to the real subject. "It might be rubbish. But if so, the question remains as to what she does in Pimlico several afternoons a week. There's nothing for a lady to do in Pimlico. It's not as though she could be shopping or visiting friends."

"What about charitable work?"

"Mrs. Thorold?"

He shrugged. "It's a possibility, however remote."

"All right, then. It's not absolutely impossible that she might be engaged in some missionary scheme or seeing a homeopathic physician. But I'd like to be certain in case she's linked in some way to this scheme of Thorold's."

"That seems even less likely than the charitable work."

"I know," she conceded. "But I won't feel easy until I've seen it myself."

At the junction of Vauxhall Bridge, a brewer's cart toppled over. Carriages, hansoms, carts, and drays from all directions juddered to a halt as ragged men and women, street urchins, and girls carrying babies all scrambled to nab a share of the spilled beer. One particularly large laborer applied his mouth directly to the leak in a cask, cheered on by his mates. The cart driver made no attempt to clear the thoroughfare. Instead, he mounted guard in front of the intact beer casks, using his horsewhip and a steady stream of colorful threats to fend off those who approached.

"For pity's sake," muttered Mary.

"I don't suppose you could be persuaded to abandon Mrs. Thorold?" he muttered.

"Absolutely not. Besides, we can't even turn round."

He craned his neck to look and groaned. In just under a minute, traffic had become jammed for hundreds of yards around.

"Would you rather get down? We could follow her just as easily on foot."

He looked at her dress: another frumpy brown sack. "We'll be covered in dust. How will you explain that at home?"

They sat. After some time, a reluctant coachman organized a small gang of men to help shift the debris. But despite these efforts, it took nearly three-quarters of an hour before the road was clear. The driver of the tipped cart was no help. He spent the interval gibbering with rage and bemoaning the damage to his axle. Eventually, a narrow route was cleared through the broken casks and spilled ale, but even then it took several minutes for traffic to resume movement.

At the first opportunity, Mrs. Thorold's carriage nipped precariously through a narrow gap on the edge of the pavement, very nearly crushing a dirty toddler and the basket of watercress to which it was strapped and causing another temporary stoppage as the indignant cresswoman rescued her child. For a few minutes, Mary was sure they'd lost her. As they cleared the junction, though, she caught sight of the familiar carriage disappearing round the corner of a side street. Their driver made a sharp right turn and urged the horses to a trot.

The Thorold carriage turned left into Denbigh Place, a narrow street of terraced houses. The road was remarkably empty: no children playing outside, no vendors going door to door. In a perpetually loud and active city, the effect was chilling. It was as though the entire area had been evacuated.

Mrs. Thorold's carriage halted halfway down the street, and the door flew open even before Brown had clambered off the driver's seat. He did manage to fumble the steps down, but with a sharp gesture the lady in the carriage dismissed his attempt to help her down. Her build was substantial and familiar, and she was wearing full matronly gear — wide crinoline, multiple skirts, bonnet. Her step was sure, and she descended with a matter-of-fact confidence completely unfamiliar to Mary. The distance from curb to front door was only a few paces.

Yet it was enough to note the woman's upright posture and brisk stride. She opened the door using her own key and vanished inside.

James and Mary exchanged incredulous looks.

"Did you . . . ?"

"Was that . . . ?"

Glancing toward the house again, they were in time to see Brown drive on and turn into the back street. Apparently, she was staying awhile.

"What are the chances of another lady using Mrs. Thorold's coachman?" asked James.

"Another lady with her figure?" Mary shook her head. "It's almost impossible."

"Charming family," he drawled. "Papa's corrupt, Mama prowls London on the sly. . . . Is there anything George and I ought to know about dear Angelica?"

Mary kept silence. There was indeed, but she'd promised not to tell. And, truthfully, she didn't want to tell. If he knew the latest developments, he'd have no reason to keep working with her. He was useful to her. And she'd actually come to enjoy his company, arrogant as he was.

He was watching her expression intently. "Is that a yes?"

"It can wait." She jumped down from the cab and waited impatiently while he paid the driver.

"All right," he said as the cab rolled away. "How do we learn more about Mrs. Thorold's business here?"

"We ask the neighbors."

"We just ring the bell and say, 'Beg pardon, who's that lady and what does she do?'"

She rolled her eyes. "We ring the bell and explain that I'm feeling faint from the heat, and may we come inside for a moment." She took his arm and leaned on it dramatically.

"And I just stand there like a dolt?"

"You're my brother, who's extremely concerned for my health."

James shook his head. "I've a better idea. I'll do that while you explore the back street. See if you can't get a look in the windows."

"But ladies won't talk to you as freely as they will to me."

He grinned. "I'm not going to the front door. I'm going to charm a pretty housemaid into telling me all."

"You seem very certain of your charm."

He tried to look modest and failed. "It worked on Angelica . . . and I wasn't even trying with her."

Mary's exploration of the back street was brief. The rear of the house was tidy and blank, the windows tightly covered from prying eyes. There wasn't a single clue for the eager sleuth. She prowled the length of the alley for ten minutes or so, then returned to the corner of Denbigh Place to await James. He was some time—at least half an hour by her estimate, although she had no watch—and it occurred to her that, purposely or not, he was repaying her for his wait outside the Lascars' refuge. The only other human in the street was a boy of about ten, idly kicking a ball.

"You look smug," she said to James when he finally appeared.

He grinned. "The housemaid, Janet, is a charming girl. Served me tea and told me every detail of her life, from dawn to midnight. Apparently, I remind her of the hero of some novel she's reading, but I'm better-looking."

"Why is modesty never one of the hero's attributes?"

He took her arm. "You're only envious because I had tea. And some rather nice scones with jam and cream."

"Is this a sample of your famous charm?"

"Oh, I don't waste it on just anyone," he said with a grin. "For example, ladies met in wardrobes, ladies who punch me in the nose, ladies who—"

Mary had to laugh. "Very well. Tell me what you learned."

He turned serious. "Mrs. Thorold lets the house under the name Thorpe and she comes by in the afternoons. She has a gentleman friend, a Mr. Samuels, who calls in two or three times a week."

"Has anybody seen inside the house? Does 'Mrs. Thorpe' keep a maid?"

"No; it's something of a local mystery how they keep the house clean."

"Well, what about any unusual deliveries? Anything that could link them to Thorold's cargoes?"

He shook his head. "Nothing of the sort. These two keep a low profile; Janet doesn't know where Mr. Samuels comes from either, and she's as nosy as they come."

Mary digested this. "It certainly sounds like an adulterous affair."

James nodded. "Janet thinks so. Apparently it's a favorite topic for all the local housemaids when they see each other."

They walked on a little farther, to the edge of a small garden square. The boy with the ball suddenly booted it toward them. "Pardon, sir!" cried the boy.

James caught the dirty ball almost as a reflex. "Excuse me a moment, will you?" He motioned for Mary to walk on and dragged the boy about twenty feet off. At first it looked as though he was scolding the child, but then as the boy began to speak, James began to listen intently. Mary watched this byplay without particular interest until she noted the sudden change in James's body language. He stiffened, glanced over at her, and spoke to the boy again. The whole exchange took only two or three minutes, but when it was over, James gave the boy something—money?—and rejoined her.

"Who was that?" Mary asked.

"Funny you should ask." James's grip on her arm was tight and he stalked along with long steps, forcing her to scurry to keep up.

"What's happened?"

He stopped short. "When were you going to tell me?"

Mary felt that moment of dread again; the knowledge that she was caught. "Tell you what?" she said
cautiously.

His grip on her arm tightened. "This morning you
witnessed the marriage of Angelica Thorold and Michael
Gray. Why didn't you tell me?"

"I—I promised."

"You promised." His voice was contemptuous.

"Michael and Angelica. I promised them not to tell
anyone."

"You should never have made that promise. You had
already agreed to work with me, and our agreement
should have prevented such a promise." He glared at her
for a minute longer, then suddenly released her arm. The
movement was so sudden that she stumbled backward.
"You went back on your word!"

Stung, she defended herself. "You had me followed,
so clearly you don't trust me anyway! You're so outraged
now, but you're the one who's been spying on me!"

"I have no need to justify myself to you," he muttered,
"but that boy was shadowing Gray. Not you."

Mary blanched. Her righteous anger evaporated, to be
replaced by cold nausea.

"That boy only reported what he saw in the church
this morning. You witnessed the marriage." James stared
at her for a long moment. "How old did you say you
were?"

"I—I said I was twenty."

His eyes narrowed. "You *said* . . ."

She couldn't manage another lie. Not now. Not to him. "I'm seventeen," she admitted in a small voice.

"So the marriage isn't even legal."

"No," she whispered.

"Is this your idea of a joke? And if so, who's it on? Angelica, Michael Gray, or George and me? Or maybe your plan was to deceive all of us for some reason of your own."

She couldn't speak.

He looked as though he'd tasted something rotten. "I hope to God no one else finds out."

She was shaking now. "They won't!"

He only stared at her again, shook his head, and turned away.

Mary stared after his receding form. When it was clear that he wasn't going to stop, she hurried after him. "Wait—where are you going?"

He swung round to face her and spoke formally. "I regret having urged this so-called partnership upon you. Consider yourself rid of me."

Stupidly, she gaped at him. "I beg your pardon?"

"Good-bye, Miss Quinn. I wish you well." He turned on his heel and strode away.

Twenty-one

Sunday, 16 May

Another sweltering, foul-smelling day. Sunlight glowed round the edges of the curtains. Mary lifted one eyelid. Why did she feel so . . . ? Even before she could frame the question, the events of yesterday came back. They didn't rush or ebb so much as cudgel her brain. James. Their argument. Their separation. It ought to be for the best, but she hadn't yet persuaded herself of the fact. Had she no shame? He was arrogant and hot-tempered, but her behavior had been worse: dishonest and foolish.

On her return yesterday, she'd taken refuge in that classic lady's complaint, the headache, in order to avoid dinner and a family evening. Cass had taken it upon herself to smuggle up a supper tray: a lukewarm cup of tea, three door-stopping slabs of bread and butter, and a wedge of slightly stale Madeira cake. Even in the hard grip of self-loathing, Mary had to smile at the girl's idea of comfort and easily persuaded her to consume most of it. This morning, however, she felt hollow as a result of the missed meal.

Was it even worth getting up today? She wrinkled her nose. Such a question was embarrassing, even when unspoken. And — how had she managed to forget? — the conclusion of the assignment awaited. Her first assignment. Her much-compromised assignment. After which she could finally go back to the Lascars' refuge. And here she was, feigning illness over a man who despised her.

Spurred by that thought, she sat up in time to hear the clock on the landing toll nine. Nine! Where was Cass? No tea, no bathwater, and it was two hours past her usual rising time. She was becoming quite a lady, marooned in her room by the absence of the maid. She washed using the water from her hand basin, dressed quickly, and went down to the breakfast room. It was deserted, and she was just sitting down to coffee, eggs, bacon, tomatoes, and toast when, from the back of the house, she heard a muffled but distinct crash and an outbreak of shrill scolding.

With an inward sigh, she went into the corridor. It was easy to determine the location. Even from the top of the servants' staircase, Cook's voice was enough to make her wince. Mary hesitated; she had no authority there, of course. But even as she paused, she heard the meaty slap of flesh against flesh. That decided her.

The trouble was in the larder. Rounding the corner, Mary saw fragments of glass strewn across the stone flags.

Sprawled on the floor among the shards was the cringing figure of Cass Day, protecting her head with her arms.

"Good morning, Cook," Mary said coldly.

Cook, a brawny woman in her early forties, glared at her. She was breathless. "What d'you want down here?" On the floor, Cass did not move.

"Miss Thorold is much concerned by the din," Mary improvised. "She sent me to assist you."

Cook wiped her forehead with her apron. "It's that lazy, thieving brat," she spat. "Caught her nicking those lamps."

The remnants of a pair of oil lamps lolled drunkenly in a corner. "I see." Mary swung her gaze from the lamps to Cass's still form and back to Cook.

"She's sacked, o' course. But she needs a good lesson first, the sniveling weasel." Cook's sleeves were rolled up well past her forearms, and she was still enraged.

The two women stared at each other for a minute, weighing their choices. It was certainly within Cook's powers to fire Cass and even to beat her. In the taut silence, a violent tremor shook Cass's curled-up body.

"You're busy. I'll see her off the premises." Mary glanced down at the girl, her voice cool and neutral. "Stand up, Cass."

Cook's eyes narrowed. "And just who'll clean up this mess?"

"Cleaning and trimming the lamps is William's

responsibility." Mary tucked Cass behind her. "I'll inform him of the damage."

For the first time, Cook shifted her weight. There was another tense silence. Then she twitched her apron defensively. "Get her out of my sight," she snarled.

Mary's palms were clammy with relief as she pushed Cass gently into motion. "Get your things."

Neither spoke as they threaded their way through the kitchen to Cass's "room" at the end of the scullery. It was a small space, unventilated and low-ceilinged, with a dirty straw pallet on the ground. The stone-flagged walls were slimy with mildew, mouse droppings made for a gritty footing, and the musty tang of urine permeated the air. Cass shuffled forward with a practiced stoop and retrieved a ragged nightdress from beneath the flour-sack bedsheet. This she rolled into a tight ball and stuffed into an equally threadbare nightcap. From a makeshift washing line strung between two beams, she took a much-patched petticoat and a pair of coarse black stockings. Finally, she groped in a crevice between wall and floor and, after a little fishing, retrieved a tiny memorandum book. The cover had been chewed by mice, but from the way Cass tucked it into the folds of her skirt, it seemed to be her most prized possession.

"I'm ready," she mumbled. There was a small, bleeding patch on her scalp where the hair had been torn out.

Mary looked at her for a moment. "Come upstairs."

Cass meekly followed her up the servants' stairs,

belongings tucked beneath her arm. When Mary turned the corner and began the climb up to the second floor, Cass hesitated only for a moment. Once in her bedroom, Mary closed the door firmly. "Now," she said, "I believe you have something to tell me."

Cass half lifted her head but dropped it again before Mary could catch her expression. "I—I don't understand, miss."

Mary reached forward and lifted the girl's chin with two fingers. She wasn't surprised when Cass flinched, as though expecting to be hit. She was, however, surprised by the tears glinting on her cheeks. "You didn't try to steal those lamps. I know that as well as you do."

Cass's face twisted with surprise, but she neither confirmed nor denied the remark.

"You haven't told me your side."

Cass scrubbed her sleeve over her face. When she finally spoke, her voice was barely audible. "What good would that do, miss?"

"None, as far as Cook is concerned," acknowledged Mary, passing her a clean handkerchief. "But the truth is important. Would you really want me to go on thinking that you were a thief? And a stupid thief at that?"

Cass half sobbed, half laughed. "No."

"Well, then, why don't you tell me what happened?"

She spoke slowly. "Cook made me clean the lamps this morning. It's 'cause William drank too much last night and he's behind today. I was taking the last two up

245

to the dining room when I fell and smashed the lamps."
She twisted the handkerchief nervously. "That's all."

"So to cover for William, she accused you of stealing
the lamps?"

Cass nodded.

"Well. Cook's responsible for engaging her own help,
and I can't help you get your post back. But even if I could,
I don't think I would."

Cass looked hurt. "But why?"

"I want to help you, Cass," Mary explained gently,
"but not to a place that's dangerous to your health."

Cass's jaw took on a stubborn shape. "Any place is
better than no place. And now I've no letter of character.
I can't get a place without a character." The tears welled
up again, and she swiped at her eyes.

"Use my handkerchief, Cass. Please."

There was something about the handkerchief; perhaps
it was simply too fine to soil. In any case, Cass stoppered
her tears. "I'm sorry, Miss Quinn," she mumbled.

"Don't be. Listen, Cass, do you really want to be a
scullery maid?"

A shrug. "It's what I know, miss."

Mary waved one hand impatiently. "But do you
remember when we talked about being a lady? Not a real
lady, but one like me?"

"Ye-e-s. . . ."

"Well, would you still like to try to be one?"

Cass blushed. "That was just dreaming, miss."

Mary took the girl's thin hands in hers. "What if I told you it wasn't a dream, Cass? What if I said it was possible for you to go to school and meet other girls your age?"

Cass frowned, more in bewilderment than refusal.

"Lessons are work, too," warned Mary. "You won't enjoy all of it. But you could learn."

She shook her head, as though to clear it. "Miss, you're not . . . I'm a scullery maid. That's all. You're very kind, Miss Quinn, but I can't. I can't even understand what you mean."

Mary stifled a sigh. "I know this is sudden. What I mean is that I know someone who can help you. She's a teacher at a girls' boarding school, and she's interested in—" She broke off. Cass's face had gone still and rigid and she was edging toward the door, shaking her head. "What's the matter, Cass?"

Cass continued to shake her head. "You're very kind, miss, but please, I must go."

"Let me give you a letter—it's like a character, but for school instead of working in service. You can take it to this school . . ."

Cass blinked, then nodded once, sharply. It wasn't the eager acceptance she'd hoped for, but Mary immediately sat down and lifted the writing desk onto her lap. It took her a minute to find pen, ink, and paper. *Dear Miss Treleaven,* she wrote, *Cassandra Day, the bearer of this letter . . .*

The door clicked, and Mary looked up. By the time

she'd reached the doorway, Cass was already half-way down the hall, sprinting, her squashed bundle of clothing clutched hard against her side. Mary's first impulse was to give chase. But what good would that do? Even if she caught Cass and personally delivered her to Anne Treleaven, the Academy wasn't a prison. Reluctant pupils were always permitted to go. She listened to the receding clatter of Cass's footsteps and rubbed her face wearily. Her fingers were slightly greasy—probably from touching Cass's. She washed her hands and went back down to the breakfast room.

It was becoming a morning of domestic crises. Half an hour later, when Mary happened to pass by Angelica's bedroom door, she couldn't help but hear a smothered sort of wailing. She hesitated. Angelica had never welcomed her concern before, and she couldn't imagine that changing now, but yet after yesterday's escapade, Mary felt responsible for her.

She equipped herself with a tea tray and knocked at the bedroom door. It required persistence, but after several minutes, she heard a muffled "Come in." The bedroom was in darkness and the air was thick with sleep and stale perfume.

"I brought you a cup of tea," Mary said to the lump under the bedsheets.

Angelica continued to sob into her pillow.

Mary was genuinely alarmed. This was, after all, the

day after the supposed happiest day of Angelica's life. "Angelica? Are you ill?"

Long silence. "N-no."

"Did you fall out with Michael?"

Angelica's face appeared, puffy and red and grotesque. "N-no. Yesterday was lovely—Michael was lovely—everything is love—lovely. . . ." She melted once again into tears.

Mary didn't know how to respond. "So—yesterday was lovely but today is not?"

Angelica made a mewling sound that seemed like agreement.

"But you don't know what's the matter?"

Angelica shook her head and bawled. After several minutes, exhausted and hiccupping, she stammered, "I—I'm like this. Sometimes."

Mary remembered the morning after the party. Angelica should have been triumphant, but instead she'd seemed utterly miserable. "Why don't you sit up? You'll breathe more easily." She poured a glass of water.

Angelica struggled up clumsily and blew her nose. "You must despise me," she said eventually. "My life is so easy compared to yours, but I'm the one crying over nothing."

"I don't despise you." Mary said the words automatically, but realized that she did mean them. Angelica was a selfish brat. But for all her wealth and privilege, she was as powerless as Cass Day in the ways that counted.

Angelica sighed and looked down at her hands. On her left ring finger was a plain gold band, so thin it was barely more than a shadow. Her face clouded again.

"You don't regret marrying him, do you?" Mary asked. "You seemed quite sure of yourself yesterday."

Angelica's face crumpled again, as if to cry, but she managed to control herself. After a few minutes, she spoke. "I thought marrying him would make me happy. It did make me happy for a few hours. And then—we came sneaking home yesterday to dinner as usual—it was as though nothing had changed." She gestured feebly. "It's all the same. I'm still here. He's still the secretary. I thought I would feel different."

"Things will be different as soon as your parents find out you're married. Perhaps you and Michael should tell them."

Angelica drank some tea. "I lay awake all night thinking about that. But it's more than that. I expected getting married to change everything, but it's made the same things more complicated. I feel trapped—not by marriage but by everything else. I—I don't know how to explain it."

Mary looked at Angelica for a minute. Then she said, "I know you don't like me much, but may I offer my opinion?"

"It's not that I don't like you . . . but I had decided not to like you." She half smiled. "I don't suppose it matters to you, but I think you're interesting."

Interesting. It was a painful reminder of James's

assessment of her—and his later disdain. Mary drew a deep breath and focused on Angelica's situation. "I think," she said carefully, "that there are some women for whom marriage and children are the most important objects in life. But I think there are others who long for more. Your unhappiness reminds me of that sort of need."

Angelica's brow wrinkled. "Marriage is what I was raised for."

"You're a gifted pianist, Angelica. Have you ever thought of doing more than playing for your family and friends?"

A faint blush tinted her cheeks. "My music teachers always said so. . . . I never thought—never allowed myself to think. . . . And I'm married now." Her shoulders slumped. "It's too late."

"Is it?" Many actresses and opera singers continued to perform after they married. "Couldn't you be a musician and a wife?"

"I can't do that!" Angelica looked genuinely scandalized. "And poor Michael . . ."

"He seems a reasonable man, and he wants you to be happy. He would probably be proud to have a talented wife."

Angelica shook her head, agitation visible now in those round blue eyes. "It's not done. It's just—it's not . . ."

"I'm not trying to tell you what to do," said Mary quickly. "Only suggesting that your unhappiness might be due to your lack of choices." She couldn't gauge

Angelica's response. "Only you can know that, but I didn't want to go away without saying this." And it was true. At some point in the last half hour, she'd gone from being Angelica's dutiful companion to a concerned acquaintance. In Angelica's misery—as in Cass's—Mary saw her own history.

"I'll leave you to think about that," she concluded. "Do you need anything else?"

Angelica was already lost in thought. "Hm? Oh—no. But Mary?"

She paused at the threshold. "Yes?"

"Thank you—once again."

Twenty-two

As no one desired Mary's company that morning, she quickly announced her intention of going for a walk and caught an omnibus to St. John's Wood. How ironic that she'd made a hash of everything except her bolt back to the safety of the Agency. On Acacia Road, the brass plaque that announced MISS SCRIMSHAW'S ACADEMY FOR GIRLS seemed almost unbearably comforting. She unlatched the wrought-iron gate and slipped inside, steeling herself for the worst. Her need for counsel was great, and if the advice was unsparingly harsh, so be it.

Anne's office was on the ground floor. It was surprisingly modest, both in size and decor: no sprawling mahogany desks, smoky oil paintings, or crystal decanters here. Instead, the room was as spare and trim as the woman herself, softened only by the profusion of potted plants. The door was ajar. At Mary's light tap, Anne looked up instantly. Her eyelids barely flickered at the sight of Mary but, for her, the tiny movement represented a significant display of emotion. "Hullo, Mary."

Mary was horrified to find herself blinking back tears — yet again. First at the Lascars' refuge, then nearly before James, and now . . . "I'm sorry — bursting in on you like this — I couldn't think what else to do — I've made such a mess — I know it's the final day tomorrow . . ."

Anne shut the door and enveloped Mary in a fierce hug. She was remarkably strong for one so bony. "It's all right; don't try to talk just yet."

Mary wasn't quite sure why she was crying: for her abject failure as an agent-in-training; for disappointing Anne; for betraying James; for not reaching Cass; even for Angelica, who cried so easily. Once permitted to let go, it was some time before her tears slowed. Eventually, as they tapered and she began to hiccup, Anne produced a hand-kerchief and a glass of brandy. "Drink that."

Mary sat and drank. She mopped her face, blew her nose, and attempted a shamefaced smile. "I'm sorry."

"You needn't apologize for crying. Suppose you tell me what you've been doing?"

Mary told her story with logic and economy, excluding nothing — except, of course, her private conversation with Mr. Chen. While she was tempted to tell Anne about her father, it was all too new. Too raw. And some part of her wondered whether it was even safe. . . . Unconsciously, she touched the jade pendant, which lay concealed beneath her dress.

Would Anne and Felicity despise her if they knew the truth? Would they be like so many other Englishwomen and men, priding themselves on being fair and modern but secretly fearing and loathing her? She'd heard the full range of epithets in her childhood. Although the hate words were ugly, the problem was larger than that: it was that she couldn't bear to hear them from her benefactors.

Yet even while common sense told her that Anne and Felicity would never insult her with those names, she continued to shy away from the truth. If she did tell them—even if they didn't abhor her—she would cease to be simply Mary Quinn. She would always be the half-caste, the Chinawoman, the different one. Neither fish nor flesh nor fowl, as the proverb had it, but she would become a thing. She would belong nowhere and be like no one.

When Mary finished her tale, Anne was silent. Mary tried not to fidget. Whatever criticisms Anne made, she would accept. She would demonstrate that she was capable of learning from her errors.

Anne's quiet voice cut through her thoughts. "Why did you come here today?"

She wasn't prepared for that question. Floundering for a moment, she pulled herself together. "I need your advice."

"What on?"

There was no short or pleasant answer possible. "I don't know what to do next. I haven't overheard any discussion of the shipment from India. I have made a series of errors, some of them very grave. I have been reckless. I have broken my word." Here, she halted.

"All that is true. You also overstepped the bounds of your assignment. The primary agent was most displeased with your attempts to search the warehouses. By breaking in and nearly being caught, you made her task much more difficult than it need have been."

Mary's face burned. She hadn't even considered that possibility.

There was another pause before Anne's cool voice reached her ears. "Do you wish to be relieved of your responsibilities?"

Mary flushed scarlet. "That is the most sensible course of action," she said slowly.

"But?"

"I've given you no reason to believe in my abilities," she said shakily. "I've been headstrong and arrogant and a danger to my colleagues. I've made the worst start possible. . . ."

"But?" Anne sounded genuinely curious.

"But I should like to continue with this assignment." She drew a long breath and met Anne's gaze with an imploring look. "I need to justify the faith you've had in me for all these years."

Anne's fine brows drew together in a slight frown. "You mustn't do this for me or for the Agency, Mary."

She shook her head vehemently. "It's more than that,

Miss Treleaven. I want to do my job. I want to meet my responsibilities. I want to see this task through to its logical conclusion. I want a chance to put things right."

Anne's expression was neutral. Mary held her breath. The small, squat clock on the desk rang the hour, followed by twelve silvery chimes. She would have to leave shortly in order to catch an omnibus back to Chelsea.

Anne, too, glanced at the clock. "You may continue with the assignment, Mary." She cut off Mary's thanks with a swift gesture. "Now. It seems to me there are four main threads in your narrative; I shall address them in order of importance.

"The transcribed documents you mentioned may be useful, but we have other resources. If only Michael and Angelica Gray know their location, they are unlikely to be lost, and Scotland Yard can compel Gray to turn them over if need be. If you haven't located other documents at this point, you likely won't." Anne fixed her with a stern look.

Mary nodded. Her cheeks and ears were scarlet.

"As for Mrs. Thorold's activities, you should remain alert for irregularities. I will arrange to have her placed under surveillance, but keep track of her movements today. Concerning James Easton: will you have further contact with him?"

When Mary tried to speak, only air came out. Eventually, she croaked, "No." At Anne's raised eyebrows, she managed some further explanation. "His brother was courting Angelica. Now that she's married, they are out of the picture."

Anne began to ask a question, then appeared to change her mind. Instead, she said carefully, "Your loyalty to the Agency comes first in this case. Remember that, should you see him again."

Mary nodded, feeling oddly uncomfortable. Was that all Anne intended to say on the matter? She considered framing a question . . . but what?

"Finally, the question of Cassandra Day: You aren't responsible there, Mary. She is free to decline our assistance."

"But I don't understand what terrified her so. She trusted me, to a certain extent, until I mentioned going to school."

Anne sighed. "Some girls simply hate the notion. They dislike what they perceive as imprisonment."

"Life as a kitchen maid is preferable?" Mary couldn't keep the frustration from her voice.

"She clearly believes so." Anne paused, then leaned forward once again. "We must return to the Thorold case. Our agent completed her investigation last night and retrieved the relevant papers from the warehouses. The shipment is due to be unloaded tomorrow. We are now waiting for Scotland Yard to confirm that they will move then in order to secure the physical evidence."

"I'm to keep an eye on the rest of the household until then?"

"Yes. The secret marriage is likely to be revealed in the confusion surrounding the arrests. You'll be able to leave your post quite naturally."

Mary nodded and rose. "Miss Treleaven . . ."

Anne shook her head. "No thanks and no apologies."

Mary ransacked her brain for something appropriate that was neither thanks nor apology. "Will you wish me luck for my last day?" There was a slight quaver in her voice.

A rare smile softened Anne's lips. "If you keep your head, you shan't need it."

Twenty-three

James's plans for a leisurely Sunday afternoon were a loss from the start. He'd put in a long Saturday night at the office, catching up on work that he'd neglected in favor of tearing about London with that woman. He really ought to have known better: any person encountered skulking in a wardrobe was going to be trouble. That went double—no, treble—for any tomboy who claimed to be a lady but whose behavior proclaimed otherwise at every moment. The damned minx was a practiced manipulator. He and George were fortunate to be free of the Thorolds and their dependents. Not that George would agree.

Then, just as James managed to distract himself with a book, the housekeeper brought him a note from Alfred Quigley. It wasn't the lad's fault: he had no idea the "case" had collapsed. But it was another unpleasant reminder of how much time and energy he'd wasted over the past fortnight. James crumpled the note into his pocket and began brooding about Quigley instead.

He ought to find something else for the lad to do. A bright child like that was wasted on simple errands. Yet at his age, it was the only sort of paid work he was likely to find, and he had to support his widowed mother. Could Easton Engineering engage the lad as a sort of apprentice assistant? Or perhaps find him a place in a decent school. . . . He'd need more schooling if he was to exploit his talents properly. Either way, the lad was a new responsibility James would have to sort out, thanks to the damned Thorolds.

Such an internal monologue was far from relaxing, and it was with almost a sense of relief that he heard the library door open. "What is it, Mrs. Lemmon?"

"I beg your pardon, Mr. Easton. There is a policeman asking to speak with you or Mr. George."

"Did he say what he wants?"

"He wouldn't explain himself to me, sir. He only declared it to be urgent."

On a Sunday, as well. "Very well." James stood. "Where have you put him?"

Constable Thomas Huggins was trailing an idle finger over the carved frame of a painting in the breakfast room. Young, with anxious, wide-set eyes, he whirled about guiltily at James's entrance. "Mr. Easton?"

"Yes." James sat down and invited the man to do the same.

"Very sorry to disturb you of a Sunday, sir." Huggins remained standing, hat awkwardly in hand. "Some rather unpleasant news, I'm afraid."

"Concerning me?"

"It appears that way, sir."

James merely waited, stone-faced.

"There's been a body discovered on one of your building sites, sir."

A body. James experienced a sudden certainty. He could see the slight, crumpled figure, its edges defined by a narrow crinoline, a mass of dark hair. "How? Where?" His voice sounded harsh, overloud.

Constable Huggins wiped his forehead. "Hard by the river, sir."

James was very glad he was seated. After a moment, he asked, "How can I help you?"

Huggins nodded, on firm ground once more. "Looks like an accident, sir. He must have lost his footing and tumbled into a pit, but we—"

Through his fog of nausea, James grasped the essential word. "*He?* It was a man?"

Huggins nodded. "Building sites are so tempting to beggars and mudlarks, you know. . . . They think it's all treasure trove."

Not a woman, then. Not— He drew a long breath.

"And so I've been sent to ask if you would come to the scene."

"Of course." James rose. "I doubt that I'll be able to identify the body, though, Constable. A vagrant, did you say?" Now that the first shock was past, he was annoyed at having jumped to conclusions. If Mary were to turn up dead, it certainly wouldn't be on one of his sites. He would banish her from his thoughts, beginning now.

"Yes, sir. It's hardly a nice subject for a Sunday, but a body's a body, even if he looks to be a ruffian. Probably mucking about with the machinery and all."

They took the waiting hansom down to the site of the future railway tunnel. It was a relatively unsmelly afternoon, for which James was grateful. The men could work efficiently tomorrow if this cool weather held.

Descending from the cab, he noted a small cluster of people. The site was guarded by a harassed-looking policeman who introduced himself as Sergeant Davis. The others were scavengers, mudlarks, and rag-and-bone men eager to strip the corpse.

James glimpsed a small heap at the far end of the tunnel mouth. "Any idea how the man got down there?"

"Fell, I s'pose."

James looked at the police sergeant sharply, but he wasn't being sarcastic. "Have you even sent for a surgeon?"

Sergeant Davis looked sullen. "What for? Christ himself couldn't raise this one."

A snigger rose from the audience.

"Get them away from here," growled James. He stripped off his jacket and scrambled into the pit. It led down from the entrance of the tunnel, and he almost slipped, skidding down crablike on his hands and feet. At the bottom, he stood and walked squelchily across its base. The dank river smell was heavier here, almost like a fluid trickling into his lungs.

The corpse's feet were small and—oddly, for a beggar—wearing shoes. Its face was pushed down into the mud, the arms sprawled carelessly. James's step quickened as he neared the body, and he turned it over roughly. It was short and slight, not a full-grown man at all. A boy, then. Why did that make it so much worse?

He scrabbled at the muddy throat, irrationally searching for a pulse point, but almost immediately realized it was futile. The flesh was cool. James squatted beside the body. A glance at the tunnel mouth showed him Huggins and Davis trying to contain the crowd. Neither seemed very authoritative.

With his handkerchief, James began to wipe mud from the features. It was unlikely the child would ever be identified, but he had to try. His stomach pitched slightly as he uncovered a few freckles. The glassy eyes seemed to focus on a point just behind his head. The eyelashes were caked in mud.

His handkerchief was soon sodden but it was enough. James's lips tightened as he looked down at the boy before him. The face was contorted and mud-smeared, the lips blue. But it was unmistakably he.

Neither a mudlark nor a beggar.

Not just any child.

Alfred Quigley.

His gut churned suddenly, and he turned aside just

in time, vomiting his Sunday luncheon into the mud. The retching didn't stop when his stomach was empty; violent convulsions shook his frame. He wasn't sure how much time passed before Constable Huggins touched his shoulder, embarrassment dyeing his freckled face scarlet.

"I'm sorry, sir. If I'd known it would bother you so . . ."

James took the handkerchief Huggins offered. Tears mingled with sweat on his face. Now that the roar in his ears was fading, he could hear the audience jeering—from a safe distance, of course. "Thank you," he said when he could speak.

Huggins blushed and looked away. "Take your time, sir."

James straightened. "I can identify the boy. He worked for me." Huggins's mouth opened in a small circle, and James hurried on. "You think it was an accident?"

Huggins looked about helplessly. "No reason for doing away with a boy, sir. I mean, if it were a girl, it'd be something else, 'specially if she was—you know. But a boy? And still in his clothes? Can't see another explanation, sir." At James's frown, he rushed on. "I'll check back at the station, of course, but I'm afraid we're a bit shorthanded at the moment. This—this is my first suspicious death, sir." He blushed again.

James nodded slowly. "The boy's named Quigley. He lived with his mother, a widow. I can give you their address."

Huggins nodded, relief evident in his posture. "The

sooner it's done the better, sir." He looked back at his sergeant and gestured meaningfully.

"You're moving the child now?"

"Sooner the better," Huggins repeated. "That lot'll have its teeth out the minute we turn our backs."

So Alfred Quigley was already "it." James bent and closed the staring eyes.

Huggins didn't seem to object. "Good idea, sir. Bit nicer for the mother that way."

Nicer. Of course. Definitely nicer, being a widow with a dead child. He fished out his wallet with a grimy hand and thrust its contents into Huggins's startled hand. "For the mother," he muttered. "Funeral." *Blood money.*

James watched the tragicomic procession: the sullen sergeant with the boy's body humped over his shoulder, followed by the timid but comfortingly human Constable Huggins. Flies were already swarming around the pool of vomit. He cast a final look at the ground and the patch where Alfred Quigley had been smothered. Then he turned and followed Huggins up out of the pit.

Murderer. Murderer. Murderer. James was unaware of how long he'd been standing at the edge of the building site, staring at the river, with that taunt running through his head. Alfred Quigley's death was his fault. There was no room for argument there. And instead of having the courage to tell Mrs. Quigley the news himself, he'd given

266

Huggins the address and left it at that. There was no particular reason for him to remain on site except that he couldn't think what else to do. Going back to the comfort of his house would be a retreat he didn't deserve.

His gaze passed over the knot of people on the sticky riverbank. Disappointed scavengers, most of them. Except for—his eyes noted a familiar figure gliding past the embankment. What the devil was she doing on his site? Sudden anger fired him, and before he remembered that he'd sworn not to think of her again, he ran across the churned-up mud to intercept her.

"What the blazes are you doing down here?" He barked the question as soon as he was within earshot.

Mary turned, then looked around and down. She seemed surprised to see him. "Good afternoon to you, too."

He scrambled up the bank, wiped his palms on his ruined trousers, and glared at her. "You should be safe at home. Don't you have a job to do?"

"Listen to me," she said quietly. She stepped closer, wrinkling her nose slightly at the fetid mud that coated him. "There are new developments."

He didn't want to talk about new developments. All he wanted was to roar at her until she cried and then pack her off somewhere safe—wherever that might be. He opened his mouth to begin, but she was already talking.

"Thorold's been arrested. The police raided one of

his ships near the warehouses." She had no idea why the schedule had been pushed forward from Monday to Sunday.

He froze, suddenly alert. "Go on."

"Two detectives from Scotland Yard came to the house during luncheon. They took him away. The warehouses are being searched and his files seized. It was a complete surprise—even Thorold hadn't an inkling. He thought they'd come to interview him about the warehouse break-ins!"

"What was he charged with?"

"Smuggling stolen goods." In a low tone, she summarized the matter of the Indian artifacts. He listened intently, frowning at the ground. Finally he asked, "Where is Gray?"

"At the house. The detectives told him to present himself at the Yard tomorrow."

"And Mrs. Thorold?"

"I was following her carriage. She called on a solicitor—I assume to arrange for Thorold's bail and defense. I stopped when you hailed me, but she was on her way home."

He considered her in silence. She seemed pleased—even blooming—with the adventure of it all. "You're certain she didn't see you?"

"I was careful."

"I hope so, for your sake."

She frowned at his tone. "What does that mean?"

An image of Alfred Quigley's dead face, muddy and

blue-lipped, flashed before his eyes. He had to protect Mary from the same fate. "I can't explain," he said in a tense voice. "But listen to me, Mary. We're clear of this situation. Thorold's affairs will be thoroughly investigated. There's nothing left for you to do. Get yourself a new post, and don't think about it any further."

"But—"

"If a trail exists for that lost parlor maid Thorold made pregnant—and I very much doubt it does—the police will find it. The best thing you can do is keep yourself clear of this mess."

"That's what you've decided?" Oddly, she wasn't outraged. Her eyes were distinctly green today and bright with excitement.

He worked to keep his voice level. Cool. "Yes."

"All right, then. What's your plan?"

He shook his head. "You're not listening to me. There is no plan. You need to get away from the Thorolds—the whole damned household—as soon as possible and before Thorold is released on bail. *Today.*" He watched her open, eager expression dissolve as she grasped his meaning. Finally.

She closed her eyes for a long moment, and he was glad for the chance to study her face. To take a lingering look. To memorize its contours. The moment didn't last long. "Let me understand this clearly: You're telling me to quit? To—to run away and mind my own business, like a good girl?"

He shifted his weight. "I didn't mean it like that." When her eyes were open, he was always on the defensive.

"You arrogant swine! You're telling me what to do—making all the decisions—after we agreed to be partners! *Equal* partners. We shook hands on it!"

"I know. I would explain if I could. . . ."

"But you can't or won't or don't have a good reason, so I'll just have to take your word for it!"

"Yes, but I wouldn't say that if it weren't extremely important. Don't you see that?"

She stared into his eyes. "Tell me." He began to open his mouth, and she added, "And *don't* say you can't, for my own good."

He closed his lips. For once, he was at a loss for words. What could he tell her? *Thorold will stop at nothing. He's murdered an innocent child and now I'm afraid for your life?* The situation seemed so far-fetched, and she was so reckless. Fired by her sense of justice, blinded by her fearlessness, she wouldn't listen to him. If anything, she'd set out to avenge Alfred Quigley. And run straight into danger. He groaned. It was hopeless.

"I would say take your time, but you did say that matters were pressing . . ."

He felt trapped by her gaze. Pinned to a card like an insect in a specimen case. The seconds—and then a full minute, and then two—ticked by.

Her eyes narrowed. "No? Then perhaps you can answer this: who are you to decide what's best for me?"

That was simple, wasn't it? A collaborator, originally. A coconspirator, certainly. A *friend*, surely. But suddenly all those seemed such weak descriptions compared with how he felt. And that realization frightened him as much as anything else he'd seen today.

"James . . ."

His heart was going much too fast. He could feel it in his throat. "It's too dangerous. That's all I can tell you. You must do as I say." His voice was overloud.

She flushed with temper. "Because I'm a mere, weak woman?"

"No. Because you're a novice, and a reckless one at that, and there's nothing you can do to help anybody." He tried to sound as cold and matter-of-fact as he could.

Her eyes widened with hurt.

"Mary?" He hated playing the brute. "Don't look like that."

She didn't move or reply.

"You'll be fine, Mary. You'll find another place. You can still get a letter, a character, from your old school, can't you? You were only with the Thorolds for—"

Angrily, she shook off his hands. "Don't touch me."

He hadn't realized he'd reached for her. "Very well. But tell me . . ."

"I have to go."

"At least let me take you home."

She straightened and met his gaze, and now instead of distress, he saw anger. "As you pointed out, Mr. Easton, we are both well rid of this mess. Therefore, there is no reason for us to continue this conversation or for you to be concerned for me." She waved away his attempt to speak. "Thank you for your assistance. I wish you well in all your business endeavors."

"So . . ." He studied her face carefully. "This is farewell forever?"

She lifted her chin. "Aren't you pleased? I know I am."

Twenty-four

In a day that had already exceeded itself for melodrama, the first thing Mary encountered back at Cheyne
Walk was another scene in the drawing room: Mrs.
Thorold, tragic and weak, leaning against the back of a
chair for support; Angelica, pale and tearstained, clutching Michael's hand; Michael guilt-stricken but resolute.
As she entered the room, only their gazes swerved to meet
her. Their bodies remained otherwise frozen.

Mrs. Thorold returned her attention to the guilty
couple. "Miss Quinn . . . would you be surprised if I told
you that my daughter is married?"

"No, ma'am."

"Or if I told you to whom she is married?"

"No, ma'am."

The woman turned to Mary. Her face was flushed
with rage, and her pockmarks stood out more than ever.
"I take it, then, that you helped them in this pathetic little
scheme."

"Yes, ma'am."

A sound of protest came from Michael, but Mrs. Thorold silenced him with a curt gesture. "Who else in the household participated in this deception?"

"No one else, ma'am."

A heavy, skeptical silence followed. "I see." She spoke to Mary with a serene air. "You, of course, are dismissed."

There was a brief pause, during which she considered her new son-in-law. "You'll soon be arrested."

Angelica gasped, but Michael didn't flinch.

Mrs. Thorold's gaze traveled to the trembling figure of her daughter. "As for you, my girl . . . my only child . . ." She smiled. "Not a penny. Nothing but the clothes on your back."

Angelica's mouth fell open. She had been pale before, but now all hint of color rapidly drained from her face, leaving even her lips chalky.

Mrs. Thorold observed the effect of her words with apparent satisfaction. "William will escort you both from the house. Ring the bell, Miss Quinn."

"Mama?" whispered Angelica. "Please. . . ."

Mrs. Thorold's glare fell on her like a blade. "You'd have done better to elope," she said with crisp relish. "You could then have taken some jewels."

Michael stared at her in horror. "My God—it's one thing to cut off your only child and another to enjoy it! Are you mad?"

Mrs. Thorold flicked a glance at Mary. "I said, ring the bell!"

Mary clasped her hands before her. "No."

"How dare you? You are my servant, Miss Quinn!"

"You fired me not two minutes ago."

Meanwhile, Michael put a protective arm around Angelica. "Hold on to me, darling; I'll take care of you." He shot a dark look at his mother-in-law. "No need to ring, madam. Mrs. Gray and I will see ourselves out."

Angelica seemed about to faint.

Mrs. Thorold clutched the back of a heavily carved chair with an effort that turned her knuckles white. "Get out!" she spat. "Leave my house this instant, you ungrateful wretch!"

Mary placed herself between mother and daughter. "Mrs. Thorold, you have nothing to gain by turning out Mrs. Gray now instead of in an hour's time."

"Haven't I?" The older woman's eyes glittered as she looked past Mary at Angelica's slumped body. "I lost my son and heir years ago, my husband is a fool, and now this strumpet can't even make a decent match. What else have I to lose?"

"The neighbors will have less to gossip about if she's able to walk from the house."

For a moment, Mrs. Thorold seemed to consider Mary with new interest. Then her hand fluttered to her forehead. "All this turmoil has been terribly enervating. I shall be resting in my boudoir, and I am not to be interrupted under any circumstances. When I emerge, you will all be gone."

Once she had limped from the room, Mary went to the drinks table. She poured two large measures of brandy and handed them to the Grays. "Drink that."

In the long silence that followed, Michael swallowed his in a single gulp, poured another, and repeated the procedure. Angelica sipped hers mechanically. There was a long silence, broken only by the chiming of the clock on the hour.

A full ten minutes passed before anyone spoke. Angelica broke the silence. "This morning, I prayed to be independent. It looks as though my prayer has been granted." Her tone was dry and neutral.

Mary inspected her for signs of hysteria but found none.

Michael sat down and took her hand. "You can depend on me, darling."

Angelica turned to him. "Can I?"

"Of course you can! We're man and wife now!"

She looked at Mary. "Are we?"

Mary was startled. "I was your witness."

"I know. You signed your name in the register." Angelica drained her brandy glass. "But you look very young for twenty, Mary."

Mary's cheeks and throat felt hot. "Do I?" Her voice sounded rusty.

"Are you sure you're not younger? Quite a lot younger?"

Michael stared at them both in distress. "That's ridiculous!"

Angelica was the calmest person in the room. "If I had to guess your age, Mary, I'd say sixteen. Seventeen, at most."

Mary bowed her head. "It was wrong of me to deceive you. I was only trying to help."

Michael attempted to speak, but Angelica's cool voice sliced through his sputtering. "It was wrong," she agreed, "but I'm rather glad of it. It provides grounds for an annulment."

Both Mary and Michael swung about to stare at her.

"Anj? Darling? What are you saying?"

"Are you feeling well, Angelica?"

Angelica lifted a hand in a gesture reminiscent of her mother's. "I'm perfectly well." She took a deep breath. "After our conversation this morning, Mary, I spent a long time thinking about what I wanted. It was difficult. While I'd always known what I wanted in terms of dresses and jewelry and the most romantic marriage proposal in the world, I'd never thought about life beyond that point. You'll think that shallow and foolish, Mary."

"Darling!" said Michael. "That's what all girls think of."

Angelica smiled sadly. "So it seems. But this morning, I finally began to think again. And I have changed my mind about what I want."

Mary sudden realized the delicacy of the situation. "I ought not be here. You two need to talk about this."

As she stood, Michael's arm shot out to restrain her. "You might as well stay. It's your doing, after all." He turned to his disputed wife. "Angelica—what is this all about?"

Angelica looked steadily at Michael. "Now that my mother has disowned me and our marriage is not legal, I'm free to do what I really want."

Mary stared at her, fascinated. This Angelica was a new creature. She had the same round blue eyes, the same soft blond beauty, but there was a new kind of sharpness about her; a concentrated focus.

"My music teacher, Herr Schwartz, has long urged me to go for further training abroad. He has some professional connections in Vienna. I spoke to him this morning, asking if it was not too late to begin lessons with one of his associates."

"If all you want is more pianoforte lessons—"

Angelica's hand again stopped Michael's words. "The music lessons are only a beginning. Herr Schwartz thinks I have potential, that I might have a future as a concert pianist." She stopped and drew a shaky breath. "It's a terrifying prospect, of course. I've never really wanted to go abroad, and now I shall have to support myself by giving music lessons in a foreign city! But if Herr Schwartz is able to arrange it, that is what I intend to do."

There was a stunned silence.

When Michael spoke, his voice was gentle, cajoling—the sort of tone one might use with a sick animal or an irrational child. "Angelica, love, you never told me about all this. If you want more music lessons—even if they must be in Vienna—what has that to do with an annulment?"

Angelica blinked. "You wouldn't want to go to Vienna."

"For you, darling? Of course I would! After all, you can't very well travel alone, let alone live in foreign parts without a protector. Why, you'd be an easy mark for every crook and unscrupulous so-called gentleman. . . . You must have your husband with you, sweetheart."

"How could we live? You heard my mother disown me. Music lessons pay little. I couldn't support two, let alone three."

Michael flushed. "You wouldn't have to work, of course," he said stiffly. "I would provide for you—and our future family."

Angelica shook her head. "We've wandered from the point. Michael, my decision is already made."

There was a very long silence.

When Michael spoke again, his voice was hard. "Yesterday, you married me. You told me that you loved me and that you would be my wife. Today, you want nothing to do with me, and you're willing to flee to a foreign city in order to get rid of me. I demand to know what has happened in the meantime!" He turned to

Mary, his face twisted with anger. "What the *devil* did you say to her?"

Angelica stood. "You have every right to be angry, Michael, but you mustn't shout at Mary. This is purely my decision."

He crumpled suddenly: voice, face, posture. "Then *why*?"

Angelica reseated herself and waited for him to do the same. After a few moments, she said slowly, "Michael, you're a fine man, but I married you primarily to defy my parents. They wanted me to marry a rich and powerful businessman, and I chose the poorest man I knew." Michael flinched, but she continued as though she hadn't noticed; perhaps she hadn't. "I don't love you enough to remain married to you, now that every other aspect of my life is changed. I've always been terribly selfish; you may think I don't know it, but I do. And I shall continue to be so. I'm going to remain a spinster and study music in Vienna and disregard anyone who attempts to stop me." She slipped the wedding band from her finger and offered it to him. "It's a worthless thing to say, Michael, but I am sorry."

His gaze remained fixed on the carpet for a long time.

Mary scarcely dared to breathe.

Angelica kept her hand outstretched, offering back the thin circlet of gold.

After some time, he carefully composed his face. "I'm sure you'll manage in Vienna."

"I—I'm frightfully sorry, Michael," Angelica murmured.

"Yes, you said that before."

"You'll find someone better than me; someone who appreciates you," said Angelica with forced brightness. It was exactly the wrong thing to say.

"No, I won't. I'm going to prison."

"The police investigation should clear you," Mary said. "If you tell them what you told me yesterday. . . . You could show them those documents you copied. . . ."

He shrugged and stood. "I very much doubt they'll listen. If you'll excuse me, ladies . . ." He left the room with his shoulders slumped, a far cry from his usual suave, elegant self.

Angelica looked at Mary, eyes wide. "Do you think I did the right thing?"

"Which part? Asking for the annulment?"

"All of it, I suppose." Angelica rolled the wedding band between finger and thumb. "It's terrifying to be on the verge of finally getting what you want."

"Is it?"

"I keep wondering if I should take it all back. Of course, I don't really want to."

Mary grinned suddenly. "Well, if you change your mind, there's always George Easton. . . ."

Twenty-five

Numb.

That was the word for his hands and the curious, cold feel of his lips. Pity it didn't apply to his emotions. James stared at the crumpled bit of paper he'd just fished from his pocket: half a sheet of writing paper folded neatly in thirds and addressed to J. Easton, Esq., in painstaking, rather wobbly printing. It was Alfred Quigley's letter. James had forgotten all about it until he'd gone looking for his spare handkerchief.

It was irrelevant now, of course—along with James's plans to employ the lad properly or to help him get a decent education or any of the good intentions he'd so resented this morning. Yet what the hell was he to do with the note? It seemed to vibrate between his fingers—in truth a tremor most likely caused by the mild breeze or James's own nerves—and the movement made it seem alive. With a sigh, James unfolded the paper.

Saterday 9 pm

Deer Mr. Easton

*Ther is sumthing rong at the Saylers ~~Refy~~ House,
its to do with the Famly in Chelsy and the China-man. I
will explane all wen I see you next but I thot you shood
no now.*

Yrs sincerly, A. Quigley

James felt an immediate cold queasiness that had
nothing to do with the river's stink. Last night, Alfred
Quigley had been alive and well and making plans for the
following day. This afternoon, he was dead and cold. Certainly, life was nasty, brutish, and short—particularly if
one was poor—but this was surely too great a coincidence.
Quigley knew something about Thorold and the Lascars'
refuge; Quigley reported it to James; Quigley turned
up dead on James's building site. The boy was killed
not merely because he was in the way but because he'd
uncovered something important. And this scrap of paper
was the link between the discovery and the murder.

James ran several streets from the building site
before finding a cab, and even then, the first two declined
to drive him because of the state of his clothing. It was just
over three miles to Limehouse, and the driver, spurred on
by the promise of a tip, set a smart pace.

"Stop here," said James at the entrance to George
Villas.

"I ain't waiting here," the cabbie said sullenly. "Don't

wait for nobody in this part of town, not even the Prince of Wales."

Wise man, thought James, and emptied his pockets of coins large and small.

The front of the Lascars' home was like a blind face. He jerked sharply on the bellpull and waited. Nothing. He rang again. Still nothing. A vigorous rap on the door, however, pushed it ajar.

"Mr. Chen?" he called, stepping gingerly into the front hall. The smell of the place was thick in his nostrils and familiar from his last visit. Incense, he remembered. Mothballs. Chinese herbal medicines. Unfamiliar spices. And below all that, traditional English damp rot and mildew that caught him in the throat. His voice seemed to churn up the air in the foyer.

"Hello? Mr. Chen?" he called again, to be answered only by stillness.

The last time he'd been here, Mr. Chen had answered the door promptly. Perhaps he had Sundays off?

"Is anyone in?" he called, very loudly this time. There had to be *some* servant about. When the echo of his voice died out, James felt the first prickle of anxiety. First, Alfred Quigley. Then the arrest of Thorold. What else was wrong? Had they all cleared out? They couldn't all be in it together — all those frail old men? But Chen could. Chen could have used the place as a center of operations, and Chen could have escaped by now. That made sense: banish the old men, give the servants the day off, and disappear.

Damn it. The whole time that old man was filling him with nonsense about penniless Lascars, he'd been working with Thorold. It was a fine front, of course. Who would suspect a sweet-faced old Chinese man?

The door of the manager's office stood ajar, and when he pushed it wide, even James was startled. The room had been ransacked—although the word implied a degree of method that didn't seem quite right here. The carpet was littered with reams of paper, most of it trampled and shredded by heavy boots. All the drawers and cabinets were torn open, spilling their entrails onto the floor. The shelves were tipped over, along with their contents. He couldn't be sorry that the hideous oil painting was kicked through or its gilded frame broken. But the curtains, too, were pulled down, one side of the brass rail slumped against the ground. This was more than simple robbery. There was rage here.

James thought back to his meeting with Mr. Chen and again revised his ideas. Mr. Chen had no need to ransack his own office. Whatever he needed, he could have found. So why destroy the room? To make it look like something else? Or was it someone else entirely? Head whirling, he bent to examine a dark, wet patch on the carpet. Coffee. Not blood, thank God. And it was cold, which only meant that the mayhem had occurred longer ago than ten minutes, say. And the other wet patch was oil—the smashed globe of the lamp ground into the carpet confirmed that.

A loud *klock* made him glance up—and then freeze.

"That's right," said the figure framed in the doorway. "Keep still."

James couldn't wrench his gaze from the source of the click: a sleek handgun. One of the newer revolving pistols if he wasn't mistaken. It was the first he'd seen, but everyone knew they were more accurate than the old flintlocks.

"Now. Slowly. Stand up."

James nodded, his eyes finally focusing on the person—a woman, he realized with a sense of shock—behind the gun. She was tall and athletic, her gaze cold and direct. And she seemed extremely familiar. . . .

"Come on." She bobbed the gun at him. "It's time to stop playing about, young James."

Sudden recognition sliced through him. "Mrs. Thorold?"

She smiled grimly. "But of course."

He stared at her stupidly. She wore her usual hairstyle and type of dress, but everything else—the way she moved and spoke, even the predatory way she looked at him—was utterly different. Even that day in Pimlico, hadn't shown the full scale of her transformation. "You did all this . . . ?"

She smiled. "Aren't you a clever boy. Now turn round and hold your hands high." Questions raced through his head, but before he could phrase one, she snapped, "Do it!"

One advantage to the rubbish strewn all over the floor

was that it made it easier to track her approach. She took her time picking her way through the debris. "Now don't move." Something jabbed James's spine—the muzzle of the gun, presumably. Hands delved into his pockets, explored his waistband, his waistcoat. She extracted his wallet from his breast pocket and tossed it aside. Experimentally, he turned his head an inch or two to the left but stopped when the gun dug deeper into his back. "None of that, young man."

Another pause and then the hands searched the tops of his boots. He was strongly tempted to kick backward. His leg muscles tensed in readiness, itching to strike out, but he'd never be quicker than the revolver.

"No knife?" Her voice was mocking. "You don't look like the gun-carrying sort, but surely you aren't going to tell me you came down to Limehouse with nothing but a pocketbook for protection!" A few drops of spittle flecked his ear.

"I'm a businessman. Of course I'm not armed."

"Well, I'm a businesswoman, and I'd never be so stupid," she jeered.

"I'll bear that in mind in future."

She chuckled. "You do that. Now"—her voice became crisp and commanding—"step toward the door, nice and slowly, and climb the stairs. I'll be behind you with this pistol pointing at the back of your head."

"Hands up? Or down?" James's tone was exquisitely polite.

"Such nice manners," she scoffed. "No wonder Angelica liked you."

He relaxed his arms but jerked them back up again when she poked him with the gun. "Hands on your head."

James walked out of the room, back through the musty corridor, and to the staircase. As they turned a corner, he asked, "How did you know I would come here?"

"You're exceedingly predictable."

He was offended. "How so?"

"Well, you came running at once as soon as you read that note."

Quigley's note? "How did you know about that?"

She barked with laughter. "Can't you even guess?"

His stomach knotted. It was so obvious. "You wrote it, didn't you?"

"With my left hand. The guttersnipe spelling was a nice touch, wasn't it?"

"And that explains the time delay in the note: it was dated Saturday night, but I only received it today. You could have killed Quigley at any time, but you had to make sure I didn't come here until this afternoon."

"And here you are."

When they reached the second floor, he paused, unsure whether to turn left or right. The house felt like a tomb, or a vault. Or maybe that was just his imaginative response to being marched with a gun to his head. In any case, the residents of the Lascars' refuge were nowhere to be seen. Now he had to wonder if it was because they were all lying dead behind closed doors.

"What do you want from me?"

"Good Lord, you're tedious. Keep moving."

He started upstairs to the third story. "All right. What does Thorold want from me?"

There was a rich chuckle. "My dear boy—who ever mentioned my husband?"

"Are you denying that he's your partner?"

"In the laws of this country a wife is a possession, not a partner."

"So you're not his business partner." Once again, he had to tear down his assumptions and begin again.

She snorted. "You're a bit slow, aren't you?"

"So who is your business partner?"

"Move faster."

He waited a moment, then tried a different tack. "Do you intend to murder me?"

"What do you think?" Her voice was rich with contempt.

They were on the landing of the third floor now, and the gun poked him between the shoulder blades. "Turn right."

They entered a small room, sparely furnished with a single bed, desk, chair, and washstand. It held two further objects. The first was a large hookah standing in the center of the floor. The second was the body of Mr. Chen, bound hand and foot and crumpled in a heap beside the hookah.

James looked from Chen to Mrs. Thorold and back again. "Is he dead?"

She shrugged. "Perhaps. I only tapped his head, but he's an old man."

James knelt and touched Chen's throat. The body was warm, but he couldn't seem to find a heartbeat. Or perhaps his own pulse was pounding so loudly he couldn't detect the other. He glared up at her, finally passing from disbelief to anger. "Why him? What did he ever do to you?"

Her pockmarks were deep, making a painful-looking pattern in her pale skin. "Like you, he asked too many questions. I came here to silence him."

"So this is the grand scheme? To let people think we smoked ourselves to death? No one will believe that!"

"Come, now. You're not thinking straight. Death by opium overdose is slow. I've not got all night to wait about and see if you've taken enough."

James straightened slowly and looked into her clear blue eyes. They were exactly like Angelica's. For the first time, he felt certain that he would die in this hovel. In this room.

She removed a length of rope from her handbag and tossed it to him. "Tie your ankles together."

It was coarsely woven hemp. Strong sailor's rope. "And if I refuse?"

She sighed. "You quibbling, nosy little swine. You've a choice. In the more comfortable scenario, you tie yourself up. I knock you out. Then I light a merry little fire that burns the whole place to the ground, but you don't feel a thing."

James raised one eyebrow and considered it as though it was a business offer. "And the second choice?"

"I shoot you once or twice, but not to kill—probably in the groin. You die a slow and painful death. Then I burn the house down anyway, and no one's the wiser."

"Shooting's noisy. And perhaps I'm a coward. People will hear me scream."

She smirked. "Maybe. But in this area, they'll turn a deaf ear."

James thought about that for a moment, then sat down and began to tie his ankles. He took his time and, as he worked, said, "Does Thorold know what you do?"

She shrugged. "I'd say he knows as much as he cares to."

"Meaning as little as possible."

"Precisely."

"He knows about this place."

"Does he now?"

"He named it in his will," he said. "That's how I found it."

Her face turned ugly. "I might have guessed."

"He left it a substantial legacy, and he's also making regular donations." James watched her features carefully. "Guilt money? For what you were doing?"

Petty irritation twisted her expression. "He was always a soft touch. No guts."

He completed one final loop with the rope and knotted it. "There."

"With that slip knot? Don't play the fool with me, young James."

He shrugged. "I thought it worth a try."

"Perhaps with my husband you'd have succeeded," she snorted. "Now retie it!"

"So your husband employed Lascars on his ships—or at least he claimed he did, and Lloyd's paid up." James mused as he worked. "But the ships always sank. And he felt guilty enough about that to donate money to the refuge. . . ." The facts were before him, but he couldn't work out how to organize them. "It's as though his scheme was broken in the middle, but he couldn't fix it."

A husband and wife, emphatically not partners.

Insurance fraud.

Sunken ships.

Guilt money.

A ransacked office.

There was at least one more missing detail. . . .

Mrs. Thorold watched him struggle with the puzzle, a scornful smirk on her face. "You poor dim brat," she said, almost tenderly. "You're nearly as stupid as my husband."

Such contempt. Such arrogance. An idea flashed into his mind. "You were working against your husband! Sabotaging his shipments!"

"Ah. The male mind, sluggish and inadequate as it

292

is, finally begins its labored processes." She waved the pistol at his hands. "Don't stop."

She was arrogant, rude, decisive. She knew best. She enjoyed insulting him. With a jolt, James realized that he and Mrs. Thorold were more alike than he could have imagined. And with that shock came a heady sense of courage. His first concern now wasn't survival or out-smarting the woman. Yet it rankled to stop just short of an explanation. It troubled his sense of order and process.

Very deliberately, he ceased his knot tying. Looking up at Mrs. Thorold with his most winsome grin, he said, "My poor brain finds it difficult to reason and tie knots simultaneously. Can't you put me out of my misery—well, before you put me out of my misery?"

She snorted. "This isn't a Drury Lane comedy."

"Certainly not for me; comedies have happy endings."

"Well then?"

"It's your drama. You're the playwright and the heroine."

"Mere flattery won't save your life."

"I'm not interested in saving my life."

She mimed exaggerated surprise. "Brave words, little boy."

"I'm interested in the story; the play, if you like. You're sabotaging your husband's shipments. But that hasn't anything to do with the stolen artifacts from India, has it?"

She was watching him with amusement now, a small

smile playing about her lips, although the gun never wavered. "Save your breath, dear. I'm still going to kill you."

"I understood you the first time, believe me."

"Then?"

He finished tying up his ankles. "I'm an engineer. I like to know how things fit together. Before you kill me, won't you at least tell me about your scheme? Anything worth killing three men for—not to mention all those sailors—surely merits a little boasting . . ."

"That little brat hardly counts."

"Two men, then."

"Chinamen aren't real men."

"All right, then. One boy, one foreigner, and one Englishman. It's still a fair amount of dirty work."

She gave in to a smirk. "You're oddly persuasive."

The tension in his gut suddenly, rapidly, eased. A trickle of sweat rolled down his forehead and stung his eye. "So I'm told."

"You can have the short version: my husband is a fool who fancies himself a smuggler of precious artifacts. Yet he also makes false insurance claims that attract the attention of the authorities, jeopardizing not just the smuggling operation but our entire livelihood."

Her use of the word *our* was interesting. "That much I knew."

"Naturally, some little nobody at Lloyd's worked out the scheme and began to bleed him for it." Her mouth twisted in disgust. "Fancy trusting someone to cover your own stupidity!"

"So you stepped in?"

"It was only a matter of time until the business went under—either through blackmail or when Scotland Yard finally worked out what was happening.

"I took his plan to its logical conclusion. I run a pirate crew who attacks and loots my husband's ships. It's perfect: lower capital and running costs, and after I split the profit with my partner, the money's entirely mine."

"You don't share it with your husband?"

She laughed. "Give me one good reason why I should."

He blinked. It was an excellent question—and one that he'd entirely overlooked. Why should Mrs. Thorold work for the benefit of her family if she cared only for herself?

She was watching him with a bemused smile. "I thought not."

He tried to rally. "How do you silence the Lascar crews on the ships you raid?"

She shrugged. "Pirates are bloodthirsty men. I imagine any useful survivors are sold as slaves in the Far East."

James nodded, although his head was spinning. It was too much to process just yet. But he had to keep her talking . . . at the very least he had to learn whether Mary was in danger.

"That's enough chitchat. Hands behind your back." Her voice was crisp and businesslike once again.

"The house in Pimlico," he said hastily. "Your headquarters?"

She only smiled and brandished another length of tough hemp rope.

"And your colleague—that Mr. Samuels. He runs the pirate crew?"

"I'm tired of talking to you. The play is over, young James."

To his shame, he began to panic and thrash, kicking out at her with his bound legs. A few well-placed kicks in the ribs put a stop to that, and she knelt heavily on the small of his back. The binding of his wrists was swift and painfully tight.

"One last question," he wheezed, as she stood to inspect her handiwork. "Aren't you afraid my confederates will be looking for me?"

She only laughed. "That was feeble; unworthy of you, I'd say."

"Why? You don't think I have a colleague?"

"Who'd want to collaborate with you?"

James went limp with relief. His last vision was of a leering grin rushing toward his face. And then there was only blackness.

Twenty-six

Mary was packing her trunk when a handful of gravel pattered against the window. Her breath caught, foolish though that was. James had made perfectly clear what he thought of her. She hesitated, uncertain how to respond. After a few seconds, another round of small stones struck the window. She flung the window open and looked down onto the pavement, eager despite herself. But instead of a tall young man, it was a scrawny child. A haze of mousy hair obscured most of its face. There must be some mistake. Yet as Mary peered down, the little body beckoned furtively. After a moment, Mary nodded and pointed to the service door.

A final look around the bedroom showed everything in order. Her trunk was neatly corded and labeled, and one of the footmen was charged with its delivery. As she descended the Thorolds' staircase for the last time, she felt haunted by the ugliness of the day: Thorold's indignant denials of guilt; James's anger; Angelica's sobbing, followed by Michael's heartache; Mrs. Thorold's glee. Mary couldn't wait to return to the calm of the Agency.

Ignoring Cook in the kitchen, she opened the area door and blinked in astonishment. "Cass?" Their gazes locked for only a moment, after which Cass fixed hers firmly on the ground. Any number of questions raced through Mary's mind. *Why are you here? Are you hurt? Have you changed your mind? What's wrong?* She settled for, "Hello."

"Miss." Cass's voice was barely audible.

Mary waited, but nothing else was forthcoming. "We can't talk here," she said quietly. "I'll meet you at the back of the stables." She waited again. "All right?"

A mute bob of the head signaled Cass's comprehension. As Mary retraced her steps though the house, she suddenly realized that she'd done the wrong thing. It was unlikely that Cass would go round to the stables. Not only were Brown and the footmen prone to hanging about there for a smoke and a gossip, but Cass was likely to have second thoughts about speaking to her and take flight. *Damn.* Her second chance to help the girl and she'd bumbled it again. The idea sent her scurrying through the kitchen and out the back door. On her way through the courtyard, she noted mechanically that the carriage was not in the carriage house. The significance of that was lost on her for the moment.

Luck was with her in a small way today. There was

no sign of the male servants, but in the darkest corner of the mews she spotted the waiting figure of Cass Day. Mary moved toward her slowly, as though approaching a frightened animal, and waited for Cass to speak first.

"I'm sorry I ran away, miss," she said eventually, in a rusty voice.

"Did I frighten you?"

Cass's eyes darted nervously to one side. "Not you, miss. I mean—that is, nothing you did. I was just stupid." After an anguished pause, she blurted out, "The other maids kept whispering about the white slave trade, miss, and reading picture-papers about it, and going on about how respectable-looking ladies are running it. They're full of it, they are, and when you—I mean, when I—that is . . ."

Mary's eyes widened. "You thought I was trying to kidnap you?"

Cass's face was beet red. "I thought that was why you were kind to me. I couldn't think why any lady'd be kind to me except for that."

Mary felt a pulse of sympathy. Hadn't she said much the same thing to Anne Treleaven all those years ago?

"I expect it shows I'm too stupid to go to school . . . doesn't it?" The girl's tone was hopeful, despite her words.

"Have you thought more about going to school?"

She nodded so vigorously that her hair flopped about. "I do want to go . . . if I still may. If you're not too cross."

"I'm not angry, and there is still a place at this school I mentioned."

"I'll work hard. I promise. I'm not clever, miss, but I'll do my best, I swear. . . ."

Mary took her by the shoulders. "Don't promise me, Cass. Promise yourself."

Cass's eyes widened as she absorbed that. Then she nodded. "You're very good to me, Miss Quinn."

"Are you sure I'm not a white slaver?" Mary smiled.

Cass blushed furiously. Then she laughed, falteringly, at herself. It was a thin, tentative squeak, a noise that suggested its maker was unfamiliar with the technique. All the same, it was the first time Mary had heard her laugh. "Yes, miss."

They were in a hansom bound for St. John's Wood when Cass produced the notebook. "I think I must be very thick, Miss Quinn, 'cause I know my numbers and some letters, but I can't make any sense of this."

Mary reluctantly accepted the object. Now that the assignment had ended, she was tired. Her brain was whirling with random bits of information, none of which she could assemble into a coherent whole. And she wanted to be left alone to think about her father.

However, Cass was watching her expectantly. Mary flipped open the notebook and scanned its pages of minutely printed columns of figures. "This is a balance sheet, Cass. It shows sums of money coming in and going out of a business." She showed her a random page. "Look: there's a date here, followed by various entries of credits and debits, for a total profit of four hundred and sixty-two pounds, eight shillings, and four pence. It only really makes sense if you know a bit of bookkeeping."

Cass looked dismayed. "Will I have to learn that, too?"

"If you like," she murmured absently, turning over a page.

"Do all ladies know it?"

"Most ladies don't. It's mainly a clerk's job, and there still aren't many female clerks."

Cass still looked perplexed.

Mary flicked through several more pages, then looked at the first and last written pages of the book. The financial entries spanned more than two years, and were kept with meticulous care. Someone would be searching frantically for this item. "Cass, whose notebook is this?"

Cass looked instantly guilty. "I—I don't know, miss."

"But you just asked about ladies knowing book-keeping . . ."

"I mean that I f-found it, miss."

"Where?"

"B-beside the front steps, miss. When I was whitening them."

Mary forced herself to speak gently. "At the Thorolds' house?"

"Yes, miss."

"When?"

"I can't remember exactly. A week ago? Perhaps less?"

"Did you mention finding the book to anybody? Cook, perhaps?"

Cass shook her head.

Mary considered the object in her hand. It was small and weathered, and some of the gilt had worn off the pages, but it originally had been an expensive item. "Did you see the person who dropped this, Cass?"

At this, Cass seemed to shrink back into her seat. "I—I don't know, miss."

Mary considered her carefully. "Are you quite certain?"

Cass's gaze was fixed on the book. "It's very important, isn't it, miss?"

Mary nodded. "Much more than you'd expect."

Cass stared for a second longer, then took a deep breath. "I didn't see exactly, miss, but I think it was Mrs. Thorold. She came out of the house as I was whitening the steps, and so I had to do them over. When I started again at the bottom, it was lying on one side. It wasn't there before." She paused, then rattled on defensively, "But it can't be hers, right, 'cause she's a lady, and not a clerk or anything?"

Mary thought back. Yes, that too made sense. Mrs. Thorold had gone out in a rush on Wednesday morning— the day Mary had overheard Angelica and Michael talking in the drawing room—and she'd been in a foul mood on her return. But if this belonged to Mrs. Thorold, it put a whole new interpretation on the Pimlico affair. Was it even possible that instead of consulting physicians and instead of carrying on an adulterous liaison, Mrs. Thorold was clandestinely running a business of some sort? And what type of business, exactly?

Mary leafed through the pages once more, any scruples she might have had about reading someone else's private affairs long evaporated. A fresh balance sheet was drawn up for this month, but lacking specific dates. There were often long gaps between transactions — sometimes of several months — but there were also clusters of entries. So it was a business that was seasonal or otherwise dependent on external pressures.

If only she had a little more information. . . . She flicked through the blank pages, of which there were many; the notebook was only half full. And then, at the very end of the book, she saw a tiny pencil annotation, half erased: C: 7, G.V., Lh.

She sat back in the seat, stunned. Of course!

What a blind, obtuse, hare-brained ninny she'd been. And the carriage was gone now! Mrs. Thorold had *said* she'd be in her room, but in all the turmoil no one had checked.

Mary leaned out of the hansom and gave the driver a rapid series of instructions. Reseating herself, she said, "Listen, Cass. You've just told me something very important, and I must attend to it immediately. The driver is going to take me to east London. Then he will take you to the school in Acacia Road, which is called Miss Scrim-shaw's Academy for Girls.

"You will ask to see Miss Treleaven. Tell her that I have sent you as a new pupil, and then give her this notebook. Tell her I am meeting Mrs. Thorold at 7 George Villas, Limehouse, and to start immediately for that address. Do you understand me?"

Cass looked troubled. "Yes."

Mary laid a hand on her shoulder. She pretended not to notice that, once again, the girl had flinched in anticipation of a blow. "You've done nothing wrong, Cass; nothing at all. And you've helped me immeasurably. I'm sorry I can't introduce you to Miss Treleaven myself, but please understand that I have something very important to do now."

Cass nodded cautiously. "I understand."

"Good."

Even as she paid the driver to see Cass safely to the Academy, Mary began to second-guess what she was doing in Limehouse. She'd been wrong so many times in the past few days, and her sense of conviction began to evaporate as her boots touched the squelchy, rotting roadway near George Villas. Mrs. Thorold's notebook—if it could be proven to be hers—was only a record of business transactions. It was devoid of specific references, and there was nothing to tie her to the Lascars' refuge except that scrawled pencil address. Yet elsewhere—in the back of her mind—things clicked together. Even now, she couldn't say why she was so certain that the answer lay here. But here she was, heeding instinct above conscious logic, gut over instruction.

She spotted it the moment she rounded the corner: a plume of smoke wafting from one of the tall, narrow houses toward the end of the row. A small crowd clustered round the front of the buildings, more intent on watching the spectacle than putting out the fire.

Mary broke into a run. "How long has it been burning?" she demanded of the stocky, middle-aged woman closest to her.

"Just got here myself." The woman's voice was placid, unhurried. She folded her arms over her stained apron and appeared to settle in for the show.

Mary pushed her way toward the front of the crowd. "Is anybody inside?" she shouted.

The faces around her merely looked blank.

"You." Mary singled out a girl in a shawl and bare feet who looked as though she'd just tumbled from bed. "Has somebody gone to see if anyone's still inside?"

The girl shook her head. "Too late for that." She pointed. "See how fast it's spreading?" Sure enough, smoke and flame were visible in the next window over.

"Who lives next door?" Mary asked desperately. "Surely they want the fire put out?"

The girl looked at her with sleepy, intelligent eyes. "In this hole? Why should anybody care?" As though to illustrate her meaning, someone heaved a brick through a ground-floor window and a ragged cheer broke from the crowd.

Mary looked at the building in despair. Surely nobody was still inside. The old sailors, at least, were turned out each morning, and Mr. Chen was competent and sensible. He wouldn't risk his life trying to save mere possessions—not even the cigar box. Yet . . . despite this rational assessment, that sense of conviction prevailed. She turned one last searching look on the crowd—not a policeman in sight—and ran into the building.

Twenty-seven

Inside, it was not yet an inferno. The dank, gloomy entrance hall and corridors looked much as she remembered but for a light haze of smoke. The fire must have begun near the top of the building. She began with Mr. Chen's office, noting its ransacked state quite mechanically. Swiftly, she scanned the wreckage for a glimpse of the cigar box but soon realized it was futile. She ought to have felt despair and outrage and frantically begun to search the room. But there wasn't time for that. She had to check the rest of the building for people before she could worry about papers—even such important ones—and she was glad for the numb common sense that seemed to prevail within her.

Up on the second floor, the smoke thickened and she crouched low, holding her handkerchief over her nose and mouth. She would search here last. If the fire was at the top, she had to begin there while she had time. The third story was thickly shrouded with smoke, and she was forced to crawl now, cursing her crinoline as, with each movement, it scraped her knees. The front rooms were the ones with smoke pouring from the windows. Nothing in the first room. Nothing in the second. The smoke stung her eyes, her lungs. She'd lost her handkerchief somewhere, some time ago.

Working her way to the back of the building, she found a closed door from beneath which smoke billowed. The doorknob was warm, but possible to touch with her gloved hand. As she pushed the door open slowly, she braced herself for a blast of heat, a surge of flame. Instead, she was nearly knocked over by a stream of thick gray smoke. Coughing, crying, she waited for a minute, then turned back to the room. As the smoke flooded into the corridor, she could make out a prone form on the floor. Forgetting her running eyes and battered knees, she crawled over to the body.

James.

She wasn't even surprised. At some level, her certainty had been focused on this. On him. He was bound, lying with his face turned toward the door. She stripped off a glove and felt his cheek: warm. A strong, steady pulse throbbed in his throat. Merely unconscious, then. But how would she ever drag him out? He easily outweighed her by fifty pounds.

She shook him vigorously. "James!"

Nothing.

Shook again, harder. "Get up! James!"

Still nothing.

She slapped his face once, twice.

Miraculously, his eyelashes fluttered slightly.

"James!" she rasped. Her throat was hoarse with smoke. "Wake up!"

His eyelids opened, and he smiled at her as sweetly as if he'd awakened from a nap. More sweetly than he'd ever looked at her before. "Mary." His voice held mild surprise. "What are you doing here?"

She grinned despite herself. "It's a long story."

When he tried to move, he seemed surprised by the ropes at his hands and feet. Slowly, memory seemed to flood back, and he grimaced. "Damn." He struggled, then winced. "You need to get out."

"I know. The building's on fire." A hysterical laugh rose in her throat, but turned into a cough en route. "We're both getting out."

He glared at her—a confused, vague glare, but familiar all the same. "Forget it. Escape while you can."

"James. Do you have a knife?"

"No."

She looked about, her frantic gaze bouncing off bedstead, washstand, hookah. "There must be something sharp. . . . I can break the windowpane."

"God damn it! Get out, Mary!" A fit of choking caught him, and when he finished, he croaked, "You're damned stupid for a clever girl."

"That's the nicest thing you've ever said to me," she

quipped, crawling round the bed toward the window. Then, in quite a different tone: "Oh, dear God."

He grunted. "Is he alive?"

There was a long pause.

"No." When she crawled back, her expression held an odd blend of dismay and perplexity. She clutched an object in her hand. "A knife," she said to James. Her voice trembled. "He had a penknife in his pocket."

James stared for a moment. Then, as she began to saw at the cords binding his wrists, he suddenly understood. "She knew he'd be no match for her strength."

It was a small knife, and the hemp fibers were coarse and strong. She gasped with frustration as the knife bounced off the rope once, twice, three times.

"Mary?" He sounded dazed.

"Yes?" Drops of salt water stung her eyes. She hadn't realized she was sweating.

"Mrs. Thorold. She did this — she was working against her husband, not with him."

"What?"

"She's a pirate!"

"Not an *actual* pirate?"

"Well, I doubt she has a parrot or an eye patch, but she's running a pirate crew!"

"So all those ships that went down . . . Thorold's cargoes . . . ?"

He nodded. "All her work."

She sighed and swore quietly.

"What's wrong?"

"You worked it out first."

He laughed at that. "I charmed it out of her."

"You can't have been that charming; she still left you here for dead."

Finally, the rope gave way. As James winced and flexed his chafed and bleeding wrists, Mary set to work on his ankles. They'd already had more time than she could have hoped. But what if the fire had moved into the stairwell?

Finally. "Sit up," she ordered.

He raised himself with a groan, but slowly managed to push himself to his feet. He grinned cockily. Almost immediately he wobbled and his knees buckled, sending him crashing to the floor with a slurred curse.

"Is it the smoke?"

He grimaced. "Concussion, I think."

She slid her arm about his waist, looping his arm over her shoulders. "Come on, then." She braced herself and stood, taking some of his weight. He was able to help, but still leaned heavily on her shoulders.

He glanced vaguely toward Chen's body. "What about . . . ?"

"The fire seems to have slowed in here, but I don't want to risk another minute."

They set off, lurching and staggering. The heat seemed less intense, but sweat poured down both their faces: James's from pain, Mary's from the strain of holding him upright. The smoke was collecting in the corridor, and they both began to cough furiously.

Mary couldn't afford breath for speech. She could only hope that he stayed conscious. At the head of the stairs, she slapped his cheek lightly. "Down," she ordered.

In response, he gripped her shoulders tighter. At the first landing, the smoke eased a little and Mary glanced up at him. His face was black with soot. Hers must be the same. How had he ever recognized her?

They turned onto the second-floor landing, and James ducked as they passed under a low doorway, tipping them off balance again. They lurched and staggered against the wall.

"Mary."

"What?"

He tilted her face back and kissed her.

Her eyes widened. "What—what was that for?"

For an answer, he kissed her again.

She pushed him back breathlessly. "You really must be concussed."

"I'm perfectly lucid."

"You don't even like me!"

They began moving downward again. "That's your main objection?"

"It's rather a good one."

"Well, as it happens, I do like you."

"Telling me to clear off? You have a funny way of showing it."

He stopped again. "For God's sake," he said in exasperation. "I was trying to protect you. Foolishly and pointlessly, as it turns out." It was the most James-like speech he'd uttered so far, and for that reason it unnerved her all the more.

"Shall we focus on leaving the burning building?" she snapped.

They descended the remaining stairs and burst out through the front door, disheveled and reeking of smoke. They collapsed against the nearest lamppost, clinging to it to remain vertical, swallowing huge gulps of air that under any other circumstances would seem impossibly foul.

Some time later—she couldn't have said how much—Mary looked about her. Something was different, although her dazed senses couldn't work it out. The streetscape, the buildings, the relative quiet of a Sunday afternoon . . . and then it struck her. The crowd, small as it had been, was gone. Only one person remained, watching her and James with mild interest.

She tried to speak, but only a rattle emerged. She cleared her throat and tried again. "Where's the crowd?" Her voice was a foghorn, two octaves lower than her usual pitch.

The barefoot girl smiled wryly. "Bloodthirsty buggers; they're only interested in total destruction."

Mary looked up at the Lascars' home, the windows of which still belched smoke. "A house fire isn't enough?"

"Didn't you know? I thought that's why you went in."

Mary shook her head, thoroughly puzzled. "What do you mean?"

The girl—or rather, woman—grinned again. Seen in the late-afternoon light, she was older than she first appeared and a number of her teeth were black or missing entirely. "The fire's near put itself out." At Mary's frown, she sighed and leaned in. "The house. It's too damp to burn, love. How else d'you think you came out alive?"

Twenty-eight
Tuesday, 18 May

After breakfast, Mary was summoned to the teachers' common room. It promised to be another warm day. Her heart thumped hard enough to make her breathing shaky and her lips tremble. She knocked on the door, two crisp raps, and was pleased to be able to control her nerves to that small extent.

"Come in."

She entered and sat on the blasted horsehair chair, daring it to slide her onto the carpet. "Good morning, Miss Treleaven, Mrs. Frame."

Greetings were returned, tea poured. Not Lapsang souchong. Mary immediately set hers on a side table so that the cup wouldn't rattle in its saucer.

Anne sipped her tea, set down her cup, and fixed her sharp gray gaze on Mary. "We hope you are feeling better after the events of Sunday."

"Entirely, thank you." She'd nearly gone mad after

thirty-six hours of enforced bed rest and barley water to soothe her smoke-scorched throat.

"We have asked you here this evening, Mary, to present your report on the affair of Henry Thorold. As you know, his case is now concluded, and he is in police custody."

"And Mrs. Thorold?" The question slipped out before she could think to repress it.

"Still at large." Anne's clipped tone was the only indication of her frustration. "Scotland Yard believes she may have fled the country."

Mary's eyes widened. "She must have left on Sunday— immediately after setting fire to the refuge. Perhaps that's why she didn't use enough paraffin to burn down the house; she was in a hurry."

"All possible," said Felicity. "And if she had had a false passport ready, she could easily have been in France on Sunday night."

"In the future, the Agency might have an opportunity to help Scotland Yard find Mrs. Thorold," said Anne. "But we are meeting here now to discuss her husband. Before I present our final report on him to Scotland Yard, there are a number of details I should like to confirm with you and which should prove useful to the prosecution. You may begin whenever you are ready."

Mary shouldn't have been rattled by Anne's formality, but she had to swallow hard before finding her voice. "As you know, I first went to Cheyne Walk to observe the Tho-rold family without expecting to be an active participant in the case." Her voice was still huskier than usual, but at least it was steady. "I eventually learned that the secretary, Michael Gray—whom we'd suspected as part of the ring—was also suspicious of Thorold. Gray informed me that he'd taken secret copies of some relevant documents and hidden them safely. I believe the police retrieved the relevant documents from him?"

Anne nodded. "I understand that he was very cooperative. He is, however, still under investigation. Your report may certainly help to clear him of any wrongdoing."

"I hope so." Mary took a deep breath. "While I was searching Thorold's files, I met James Easton, who was searching for related information." She couldn't control the blush that stained her cheeks, but pushed on. "Working together, we discovered the Lascars' refuge in Limehouse and Mrs. Thorold's house in Pimlico. At that point, I had nearly all the information I needed, but couldn't see how to put it together until it was nearly too late. The missing link between Thorold, the Lascars' refuge, and the Pimlico house was, of course, Mrs. Thorold. I should have known better than to underestimate a woman," she added, "even one pretending to be an invalid.

"But I did underestimate Mrs. Thorold. She was clever: she disguised her business as an illicit affair. It was a perfect stereotype. And in a sense, it was also the truth. Mrs. Thorold was betraying her husband's confidence, but instead of committing adultery, she was running her own business.

317

"In hindsight, I ought to have been more suspicious of Mrs. Thorold. Her performance didn't quite cohere; she was weak and passive at some times and quite assertive and strong-willed at others. In fact, Thorold was much the better actor: he seemed to be a very ordinary, slightly stressed businessman, not one whose trade was being sabotaged by his wife and whose company was on the brink of failure. I allowed myself to be distracted by Mrs. Thorold. It wasn't until the last minute, when Cassandra Day showed me the notebook she had found, that I realized Mrs. Thorold was actually engaged in business." Here, she paused. "You know, of course, that James Easton managed to wring a fairly comprehensive explanation from her?"

Anne raised one eyebrow. "I believe it was quite a classic, theatrical villainous confession: high-seas piracy, revenge, marital discord."

"He must be a persuasive young man," Felicity said with a grin.

Mary didn't take the bait. "The weakness in our theory, of course, is that it depends on that confession. The notebook is a very careful document—it contains financial information without any direct references to the business. It could belong to hundreds of other people."

"But something in it led you to the Lascars' refuge. . . ." said Felicity.

Mary hesitated. "Yes . . . there's a tiny pencil reference to the address of the refuge and the surname of the warden. But it's very cryptic. My decision to go there was partly—perhaps largely—a matter of . . . instinct."

"There's no reason why reason and instinct can't coexist," said Anne gravely.

Mary nodded, grateful for the affirmation. "I believe you know the details of Mrs. Thorold's piracy better than I; you've spoken to James yourselves?"

" 'James'?" Anne's eyebrows lifted.

"Mr. Easton," Mary corrected herself. Her cheeks were burning.

"Ah. Yes, you were excluded from those interviews for reasons of security. We didn't meet him ourselves, of course; that was a matter for the Yard. But we did read the transcripts of his evidence. Her house in Pimlico was searched yesterday and while most of the papers appear to have been burned—there were a lot of ashes in the grate—there are enough indicators for us to formulate a theory.

"We know from her own boasting that Mrs. Thorold directed a pirate crew who attacked her husband's ships on the high seas; she probably used detailed routes and cargo information stolen from his files. She seems to have had an accomplice in the firm, most likely a junior manager named Samuels, who didn't turn up for work yesterday. His lodgings are deserted, and no one knows where he is.

"We aren't certain when Thorold realized what she was doing. It may have been quite recently, since his will was revised to include the Lascars' refuge only last year. It's possible he was afraid no one would believe that he'd been ignorant for so long. A wife is the property of her husband, and what she knows, her husband knows. That is the presumption in law and in practice, and she must have counted on that to keep her secret safe. Who could have imagined that Mrs. Thorold, of her own initiative, was assembling pirate gangs, attacking her husband's ships, stealing his cargoes, and murdering his crews?"

All three women were silent, still shocked by the enormity of the scheme.

Finally, Mary said quietly, "Thorold used the cheapest foreign sailors he could find. He was proud of his cost-cutting initiative—'one of the benefits of empire' was how he described it one evening at home. His cut-rate crews would have worked to Mrs. Thorold's advantage, too, as no one thought to inquire into the deaths of a few dozen Lascars." She paused and thought of Mr. Chen. "Almost no one, at any rate. Lloyd's was interested mainly in the actual goods lost."

Felicity nodded eagerly. "The insurance company: that's another interesting point. As suspected, Thorold was indeed defrauding Lloyd's, claiming that ships were lost or capsized when they'd actually arrived safely with all goods—including the smuggled ones—intact. As Michael Gray's evidence shows, Thorold bribed a man called Mays to manipulate the internal investigation and destroy evidence of his fraud, with some success. However, he could only cover up the truth for so long before Lloyd's became suspicious of Mays's honesty.

"At about the same time, Thorold began to make genuine claims for cargoes stolen by pirates. He must have been beside himself when he learned that his real payouts were jeopardized by the earlier, false ones. And he couldn't afford to go uninsured: piracy was threatening the survival of his business.

"All he could do was try to brazen it out. His ships were being attacked with astonishing regularity, and he must soon have suspected somebody with inside information. It's not yet clear when he realized it was his wife, but eventually he did. That's probably why he named the Lascars' refuge in his will; it was his way of trying to make amends."

"And perhaps," observed Anne, "a sort of indirect confession. Was it the will, Mary, that prompted you to make the connection between Chelsea and Limehouse?"

"Yes." Mary quickly steered the conversation away from Lascars. "We knew about the house in Pimlico because she spent time there regularly, as did Mr. Samuels. But she never visited Limehouse. It was only through a series of unforeseen events—James Easton's involvement, the address in the notebook found by Cass Day—that we found the link at all." She ground to a halt and looked at her employers.

Anne nodded gravely. "Thank you for your summary,

Mary. The work you did was extremely valuable. You must have some questions of your own at this point."

Mary nodded, blushing with the pleasure of an unexpected—and from Anne, lavish—compliment. "There are a few things I don't understand," she said carefully. "How did Mrs. Thorold discover James's—I mean, Mr. Easton's—involvement?"

Anne nodded. "Mr. Easton had both the Pimlico house and the Lascars' refuge under surveillance. One of his scouts, a ten-year-old boy, was discovered dead— murdered—on Sunday morning. He must have been spotted by Mrs. Thorold. It would have been relatively easy to trick the boy into giving up information before killing him. Ironically, the reason you escaped suspicion was that Mrs. Thorold didn't believe that a young lady was capable of giving her trouble."

Irony, indeed.

"That makes sense," agreed Mary. "But why would Mrs. Thorold attack her husband's business ventures? I can understand the need for a career beyond needle-work and social visits; her own daughter found the same desire, and it's something we all acknowledge here at the Academy. But to undermine her husband's own trading operations . . . ? It seems neither intelligent nor farsighted."

Felicity nodded eagerly. "Of course. We can only specu-late at this point, but Mr. Easton's evidence indicates that she looked down upon her husband; deep-seated contempt is not too strong a phrase. Perhaps it was her way of getting revenge on him or proving that he's her inferior."

"It's possible to weave any number of explanations," said Anne with faint reproach. "But only she would be able to tell you."

"Or possibly, she couldn't. Marriages are complicated beasts," said Felicity cheerfully. "The number of apparently devoted husbands and wives who'd like to kill and dismember their 'better halves' is quite astonishing."

Mary wondered about "Mrs." Felicity Frame. She'd never mentioned a Mr. Frame. . . .

"Next question?" Anne prompted her.

"Why did Scotland Yard move in a day early? I thought they'd agreed to act on Monday."

Anne looked mildly annoyed. "That was nearly disastrous. A rather keen superintendent at the Yard thought that if Monday was timely, then Sunday would be better yet. It was fortunate that the ship was already docked, waiting to be unloaded, or else there would have been no physical proof."

Mary nodded. "I see. I hope the primary agent wasn't compromised. . . ."

"The primary agent is an extremely capable operative," said Anne. "She certainly didn't appreciate your interference at the warehouses, but she's equal to almost any surprise."

Mary flushed. "Of course."

"Think of it this way," said Felicity more gently. "You're

her colleague and thus the last person from whom she expects surprises, especially when they go against orders. Your warehouse escapade resulted in no harm, but it did cause her inconvenience."

Mary struggled to find an answer that didn't sound glib or defensive, but Anne broke in with unexpected gentleness. "We needn't revisit that now, as you've learned from the experience. Do you have further questions?"

"Only one. . . ." She hesitated. "This is perhaps inappropriate, but how do you feel about dogs?"

Anne blinked. "Dogs! As pets?"

Mary nodded.

"Here at the Academy?" Anne couldn't quite control the distaste on her face.

Felicity frowned. "Why do you ask?"

"Thorold kept a guard dog," Mary said apologetically. "Not much of a guard dog. It was more interested in playing with strangers than keeping them at bay . . . but I can't help but wonder what's happened to it."

"I suppose you got to know the dog on your nocturnal rounds?" Felicity asked.

"Not very well," admitted Mary. "But it was a lovely mongrel. . . ."

Felicity looked at Anne. "I'll make inquiries," she said firmly. "Yes, darling, I know you can't stand the beasts, but even a dog shouldn't suffer just because its owner's a criminal."

"Thank you."

324

"That reminds me, Mary. . . . This is rather a personal question. . . ."

"Yes, Miss Treleaven?" Mary steeled herself for an inquiry about her parentage. Although she dreaded what might come, there would also be a kind of relief in being able to speak of her father. . . .

Yet Anne seemed distinctly uncomfortable, and remained silent.

After a glance at her tongue-tied colleague, Felicity spoke again. "It's about your associate, James Easton."

So her secret was still safe. Even so, the new subject was also extremely awkward and there was no controlling the wash of heat that flooded her throat, her cheeks, the tips of her ears. On Sunday afternoon, Anne and Felicity had found her huddled with James against the lamppost outside the Lascars' refuge, giggling hysterically at their escape. They'd certainly appeared to be more than "associates" then.

"We would not pry into your personal friendships if you were an ordinary teacher at the Academy," said Felicity carefully. "But as a member of the Agency, we must ask you: how much does James Easton know?"

"Nothing of the Agency," said Mary quickly. "We met quite by accident under circumstances that were suspicious for both of us." Her cheeks burned as she recalled those minutes in the wardrobe. "When he demanded an explanation, I told him that I wanted to know what had become of the last parlor maid. It was common knowledge in the servants' hall that she had fallen pregnant and that Thorold was the father."

"And he believed you?" persisted Felicity.

"I think so. He then he suggested that we work together in order to pool information."

"What was his motive for searching Thorold's files?"

"His brother was about to propose marriage to Angelica. Mr. Easton worried about how Thorold's business affairs might reflect on the Eastons if the families were linked by marriage."

"Practical young man," murmured Felicity. "Not the romantic type himself?"

Mary blushed furiously again. "I don't know, Mrs. Frame."

Felicity observed her closely for a minute, then smiled. "I see."

Mary was certain she did.

Twenty-nine

She didn't want James to court her or anything ridiculous like that. They were both far too young and from separate worlds besides. She would never be able to tell him about the Agency, let alone her criminal past or family history. They were too different even to be real friends. Yet she felt a sharp pang of regret as she thought about the end of their partnership. They'd worked well together, despite the squabbling and the mistrust. And she would miss him.

No matter. As Mary stepped off the omnibus in Limehouse, she set aside thoughts of James, the Agency, and the Thorolds. She was finally free to think of her own interests today. As she neared the Lascars' refuge, the fluttering in her stomach sped up. There was no reason to think she'd find the cigar box. Mr. Chen's office had been thoroughly smashed up. But she wouldn't be able to rest until she'd searched the wreckage herself.

As Mary neared the refuge, she saw a small number

of elderly Asian men carrying pails and crates of rubbish from its front door to a large wagon that blocked the street. They moved slowly, many of them apparently stiff with arthritis. A young white man in a bowler hat was giving them orders.

The young man spotted Mary and bustled over. "Road's closed here, miss."

She fought a sudden surge of nausea. "Are you clearing out the entire building?"

He nodded. "There was a fire here on the weekend. All the contents are ruined, but by the mercy of God the building survived."

"*All* the contents? They're just being thrown away?" Her voice sounded high and thin.

"There was nothing worth saving," said the supervisor defensively, "apart from some sticks of furniture, and the salvage man's already come and gone. Why, that's our third wagonload of rubbish today! Oh, yes, we've been busy. . . ." He went on to give details of the cleanup operation, details that she heard but failed to understand.

"What a shame," she finally choked out. That was it, then: her father's legacy, lost once again. She'd never even had a chance to look at the documents in the cigar box.

"Not a shame, miss," the young man chided her. "It's a blessing in disguise. The Lord giveth and the Lord taketh away, and here He's given us a new opportunity. The house needs refurbishment and these old Lascars need employment, and here we all are, working together!"

She nodded unsteadily.

"We'll have to find some new funds, as we recently lost one of our benefactors, but . . . " He rattled on happily about fundraising and plans for a grand new refurbishment.

"What happened to Mr. Chen?" interrupted Mary.

"The old man who managed the place? Oh, that was a shame. Must have been overcome by smoke, although—between you and me—" the young man leaned in confidentially, "it wasn't too great a loss. Apparently, the man was an opium fiend."

"He wasn't!"

He looked at her patronizingly. "Well, proof is proof, no matter what you like to think, and there was an enormous drug apparatus in his room when he died. Not that he won't get a decent Christian burial, after all that."

Mary turned away.

"I say!" he called after her. "No need to be like that! What's your name, anyway?"

She ignored his cries. She walked as fast as she could, deaf and blind to everything around her. But when she came to Victoria Park, she suddenly halted, unsure what to do or where to go.

She had just won the battle against tears when there was a light touch on her elbow. Turning, she found herself face to face with the inevitable.

He was elegant in a well-cut suit and polished boots. As his dark gaze skimmed over her, she had a sudden urge to flee. She was wearing an old, faded dress; her hair had begun to slip its knot; she was regrettably hot and sweaty.

"Hello," she said, and instantly felt it was inadequate.

"I've been following you for a while, but you didn't hear me calling. Are you all right?"

She nodded.

"You were coming from the Lascars' refuge?"

"You went too?"

"I was hoping to pay my respects to Mr. Chen's body."

The silence stretched out between them.

"You look unharmed," she finally murmured. "Does your head still hurt?"

He shook his head. "The damage was minor: a few cracked ribs, a headache. Nothing serious." There was a brief pause, and he hurried on. "You look very well, too."

Liar. She smoothed her hair self-consciously. "Thank you." Another of those awkward silences loomed, and she said shyly, "You must be very busy. I ought not to detain you."

He held out his arm. "I'd rather take a walk with you. If your employers permit such things?"

"Of course it's permitted!" she flashed back, and then grinned. "You do bring out the worst in me. Manners-wise, anyway."

He grinned back. "I think I like you better when you're rude."

She took his arm, and they strolled across the park toward the small boating lake. He was silent again, and the faint frown between his brows was delightfully familiar to her. He seemed to be searching for words.

He smiled at her, but his gaze was serious. "I wanted to ask you something."

"Yes?"

"I hoped you could explain something to me." That little frown deepened, and he pushed on hurriedly. "I can understand the business with Thorold—it's precisely the sort of thing I was afraid of. But how did Mr. Chen fit into all of this? Why would Mrs. Thorold need to kill him?"

Back to business. Of course, she should have known. "Didn't she tell you?"

"She didn't think it worth boasting about." Much like the murder of Alfred Quigley. He still felt sick when he thought about it. His visit to Mrs. Quigley this morning ranked among the most uncomfortable incidents of his life.

"I'm not certain. But I do have a theory."

"Go on."

"Mr. Chen may have been on her trail. What if a couple of Lascars sometimes survived a pirate's attack, either because they escaped or were spared—perhaps to help crew the pirate ship? Even if they reported the crime, who would believe them over an English captain? Authorities would assume they were confused, or lying, or that they had misunderstood something in English. But Mr. Chen

331

knew hundreds of Lascars. What if he'd begun to suspect something—had heard similar stories, and was following up on them?"

"And thus was silenced?"

"I've no proof, of course—but yes."

They reached the lake, and James stooped to pick up a handful of pebbles. He threw them into the lake, one by one. "That brings me to my second question," he said, turning to her rather fiercely. "You couldn't have known I was at the Lascars' refuge on Sunday afternoon. I went, like a good little idiot, because Mrs. Thorold lured me there."

"I went because of Mrs. Thorold, too. Nothing was clearly explained in her notebook, but once I saw it, I became worried for Mr. Chen's safety . . . and yours."

He stared at her. "How do you mean?"

It was difficult to explain. "I didn't expect to find you there, but I also wasn't surprised to see you." He was still looking at her with unsettling intensity. She couldn't bear his gaze any longer and looked away. Shrugged. "I just . . . had a feeling. A conviction that you were . . . there."

"In danger?"

"If you like."

He tossed the last stone into the lake. "Mary? There's one more thing." He sounded nervous and his gaze didn't quite meet hers.

She waited in silence.

"I, ah—this is very sudden, and I'm not—what I have to tell you . . ." He sighed and turned to face the lake.

When he spoke again, the words came out in a rush. "I'm going away."

Mary stared. While she hadn't known exactly what he might say, this was truly unexpected. "Where to?"

"Calcutta. We—the firm—have a contract to build railways."

She tried to look pleased for him. "That's marvelous news."

He studied her face. "Do you think so?"

"Of course! It's an excellent way to build the firm."

He nodded. "I'm glad you think so."

"When do you leave?"

"I sail next week."

She drew a deep breath. "You move quickly."

"Originally George was supposed to go while I ran things from this end. But this Thorold business has scrambled everything, and he's changed his mind." Amusement crept into his voice. "Did you know that he wanted to marry Angelica and take her straight to India?"

Mary laughed. "No!"

"Ironic, isn't it? That her fate was tied to India through both her father and her suitor?"

"She's managed to avoid both fates." Mary briefly described Angelica's new plans.

James let out a low whistle. "Wonder if I should tell George that she's single once again."

"But your worst fears about Thorold have come true. Are you not still opposed to the marriage?"

He shrugged awkwardly. "Well, yes, of course . . . but if George knows the worst and still wants to marry her, what can I say? Maybe he really does love her."

She laughed. "That's a very large concession, coming from you."

"One day you'll appreciate the finer points of my character."

"Finer points? Plural?"

"So many you'll grow dizzy trying to count them."

They stood there for a long moment, smiling at each other. Then Mary drew a deep breath. "Well, I suppose this is good-bye."

"I suppose it is."

"You'll do brilliantly in India."

"Do you think so?"

"With all those fine character traits . . ."

He laughed, then became serious once more. "Mary . . ."

The expression in his eyes set her heart pounding. "Yes?"

Twice he began to frame a sentence, and twice his voice seemed to fail him.

And she thought she understood. What could he possibly say to her now, when he was on the verge of leaving forever? Even something as simple as asking her to write to him carried a distinct sort of promise, the type of promise he was ten years and half a world removed from being able to make.

She forced a polite smile and held out her hand. "Good luck, James."

Regret—and relief—flooded his eyes. He took her hand, cradling it for a long moment. "And to you."

It was foolish to linger. She slid her fingers from his grasp, turned, and began to walk away in the direction of the Academy. She'd gone about thirty paces when she heard his voice.

"Mary!"

She spun about. "What is it?"

"Stay out of wardrobes!"

She laughed, shook her head, and began to walk again. She was smiling this time.

IN HER SECOND MYSTERY, Mary Quinn must confront harrowing childhood memories as she works to discover the identity of a murderer.

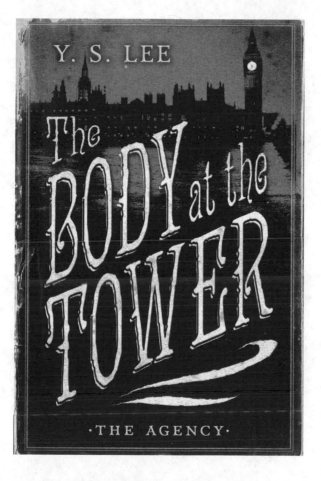

Y. S. LEE

The BODY at the TOWER

·THE AGENCY·

Available in hardcover, paperback, and audio and as an e-book

Turn the page for an excerpt. . . .

Prologue

Midnight, 30 June 1859

St. Stephen's Tower, Palace of Westminster

A sobbing man huddles on a narrow ledge, clawing at his eyes to shield them from the horror far below. It is dark, thus his terror is irrational; even if he wanted to, he could not make out what he's done, let alone note the gruesome details. Still, his mind's eye insists on the scene: gory, explicit, final. Imagination, not remorse, is at the core of his violent hysteria.

Within the hour he will exhaust himself and even fall asleep for a few minutes. When he wakes—with a start—reason will return and bring with it a degree of fatalism. Two paths now lie before him, and the choice is no longer his. He will pick himself up, carefully not looking over the edge. He will right his clothing, inspect his hands with care, and return home. And then he will wait to see what the future holds.

And he will vow to reveal the truth—but only at the time of his death.

an excerpt from *The Agency: The Body at the Tower*

One

Saturday, 2 July

St. John's Wood, London

The freedoms of being a boy, reflected Mary, were many. She could swing her arms as she walked. She could run if she wished. She looked tidy enough to avoid police suspicion but shabby enough to be invisible to all others. Then there was the odd sensation of lightness that came of having cropped hair; she hadn't realized how heavy her own hair was until it was gone. Her breasts were tightly bound, and even if they did ache a little at such treatment, she could at least scratch herself with impunity, scratching in public being one of those Boy Things she ought to enjoy while she could. It was therefore a shame that she wasn't enjoying the situation. Wearing boy's clothing was comfortable and amusing, and she'd enjoyed her escapades in breeches during her first-ever assignment. But this—today—was entirely different. It was serious, and she still had no idea why.

an excerpt from *The Agency: The Body at the Tower*

Her instructions were simple enough: to costume herself as a twelve-year-old boy and attend a meeting of the Agency at three o'clock this afternoon. No further explanation had been offered, and by now, Mary knew better than to ask for more details. Anne and Felicity always gave precisely as much information as they deemed appropriate. Of course, such knowledge hadn't stopped her from fretting about the possibilities yesterday, overnight, and all this morning. Over the past year, she'd delighted in her training: tests, lessons, and brief assignments that offered a taste of the life to come. But there was little pleasure in her this morning. What did Anne and Felicity want? And what sort of assignment could be connected with her present guise?

The Agency had been created and was staffed entirely by women, and its genius lay in the exploitation of female stereotypes. Its secret agents disguised themselves as maids, governesses, clerks, lady companions, and other humble, powerless characters. In most situations, no matter how dangerous, few people would suspect a subservient woman of being intelligent and observant, let alone a professional spy. With this as the Agency's guiding philosophy, it made no sense whatsoever for Mary to be dressed as a boy.

She raked her fingers through her hair, then stopped abruptly midstroke: that was a girl's gesture. And the only thing worse than not understanding what she was

an excerpt from *The Agency: The Body at the Tower*

doing was compounding it by doing a poor job, too. As she neared the top of Acacia Road, where the Agency was headquartered, Mary pressed her lips together and took several deep breaths. Her cowardly impulse was to turn and make one last circuit of Regent's Park, to spend just a little more time thinking matters through. As though she hadn't already been marching about St. John's Wood for the past two hours. As though physical movement might still her mind and soothe her nerves. As though she was calm enough to sort through the swirl of emotions clouding her brain.

It was time to act, not to think. A few brisk steps took her to the house with its wrought-iron gates and polished brass nameplate: MISS SCRIMSHAW'S ACADEMY FOR GIRLS. The Academy had been her home for years now. But today, looking at the nameplate, she willed herself to look at it as a stranger might — specifically, as a twelve-year-old boy might. The house was large and well kept, with a tidy garden and flagged path. But in contrast with those of the neighboring houses, the front steps were swept but not whitened — an essential task that proclaimed to the world that one kept servants and kept them busy rewhitening the steps each time a caller marred them with footprints. The Academy's irregularity here was the only sign of the most unusual institution that lay within.

Suddenly, the front door swung open and disgorged a pair of girls — or, rather, young ladies. They were neatly dressed, neither at the height of fashion nor in the depths of dowdiness. They were having an animated conversation. And they looked curiously at Mary, whose nose was still inches from the closed gate.

"Are you lost?" asked the taller of the two as they approached the gate.

Mary shook her head. "No, miss." Her voice came out higher than she wanted, and she cleared her throat hastily. "I was bid come here."

A fine wrinkle appeared on the girl's forehead. "By whom?"

"I mean, I've a letter to deliver."

The girl held out her hand. "Then you may give it to me."

Mary shook her head again. "Can't, miss. I'm charged to give it to Mrs. Frame and no one else. Is this her house?" She'd spent all morning working on her inflection, trying to get the accent right while keeping her voice gruff.

The girl looked imperious. "You may trust me; I'm the head girl at this Academy."

Mary knew exactly who Alice Fernie was. Head girl, indeed! She was only head of her year. "Can't, miss. Orders."

Head Girl's face twisted into a scolding look, but before she could speak again, her companion said, "Never mind, Alice. We'll be late if we stop to argue with him."

"I'm not *arguing*; I'm just saying . . ."

an excerpt from *The Agency: The Body at the Tower*

The second girl unlatched the gate and nodded kindly to Mary. "Go on, then."

Mary tugged her cap respectfully and dodged around the pair, leaving Alice scowling into the road. As she walked around to the side door—the front door wasn't for the likes of humbly dressed messenger boys—she grinned broadly. Her disguise had passed well enough before Alice and Martha Mason, which was a start.

Her small stock of confidence plummeted, though, as she walked down the familiar corridors, heavy boots shuffling against the carpet runners. It was one thing to slip past a pair of schoolgirls, and another to confront the managers of the Agency. As she neared the heavy oak door of Anne Treleaven's office, her stomach twisted and she felt a wave of dizziness. She'd been too overwrought to eat breakfast. Or, for that matter, last night's dinner.

As she raised one hand to knock, she had a sudden memory of doing precisely this, feeling exactly this way, just over a year earlier. That was when she'd learned of the existence of the Agency and embarked on her training as a secret agent. And here she was, not fourteen months later, feeling as confused and anxious as she had back then. The thought gave her courage. She was not the same girl she'd been last spring—untrained, ignorant, hotheaded. Over the past year she'd learned so much. But it wasn't the physical techniques—sleight of hand, disguise, combat—that showed how she'd matured. It

an excerpt from *The Agency: The Body at the Tower*

was her understanding of people, of calculated risk, that showed how she'd changed — as well as what remained for her to learn. It was all thanks to these women. She trusted them. And that trust would conquer the fear that made such a hard knot in her stomach.

Somehow.

In Mary's first assignment, she must infiltrate a rich merchant's household to navigate a nautical mystery.

Mary's second adventure sends her to investigate murder, with one catch: she'll have to disguise herself as a boy.

When Queen Victoria hires the Agency to discover who is stealing from the palace, Mary finds more than she was looking for.

Mary agrees to do one last job for the Agency, tracking a criminal she thought — and hoped — was gone for good.

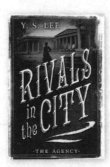

www.candlewick.com